# A SKELETON *IN* EVERY HOUSE

Isabella Duke

THE FIRST CATRIONA WINTERS MYSTERY

Also in the Catriona Winters Mysteries
*The Devil and the Deep Blue Sea*

www.isabella-duke.com

A SKELETON IN EVERY HOUSE


ISBN 978-0-6456867-7-7





12 11 10 9 8 7 6 5 4 3

# LONDON

November 8, 1880

# CHAPTER 1

The morning the body was dredged from the Thames, an impenetrable fog had rolled over London. The body was that of a man, quite evidently dead by the time he was hauled up limply, first onto a passing barge and then onto the damp wood boards overhanging the river at the dreary Limehouse docks. The initial assumption that he had fallen victim to a misstep on the riverbank, not an uncommon occurrence in such weather, quickly faded in the face of the obvious: He had been murdered. Before long, the police were summoned.

But as the same white fog swirled across her bedroom window that morning, Catriona Winters was not thinking of the murdered man. She did not yet know he was dead. She was thinking only of a letter and was putting off asking whether it had arrived.

Her house was unsettlingly quiet, her bedroom cast in the dim glow of a gas wall sconce and what meagre light had made its way through the parted curtains. Catriona usually took breakfast with her papa, but when she had gone down to the dining room just after six that morning, he had already departed.

She had asked her maid after him only to be rebuffed with the vague reply that he had left early on personal business. Sturdy, competent, and exceedingly practical, Emily was not one to speculate about exactly what sort of business this may have been. Her discretion was a quality for which Catriona had been grateful on several occasions, but today she gathered the maid had observed a little more than she was letting on, and the realisation annoyed her.

"Then I must catch him up at the office," Catriona conceded, staring absently out the window, which overlooked Thurloe Square and the surrounding houses. "He may even wish to print my story on the lecture of last night."

If she had expected Emily to enquire about the lecture or the meeting at which it had been delivered, she was to be disappointed. The maid simply stepped back, her fingers not having missed a beat with the hairpins, and surveyed her handiwork as she waited to be dismissed.

Catriona at last looked away from the window to the mirror above her dressing table. Her hair was piled atop her head in loose black curls, and her day dress, grey-blue with lace at the neck, complemented her colouring. In certain respects, she believed she took after her papa, but in her dark eyes and complexion, she undeniably resembled her mother.

"That will be all, thank you," Catriona finally said. However, as the maid turned to leave, she could not stop herself. The words flew out: "Did a letter arrive for me this morning?"

"I do not believe so," Emily replied. Instead of departing immediately as Catriona thought she would, she ventured, "A letter from Mr Hampstead?"

The anticipation had been broken, replaced by embarrassment.

"Emily, really," Catriona said, a wave of heat suffusing her face. But she said it with little feeling, knowing it would sound like an admission, and Emily slipped out, satisfied, without another word.

Mr Sidney Hampstead, an acquaintance of several years, had set off by steamer back to Boston, his home city, three months earlier. Despite their casual flirtation, the occasional unchaperoned walk, shared glances of amusement across crowded rooms, Catriona thought of him only as a comfortable friend. In his letters, which arrived like clockwork every ten days, he regaled her with the intrigues of life in an American city, and she clung to his adventures vicariously, because in London the season was over, and with it had gone her splendid fetes and leisurely afternoons strolling the green. Society had descended into a dull autumn, grasping for a scandal. Each day blurred into the next.

But the letter she awaited was not one from Sidney.

Having caught the train to Charing Cross, Catriona walked the familiar route to Covent Garden, to the offices of the *Messenger*. The staff had grown used to her comings and goings, and she believed they tolerated her presence, even indulged her occasionally, as when she wished to try to operate a Remington typewriter or observe the mechanics of the printing press on the lower floor. In reality, she knew they had no choice but to put up with her. Her papa owned the paper and she had decided to make herself useful there, given his decline in health as the cold set in, so nothing further was to be said on the matter.

Sir Frederick Winters was of that singular class of man who had made his own way in the world. Knight commander by merit of his military accomplishments, he had returned to England from his final posting in the West Indies with a daughter in tow and a small fortune on which to capitalise. In the twelve years since, he had set his sights on the *Messenger*, then little better than a scandal sheet, and transformed it into a reputable institution of investigative journalism. From the Tichborne case to the recent Afghan campaign, the *Messenger* had covered it all.

As Catriona ascended to the third storey of the building, where his private office overlooked a bullpen of reporters, she did not expect her papa to have arrived yet, still occupied with whatever business had waylaid him. In fact, she expected none of the staff to be in quite yet, as they so often spent the better part of the morning following up on leads. So the sight of two men deep in conversation caught her by surprise. One, instantly recognisable by his steely hair and aquiline features, was Sir Frederick, still wearing his coat, as if he had just come in.

The other was David Turner, Viscount Ashford, his old friend and military colleague. Lord Ashford and her papa had fought side by side in the Crimea in their youth, and it had been he who awaited them in London years later when they arrived from the West Indies. His own children, Bethany and Nathaniel, had welcomed her into their circle at once from their home across the square, and the families had been entwined ever since.

Like her father, Ashford had also had an illustrious military career. But most recently, as a personal favour to the previous home secretary, he had taken the helm as director of the newly formed Criminal Investigation Department within the Metropolitan Police. Beleaguered by scandals following a corruption trial involving several detectives, Scotland Yard was in need of a firm hand to guide it into modernity, and Ashford, the home secretary had argued, was just the man for the job.

In the dim, quiet office, Catriona could just barely hear their conversation.

"Of course, Ashford," her papa was saying. "More than happy to. I've been on the hunt for a skilled photographer for some time."

"I ought to thank you before you have the sense to change your mind," Ashford said, holding his top hat in his hands. "That son of mine brings me grief to no end."

The conversation stilled her in place. They had not heard her come in, and she did not know whether to announce herself, sensing she was overhearing something not meant for her.

That past midsummer, Nathaniel Turner, though only recently returned from his studies at Cambridge, had abruptly left London for the Ashford estate in Kent. It was no secret that there had been some strife between father and son in the weeks before his departure. She remembered how Nate had been—constantly drunk, shameless, a risk to his own reputation. The situation had been untenable, and it had been agreed, as Bethany later explained to her, her tone purposely light, that he would spend some time away from the negative influences of the city.

Yes, Catriona remembered how Nate had been.

Feeling suddenly breathless, she took hold of the edge of a nearby desk to steady herself, but her hand found a stack of reference books instead, which toppled neatly to the floor. The conversation ceased abruptly, and Ashford turned and, having spotted her, bestowed her a magnanimous smile.

"Darling, are you quite all right?" he called out.

"Yes, simply clumsy," Catriona replied, bending at once to collect the books. "Good morning to you both. I have not interrupted you, I hope?"

"Ashford was just about to head out, my dear," her papa said. "Some business down in Limehouse, you were saying?"

"Yes, a dreadful affair," Ashford said. "A man's been found dead, drifting off the docks."

"An accident?" Catriona said, joining them.

"I daresay not," Ashford replied. "The Yard is looking into it."

He hesitated before saying anything more, and Catriona thought he must be deliberating how much to share. Knowing Sir Frederick was a bloodhound for a good lead, he was no doubt choosing his words carefully.

"A murder, then?" Sir Frederick prompted. "How unfortunate."

"Quite," Ashford finally replied. Having apparently decided to share no more, he said, "I must be off. I have some matters to discuss with the detective inspector at the scene—on secondment down from Birmingham, handpicked by yours truly."

Sir Frederick, conceding their conversation had come to its natural end, began finally to undo the buttons of his coat. "Will I see you at our club tonight?"

"Would I miss it?" Ashford said, then turned to Catriona, who allowed him to press an affectionate kiss to her cheek before he swept from the room, strode through the bullpen, and descended the stairs to the street.

"There must be a report on the incident, of course," Sir Frederick said as soon as his friend had gone. He paused in undoing his coat buttons. "How typical of Ashford to hint at a good lead and then run off! A shame none of the staff are in yet. I shall head out myself."

"Papa, you must do no such thing," Catriona said, reflexively backing towards the open doorway of his office as though to stop him by force if necessary. "Remember your heart! The cold and damp at the docks could be most injurious to your recovery."

The opportunity to present him with her story on the previous evening was quickly slipping away, but she was not as sorry as she might have been. Although Catriona was not politically inclined, the lecture she had attended, delivered by Miss Frances Cobbe on the topic of women as citizens, had been of particular interest to her. The appeal had lain not in the ideas themselves but rather in the feeling they had created within her, an electric and almost frightening sense that there existed a vast world outside her own experience.

Her story had not conveyed this feeling; it had been a factual summary of the lecture, and its publication now seemed quite unimportant—when a man lay dead and there was no one to report on it.

She said without thinking, “Perhaps I could go.”

“My dear!” Sir Frederick exclaimed with such uncharacteristic vehemence that she knew at once what his answer would be. “That is out of the question. No daughter of mine shall be permitted to go skulking about Limehouse.”

“Papa, please reconsider,” she said, feeling like a child, a feeling she resented. “Lord Ashford said the police are at the scene. Surely one might rely on their protection.”

Sir Frederick looked out over the empty bullpen. As was always the case following a display of emotion, he had mastered himself quickly. “You ask because you think I cannot say no to you,” he said.

Catriona waited in silence, suspecting that if she pressed his decision, she might encourage a refusal. Sir Frederick had never limited her, never restricted her freedoms beyond what was demanded by society. In some ways, Catriona felt her papa was progressive, even avant-garde. She only hoped it might be that side of him, or the side that valued a good headline, which would win out now.

“But I can,” he said at last, “and I shall.”

“But, Papa—!”

“Do not argue with me, my dear.”

Knowing she was defeated, she decided she ought to leave quickly, but she could not help herself from making an attempt at her second objective. “Forgive me,” she said, and rose on her toes to grace him with a kiss on the cheek. “If I may, were you speaking also about Nathaniel?”

Sir Frederick regarded her with a raised brow. "I suspected you had heard that," he said. "Ashford wants to keep it hush-hush for now, but he is to return from the country within the week."

"That is…oh, within the week?" An unwelcome heat flooded her cheeks. "Bethany must be thrilled."

"I gather Ashford is slightly less so," Sir Frederick said. "You know I care for Nathaniel as though he were my own son, but you and Bethany will have to endeavour to keep him on the straight and narrow upon his return. If only your Hampstead were still in London to set him a good example!" He removed his coat and draped it with a flourish over his wingback chair.

"Yes, quite," Catriona said, willing her papa to drop the subject quickly now. Luckily, he turned to settle himself at his desk, and she took that as her cue to leave.

Having taken the Underground to its last eastwards stop and failed to hail a hansom cab willing to go any farther at that early hour, Catriona had faced a long walk to Limehouse. Even as she asked her papa his permission, she had already decided she would go. That he had forbidden it seemed somehow a necessary hurdle, and ultimately immaterial. She would write her story on the murder and present it to him, at which point she felt sure she would have come up with a good excuse as to how she had come across her information.

As she neared the river, she was met with a damp mist which seemed to creep under the skin. Missing were the sounds she had imagined, the shouts of sailors and dockworkers and the clacking of cargo carts over the cobblestones. Only the cries of gulls pierced the fog, and the buildings were so near one another that very little light penetrated their shadows.

A grim scene awaited at the docks. The police had halted all activity, and the barges in the basin were still laden with cargo, the skeletal masts of waiting ships rising from the Thames beyond the canal. Dockworkers milled about, squatting to smoke or throw dice in doorways. On the boards nearest the river lay a tattered greyish sheet. She tried not to imagine how the body might appear, waterlogged beneath it. Were the sightless eyes open? Did he still look like a person at all, or had the slithering creatures of the river got at him?

A small curious crowd had gathered near the scene, held back by a freckled young man in plain clothes, perhaps a detective constable. Pushing her way through somewhat indelicately, Catriona produced from her reticule a small diary in which she might make note of anything that stood out.

The first detail to strike her was a fine silk top hat lying some distance from the body, as if its owner had simply discarded it there. But the uniformed constables were taking care not to tread on it as they walked by, and she realised it must belong to the victim. The quality and workmanship were fine; it reminded her of the hats her papa wore but in a more modern continental style, the top a little shorter.

Nearest the dock, a patch of boardwalk was stained wine dark. Blood—it must be, and not an insignificant quantity. The victim had been stabbed or struck, perhaps even shot, before he found his way into the river. But if there had been violence at the docks, someone must have witnessed it. The place was surrounded by weather-beaten edifices, with crumbling shingles and warped leaded windows shuttered against the morning light.

She stepped towards the young constable managing the crowd and called out, "Excuse me! Catriona Winters, with the *Messenger*. I understand a man has been found dead. Any comment for the public?"

"Well," the constable began, then shifted on the spot, hesitant if somewhat flattered at having been addressed as though he were an authority on the matter. The crowd had descended into quiet murmurs, and he cleared his throat before continuing confidently: "I should say only that—"

"Whitby!" boomed a stern voice from across the docks.

Whitby started, falling silent, and Catriona turned to see whence the voice had come. Standing over the body, a man stared intensely their way. He was an inspector, she realised, perhaps the very same Ashford had mentioned that morning.

"Not a word, do you hear?" he called out.

"Yes, sir!" the detective shouted, and when he turned back to her with a sheepish, pained expression, Catriona knew she would get nothing from him.

The crowd milled around and in front of her, a blur of jostling shoulders, damp coats, and jutting shoes. These people knew the reality she had been forcing herself to ignore: that she was no reporter at all, that she was only playing at her own vague and perhaps misguided idea of what a reporter might be. She had only to turn, having been pushed already to the back of the crowd, and break free at the mouth of a dim laneway. She could only wonder what she had been thinking. She had been defeated too easily.

The laneway smelled of coal smoke, refuse and washing water, and the eternal Thames. She raised a gloved hand to cover her mouth and nose. From the windows overhead drifted scattered snippets of conversation: a man calling to his neighbour, a mother scolding a wailing child. Conditions in the district were squalid, marked by chronic poverty and want. Catriona saw why her papa had not wished her to come here. This was a side of London many preferred to pretend did not exist, and in peering into it, she felt disconcerted, as if she were not meant to have seen it at all.

Pulling her overcoat tighter against the damp cold, Catriona turned the corner—and immediately withdrew into a doorway, having spotted a shock of white hair emerging from the fog ahead. Lord Ashford stood under a stone archway at the mouth of a small courtyard. He spoke with an unfamiliar woman, Chinese and of middle age, dignified in appearance despite her surroundings. The mist hanging listlessly in the lane muffled their conversation, and within a moment, the two had passed through the archway and out of sight.

Catriona waited a minute before emerging. The laneway in which she stood was now deserted. Through the archway, at the far end of the courtyard beyond, was a boarding house of the type frequented by foreign sailors, its signpost painted in English and Chinese letters. No one else had come or gone. Had that woman or one of the boarders seen something relevant to the murder, and was Ashford making his enquiries inside?

A footstep sounded behind her, then a voice: "Hardly the area in which a lady ought to walk alone."

She whirled, and the tingling shock that had ricocheted through her dissipated. It was only the inspector from the docks.

"But by all means," he said, gesturing towards the courtyard, "do continue your attempt to intrude upon a crime scene."

The feeling of having been caught struck her intensely. She blamed him for it and disliked him immediately, having already decided that he was arrogant and even presumptuous. From his manner of speech, characteristic of the Midlands, she gathered he was indeed the inspector from Birmingham of whom Ashford had spoken. His hair was dark under his hat, and in the morning light, his eyes were a peculiar shade of grey. He regarded her with an inscrutable expression.

"Intrude?" she said. "A man has been murdered, and I am only making enquiries on behalf of the public. Catriona Winters, with the *Messenger*. And you are?"

"Inspector Thomas Marlowe, Scotland Yard," he replied, and at last gave a small bow, nothing more than the slightest incline of his head. "At your service."

"Then, Inspector, perhaps you wish to make a comment. Has the murdered man been identified?"

His mouth twitched. "Did you imagine I might be at liberty to divulge that information to a journalist?"

Catriona felt as though she had stumbled over another hurdle and barely righted herself before hitting the ground. It was not often that a man refused her anything—but in doing so, had he not referred to her as a journalist? She should have been embarrassed to cling to that so tightly. She grasped for her memory of the scene, for the picture of a fine silk top hat lying sodden on the boardwalk. "Is it not odd for a gentleman of means to have been here on a Monday morning?" she said.

"Are you sure he was killed this morning?"

"You suggest he was not?"

He glanced over her shoulder and down the laneway before surveying her again. His eyes were keenly intelligent, even perceptive, though looking into them felt like looking into deep water. "Miss Winters," he said, "morning or night, you might be surprised at why gentlemen find themselves in places like this."

Could he be trying to shock her? She had read accounts of the East End, sensationalist articles whose authors would have one believe every street corner played host to a brothel or an opium den. Had the murdered man been engaged in something illicit, something that had ended with his death in the river?

"Might I be?" she said finally, and left it at that. "You agree the death was not accidental, so was he killed on the dock or did he drown?"

"The body has yet to be brought to the police surgeon, as you well have seen," he said. "Or would you have me speculate as to the cause of death?"

"Speculation is unnecessary if there were witnesses," she said.

He gave a quick exhale, but whether aggravated or amused, she could not tell. "The inquiry has only just commenced," he said. "If you wish to follow up at an appropriate time, see me at my office at the Yard." He extended a plain card towards her.

The conversation had ended, she knew. She had coaxed nothing from him, and he was only patronising her now. A better reporter might have known what else to say, how to press him, but she simply took his card and tucked it into her diary.

He shoved his hands into his coat pockets. "If there's nothing else, madam, I suggest you not linger," he said, already half turned from her. "I hear Limehouse is not known for its hospitality."

And with that, he retreated down the laneway towards the docks. Catriona breathed deeply, long enough to quell the strange hot feeling that had crept up her neck. It was annoyance, annoyance at him and disappointment in herself for having been brushed aside. She hoped very much that she should never have cause to speak with Inspector Marlowe again.

Some distance away, a door slammed. A drunkard had stumbled out into the street, cursing and tripping over his own ragged shoes. He glanced at her, and behind the mean desperation in his eyes was something like blame. A wave of alarm overcame her, but as she turned and fled down the laneway, she quickly realised the drunk man had not followed her. Perhaps he had not seen her there at all, and she had imagined the mean look on his face. Her alarm turned into pity and disgust, for him and herself.

She had intruded into a world that was not meant for her, but had she not found what she sought after all? She had everything she needed to craft a story for the evening issue: a wealthy gentleman, a sudden bloody act of violence, and the cold, murky finality of the Thames.

# CHAPTER 2

The languid late June afternoon of her memory had found Catriona out under the sun at St James. Sidney and Nathaniel were engaged in a game of football on the green, jackets off and sleeves rolled up in the summer heat, whereas she and Bethany were content to sit beneath the shade of their parasols, playing at referee. As Catriona lifted a bare hand to shade her eyes, watching the ball weave its way across the lawn, Bethany was saying something, but she did not hear her. She was caught in an earlier memory of an evening in the gardens, an evening since which she and Nate had been orbiting one another in a different way.

Her awareness of him now seemed to collapse the world into the space between them. She was noticing things simultaneously: the way his blond hair caught the sunlight, the quick white glint of his teeth when he laughed, the high flush of colour across his cheeks, and those captivating dark eyes meeting hers for the briefest moment—a moment in which Sidney seized upon his distraction and stole the ball.

"Look alive, old sport!" he crowed as he took off towards the two trees they had designated as their goalposts.

"Kitty." Bethany touched her arm.

"Sorry," Catriona said at once. "What did you say?"

"That Sidney is trying to impress you." Bethany returned to fanning herself languorously. "You two would make a fine match, you know."

She and her brother were alike in appearance, sharing the same fair colouring, but whereas Nate was lithe and athletic, Beth was willowy, as delicate as a glass figurine.

"Perhaps we are better as friends," Catriona said. "After all, he is going back to America in a month."

"Do you imagine it is only for love of London that he has accompanied my brother on all his visits home this year?" Beth said. "He is so taken with you that I rather suspect Nate regrets having made the introduction."

"I have told him I shall write, and we must see if anything comes of it." Catriona shot Beth a glance. "But I suppose now you have the estimable Mr Bancroft wrapped securely around your little finger, you must turn your matchmaking skills elsewhere."

"Yes, my successful engagement to Henry has made me an expert at courtship," Beth said with amusement.

"You might focus on pairing off your brother, now he is back in London for good."

"Oh, I know a hopeless cause when I see one. Nate will never settle down, not if he can help it," Beth said, then shifted to make room for the two men, who had abandoned their game and were returning to the cool shade of the birch tree under which their picnic blanket had been spread.

Sidney flung himself down, legs crossed. "Gossiping about us, ladies?" he said. "Do share."

"Simply speculating as to whether our Nate will soon be a confirmed bachelor," Beth replied.

Nate gave a sharp laugh. "Ha! A shame I do not kiss and tell."

"Fine, keep your secrets." Beth diverted her attention from him and fluttered her fan pointedly. "Sidney, be a dear and fetch us some lemonade, would you? It's ever so hot today."

Catriona forced herself not to turn towards Nate, who had lowered himself to the blanket beside her. Instead, she looked across at Sidney.

He flashed her a brilliant smile, which she returned. He had been in England the past four years to study at Cambridge, as his mother, an Englishwoman who had married an American railway baron, had insisted on his receiving a proper education. The span of time had done little to diminish his charming accent and perfectly guileless demeanour, which Catriona found most refreshing in comparison to the London set. Perhaps it was that same quality in him which had encouraged his fast friendship with Nate.

"Yes, Sidney," she finally said. "Be a dear."

"Ah, the things I do for pretty girls, what?" Sidney replied.

Once he had headed off towards the refreshment stand, Beth rounded on her brother like a hawk targeting its prey. "Tell us what you think, Nate."

"About what in particular?" he said absently, leaning back on his hands and stretching out his legs. He had closed his eyes, and the sun shone over his face through the trees.

"About Sidney, of course," Beth said, "as a prospective match for our dear Kitty."

"Bethany!" Catriona said.

"Hampstead and Kitty?" Nate mused. "The possibility has not crossed my mind."

"Now it has," Beth said.

He shifted and faced his sister. "Surely you have better thoughts with which to occupy yourself these days," he said, "or is that Bancroft of yours really such a bore?"

Beth turned from him to look across the green, a little put out. "No need to be snippy," she said. "Had I known you to be so entirely against the idea, I wouldn't have brought it up."

"Who says I'm against it?" He leaned back and closed his eyes again. "I think Hampstead would make a fine husband: wealthy, well bred, and wholly predictable."

"Oh, all right, enough," Beth said with a scoff, then busied herself in adjusting her skirts to lie just so.

She was speculating about something Catriona had already noticed. It was true Sidney had been making his intentions towards her clearer, especially now, in the weeks leading up to his departure. But her own intentions lay elsewhere, in the secret of fingers brushing idly against hers, hidden in the folds of the blanket, for the briefest of moments.

Then Sidney was back with a tray of lemonades, and Beth was chatting away about something else, and it was as if it had never happened at all.

She woke at her desk when her papa emerged from his office, having turned down the last lamp inside.

"Catriona?" Sir Frederick said with a start. "Good heavens, it was so quiet I thought you had left for the evening."

"Oh!" She sat up, face still hot from the remembered summer sun, and ran a hand over her hair to ensure her curls had not fallen out of place. "I must have nodded off. I was looking over my notes, hoping I might notice something significant in them into which we might enquire further."

Sir Frederick came to stand next to her and offered his hand as she rose. "Curiosity is a sin of its own, my dear—but a sin of which I too am guilty, of course," he said. "With any luck, I can pry some information from Ashford at our club tonight, and we can follow up with another story tomorrow."

"Yes, with any luck," Catriona said. The lie she had told him, that she had simply gone to Scotland Yard and spoken with the inspector who had been at the scene that morning, collecting all the details which had comprised her story, had gone over surprisingly well. She swallowed her guilt. Nothing untoward had come of her deception.

She collected her reticule and began to pull on her coat, and when her papa turned to leave, she followed him. "But that reminds me, Papa," she said. "Do you know whether Lord Ashford does any investigative work himself?"

"I think not. He somewhat enjoys that comfortable office of his at Scotland Yard, I expect. Why do you ask?"

"Just my sin of curiosity," she said. It was not merely out of curiosity that she had asked, of course, but her papa did not need to know so.

They left the office and descended to the street, where together they made their way to the Underground station, a short walk in the brisk night air. She had recalled seeing Ashford speaking urgently with that woman outside the boarding house, and she was not sure why, but something about the scene had piqued her interest.

"Perhaps," she said, and quickly swallowed her distaste at what she was about to suggest, "depending on what his lordship reveals to you tonight, it could not hurt for me to follow up with the inspector tomorrow, see if he wishes to share anything further."

"A fine idea," Sir Frederick said. "There must be more to the story, though I confess your reporting was exceptional. Respectful of the unknown victim, yet intriguing—and you know I do not give compliments lightly!" They had reached Charing Cross station, where they would part. "Now, all work and no play makes your papa a dull boy. I shall dine at my club tonight, so no need to set aside supper."

"All right, I shall let Mrs Travers know," Catriona said, referring to their housekeeper. "Please don't stay out too late—and remember your heart!"

"Yes, yes, of course," Sir Frederick said with a wave of his hand.

"Good evening, my dear."

She knew he would watch her as she descended into the station, and afterwards he would head directly to join Ashford at Pall Mall. The goings-on at their private members club, known informally as the Flag, were quite unknown to Catriona. Founded earlier in the century for commissioned officers, it had gained an elite reputation, and, like many such clubs, it did not admit women even as visitors. She had never been inside. All she knew was that her papa often came home quite late and in high spirits.

The train to South Kensington gave her time to think. She was determined to find out why Nate had decided to return to London so abruptly and without word, but as she ascended to the street, made the short walk to the square, and called at the Turner residence, she found that Bethany was already entertaining company. The interloper in the parlour was none other than her fiancé, Mr Henry Bancroft.

Scion of the Holt & Bancroft Steam Shipping Company, which had long operated a merchant fleet between London, the Persian Gulf, and Bombay, Bancroft had been amongst the most eligible bachelors in the city. He made a good match for Beth, and Catriona had always liked him, admiring not only his sharp, handsome features but also his keen ambition, in which regard he reminded her somewhat of her papa. On this night, however, she disliked him very much indeed, as he had spoiled her plan.

Beth would be disinclined to discuss her brother in front of Bancroft, given that, for reasons Catriona did not quite understand, there was no love lost between the two. As the Turners' footman,

Arthur, took her coat and showed her through, Catriona decided she would invite her friend to luncheon the next day, where they could speak in private.

"Kitty, come in!" Beth said, rushing to her side to embrace her as soon as she set foot in the parlour.

"Miss Winters," Bancroft said by way of greeting as he rose from the settee.

"Good evening to you both," Catriona said.

"Henry and I were just discussing the evening edition," Beth said. "Is it true about the murder?"

"Your father visited our offices this morning, and I confess he tipped us off," Catriona said. Conscious of the fact that she had interrupted them, she intercepted Bethany as she moved to ring for a third cup of tea. "Thank you, but I cannot stay long."

Bancroft had turned to the fire and lifted a poker to reignite the smouldering coals. If he regretted her presence, he was polite enough not to show it and had gamely left the settee for the two women. "The docks have always played home to a certain criminal element," he said, then turned a conspiratorial glance at them over his shoulder. "But perhaps this discussion is unsuitable for polite company."

"Nothing could be more suitable," Bethany said. "Is shipping not the lifeblood of the empire? Silk, tobacco, tea—all the imports around which society is based come to us through that port."

"Perhaps someone ought to tell as much to your father and his detectives," Catriona said lightly. "Was it a very great inconvenience to your business, Mr Bancroft, that they stopped all the activity at the docks this morning?"

"Visited the scene of the crime, did you?" he said, not without surprise, and she realised she had given herself away. He pushed his spectacles higher on the bridge of his nose and, perhaps sensing her discomfort, suggested gently, "Shall we move on to more pleasant topics of conversation?"

"Indeed, I should not impose further on your evening," Catriona said. "Beth, are you free for luncheon tomorrow? It feels like ages since we have had a chance to catch up properly."

"How about that charming cafe in Mayfair?" Bethany said. "You know the one. I have errands to run in town in the morning, so I shall meet you."

"Then I look forward to it," Catriona said.

Beth accompanied her as she rose, and Bancroft rose as well, nodded to her, and said, "Good evening, madam," before turning back to the fire.

"Thank you for stopping by," Beth said as they turned and proceeded to the foyer. "I confess I have tried to catch you at home for days now."

"You must forgive me," Catriona said. "I have been at the office, trying to make sure Papa does not take on too much for himself."

"Shall I have a stern word with him?" Bethany said with a sly smile, then patted her arm, said, "Till tomorrow," and kissed her cheek before going back in to her fiancé.

Waiting as Arthur fetched her coat, Catriona stood alone in the foyer. From the parlour came the quiet resumption of whatever conversation she had interrupted with her arrival. They were not talking of murder anymore, having turned to a pleasant topic that made Bethany laugh. The sound of it should have lightened her mood, but it only made her feel suddenly and strangely alien. She felt as though part of her had remained in that shadowed laneway in Limehouse, or looking out to the grey Thames with the gulls circling overhead. It was all a far cry from a warm parlour in Brompton.

From the street beyond came the clacking of hoofs over cobblestones as a cab rolled to a stop. Catriona was not paying attention; the next few moments unfolded with stunning rapidity. From the parlour, the conversation ceased, and Beth gave a little cry as footfalls sounded on the steps outside.

Turning towards the door, Catriona felt a queer lightness, a premonition—as though she had sensed his presence.

It swung open, sweeping in the chill night, and there he was, not so changed from when last she had seen him. Paler without the summer sun, maybe, or more tired.

Nate, her Nate. There he stood, and they regarded each other across the threshold.

# CHAPTER 3

"Good morning, Papa," Catriona said the next day as she joined him at the breakfast table. "I didn't hear you come home last night. I trust your evening at your club was productive?"

"It was. Nothing like a few rounds of whiskey to get Ashford talking," Sir Frederick said with aplomb, tapping a small spoon atop a boiled egg to crack its shell. "But it pains me to tell you that apparently the drowned man was the Marquess of Stratton. An acquaintance of yours, was he not?"

"Lord Stratton?" Catriona said. "No, how devastating! I cannot believe it. What an unthinkable blow to her ladyship, and with such a young child."

"Yes, the poor girl," Sir Frederick said, "especially as rumour has it the estate has been in dire straits for some time."

Catriona turned to glance out the window at their private back garden. At that time of year, aside from the glass orangery, it was depressingly bare. "I must write her at once," she said.

"She will need all the friends she can muster," Sir Frederick replied. "Do you still plan to try for another meeting with that inspector today?"

In fact, given the unexpected return of Nate the previous evening, Catriona had altogether forgot about that. The moments following his entrance had passed in a blur. Beth had fluttered in, having spotted the cab through the window, and the commotion had given Catriona the opportunity to make her exit.

In hindsight, she supposed she had simply fled.

"Perhaps the intervening span of time will have loosened his tongue a little," she ventured, "though I do not expect so."

She had hoped her papa might discuss the murder with her further, but as he had already begun to flip through the stack of other newspapers to his right, which he referred to as the competition, she knew the conversation was over.

After writing Lady Stratton to offer her condolences, Catriona hailed a cab to Scotland Yard. She had visited several times, always with Bethany, to call on Lord Ashford in his office on the upper floor, but the impersonal purpose of her visit this day had cast the place in rather a grander and more imposing light. The reception area off the yard, across from the Public Carriage Office, was still panelled in dark wood, having been a private residence before its conversion to police headquarters. The other entrance, on Whitehall Place, which had once been the front of the home, was seldom used now.

She approached the person manning the desk only to find that he was none other than the freckled young detective she had encountered at the docks the day before. Catching sight of her, he rose, with recognition in his face.

"Good morning," she said. "Detective Whitby, was it? Catriona Winters, from the *Messenger*."

"I remember, ma'am," he said proudly. "I apologise for my brusqueness at the docks. The inspector wouldn't allow us to speak to the press."

"I completely understand," she said. "It does you credit that you so diligently respect your orders." She hesitated in producing the card the inspector had given her, feeling that if she played her hand well with the detective, she could avoid speaking with him altogether. "Might I trouble you for a moment today instead?"

"It would be no trouble," Detective Whitby replied. "I should be most pleased—"

"Whitby!"

His mouth snapped shut at once, and Catriona turned to see Inspector Marlowe stalking in from a corridor to their right.

"Not another word, Detective," he said. "Miss Winters, I gather this is not a social call."

"Social call or not, Inspector," she said, "I believe the custom is to wish a lady good morning."

Ignoring her remark, he said, "Whitby, in future, escort any unsolicited visitors from the press off the premises immediately, and do not let slip a word about our inquiry in the process."

"Yes, sir," Whitby said. His hand rose as though he were about to salute, but he seemed to think better of it, dropping it aimlessly to his side. "I apologise for the oversight, sir."

"Very good," Marlowe said. "Madam, you may follow me."

He set off immediately without turning to see whether she had obliged, and she felt she had to canter to keep up with him.

"Inspector," she said, "if you intend to escort me off the premises, as you say, after I have come all this way—"

"The *Messenger* offices are but a fifteen minutes' walk," he said. "The journey has hardly put you out."

"Getting acquainted with the city, are we?"

"Yes, with the hotbeds of trouble."

"Trouble?" she said, pressing her nails into her palm through her glove. "I respect your need to keep your inquiry under wraps, but I daresay we are on the same side."

"And which side would that be?"

"The side of justice, of course," she said. They had turned a corner and entered another corridor lined with private offices. "The press performs an important function. Someone must hold public institutions accountable."

"You need not apprise me of the role of the press, madam. What of accountability towards the victim and his family?"

"You refer to Lord Stratton?"

"I see," Marlowe said. "Revealing his identity and throwing his family to the wolves, is that your angle?"

"Inspector, the identity of the victim would make for a poor story indeed," she said. "Perhaps you are unaware of the speed at which word travels in London, but I assure you anyone of consequence will have heard the news before midday with or without my involvement. Gossip is the currency of society, after all. More to the point, I feel a very keen sympathy for his lordship's widow, so I have no wish to do his family any harm whatsoever. Quite the contrary."

"If you say so," he said. "Then to what do I owe the very great pleasure of your visit?"

"Is it so unbelievable that I might simply wish to establish a more courteous relationship between us? I could serve as an asset to your inquiry—and where are you taking me, if you please?"

"My office," he said, and apparently they had arrived, as he stopped and gestured into the room. "After you."

She entered. The desk was fastidiously tidy, the window open to admit the light and the morning air.

"If we are on the same side, as you say," Marlowe continued, pulling out the chair across his desk for her, "then how might I be of service to our common cause?"

"Thank you," she said, lowering herself into it. "Your present inquiry is of exceptional public interest, given the standing of the victim, but you will agree that the story of yesterday evening was somewhat lacking in detail."

He sat across from her. "Hardly."

"You read it?"

"I did," he said, then rested his elbows on the desk in front of him and steepled his fingers. "Do you wish to hear my opinion of it?"

"No, my purpose here is strictly objective."

"Then achieve that objective, madam, and we might both get on with our day."

From her reticule, she produced her diary and a pencil and flipped to a fresh page. "First, do you know what Lord Stratton was up to at the Limehouse docks? He was not there for business, I imagine; his family has no shipping interests to speak of."

"You cannot expect me to answer that." He leaned back in his chair. "Or do you wish me to confirm whatever rumours are flying about concerning his lordship's personal vices?"

"I wish only to know the reason for his presence there so that I might track down potential witnesses to his murder. No doubt your constables are pursuing similar avenues of enquiry."

"They are, which is why you need not do so," he said. "The matter is well in hand."

"You mean to dissuade me," she said. "But your mention of vice is a hint I intend to take."

"By prowling through Limehouse yourself in search of clues?" he said.

"Yes, if necessary."

His brow furrowed for barely more than a second before his face went impassive again. "The police presence of yesterday morning is not ordinary in the East End, madam," he said. "The area has its dangers."

An insistent annoyance was gathering within her. She set her diary in her lap and forced herself to fold her hands over it. "Stricken by an attack of conscience, Inspector?" she said. "You could spare me those dangers by sharing what you have discovered about the crime."

"Perhaps you overestimate my concern," he said.

"Perhaps you underestimate my tenacity," she returned. "Determined though you may be to keep me out of your inquiry, I am set on my course."

She stood. For the briefest moment, she was sure he would remain seated. But he did rise at last, and her anger simmered without outlet.

"Then I wish you the best of luck," he said.

"As I do you," she said. "But if you find your conscience exerts itself rather more strongly than you anticipated, you know where to find me. After all, I am but a fifteen minutes' walk."

She whirled and exited his office.

"Good day, madam," he called after her.

"Good day!" she replied without turning, then walked quickly down the corridor and out past poor Whitby at the reception desk.

As she stepped into the cool late morning of London, her face burned with a strange combination of infuriation and embarrassment. The inspector had been entirely uncooperative, yet their encounter had left her more determined than ever to pursue her own enquiries. What vice had driven Stratton to Limehouse and to his death?

The identity of the murdered man had brought her questions into sharper relief. Catriona had met Atherton, Lord Stratton, on several occasions, most notably during the season before last, when he had still been a bachelor. Though handsome and a marquess, he had been of only passing interest to her at the time. She had sensed him to be a person of insufficient substance, inclined towards the gaming tables rather than conversation.

Like many, she had been somewhat surprised when he married Margaret Cavanaugh, the daughter of a financier from New York and a stranger to the London set. She suspected their marriage had been driven by practical concerns, funds for him and a title for her, rather than by any real affection. It was not uncommon for wealthy Americans to pair their daughters off with cash-strapped aristocrats, but Catriona could not help but feel for the widowed Lady Stratton now, alone in the city with her new-born son and not even her own family there to support her.

Her brisk walk to Hyde Park left her little time for further speculation, but as Catriona neared the cafe where she was to meet Beth for luncheon, she could not stop herself from thinking the thoughts she had been trying studiously all morning to avoid: She recalled Nate and the cool manner in which his gaze had travelled over her. Seeing him had re-awakened everything within her that she had fought so hard to forget—the memory of the previous summer, which had passed as if in a fever.

"Kitty?"

Catriona opened her eyes, having drifted unconsciously into a slow blink, stilled in the middle of the footpath. "Oh, Beth," she said. "Hello."

"Are you quite all right?"

"Yes, sorry. I must have exhausted myself on the walk."

"Goodness, I thought you might faint." Bethany reached out

to take her arm, and they continued together.

"No, I feel all right now, thank you," Catriona said. "You have come to my rescue."

Alongside the path was the park, its trees mostly bare of leaves and its manicured lawns dusted with glittering white frost. Their breath misted in the cold as they proceeded towards a small cafe, a favourite meeting place. They entered and were seated, and as a waiter brought out tea and sandwiches, Beth exhaled and began to speak.

"I've had such a splendid morning at Harrods. Their winter fabrics are in, and I'm having a new evening dress made. My complexion changes ever so much in the cold, you know," she said—and then, quite suddenly, with a curious expression, "I've been thinking of putting the wedding off a little longer, till Henry is more established in his business."

"Oh?" Catriona replied carefully. She was shocked but did not mean to show it, as she sensed Bethany was unsure of her decision, and she did not wish to sway her unintentionally.

"It's been only a year since his father passed," Beth said, "and there has been rather a lot for him to take on since. I am only thinking of him, yet I suspect he thinks I have cold feet."

"Mr Bancroft would do anything for you," Catriona said. "If you wish to wait, he shall wait. And he must see the wisdom in not rushing things."

"I think he simply fears I might wake up one day and find our match unsuitable. But what do I care how his family got its money? Whether his grandfather was a dockworker or a duke makes no difference to me. I think social mobility is a wonderful sign of progress in our society." She was speaking very quickly. She stopped to take a breath. "And he must know how happy Papa is with our match, so there's no chance of my breaking it off now."

"He has certainly represented himself well," Catriona said. "The man has ambition—a commendable quality."

Beth reached for a tiny spoon and began to stir her tea absently. "If only some of that ambition could rub off on Nate," she said. As if seizing the opportunity to change the subject, she remarked, "You know he and Papa haven't exchanged more than two words since last night?"

"Is it really that bad between them?" Catriona said. "I had thought the time apart might improve the situation."

"I had hoped the same, but it seems they'll never see eye to eye. Sometimes I think Nate must be too like our mother, and Papa simply cannot bear the reminder of our loss." She set her spoon onto the saucer and delicately lifted the cup. "Regardless, it seems my brother will have to earn his way back into Papa's good graces."

Catriona glanced out the window and lowered her eyes against the bright sun. She tried to keep her expression neutral as she asked, "If their relationship is not mended, why has Nate come back?"

"Who knows?" Beth said. "Perhaps traipsing about the countryside lost its allure as the cold set in."

"Hmm, perhaps."

"Speaking of the cold, I hear Boston is dreadful this time of year." Beth shot her a wicked look. "I suspect Sidney has spent a few nights wishing he were back in England."

"Perhaps he has."

"Are you blushing?" Beth exclaimed. "I should bet he writes a pretty letter…"

"He does. Now let us speak of something else, shall we?" Catriona folded her hands on the table. "Surely two accomplished ladies have more to discuss than romance."

"Fine, if you insist." Beth gave a little pout. "I had hoped to avoid this grim subject entirely, but I heard the most awful rumour from Jessamine Parsons. Apparently, the man who was killed is Lord Stratton. Can you believe it?"

"I cannot, but I have also heard as much," Catriona said. "In fact, I have just met with the inspector leading the inquiry to confirm it. I was hoping to pry a little more information from him."

"And? Do tell." Beth sipped her tea, her dark eyes peering intensely over the rim of the cup.

"It was an unsuccessful mission, unfortunately," Catriona said, determinedly quelling the annoyance that threatened to resurge within her at the thought of it. "The man is tight lipped to the extreme."

"Oh, hold on!" Beth cried suddenly. "The inspector is that new fellow down from Birmingham. Marlowe, was it?"

"Yes, Thomas Marlowe. Do you know him?"

"I do. Papa introduced us on Saturday when I stopped in at the Yard. I gather the inspector had arrived in London that morning," Beth said—and then, with the air of one about to impart a choice titbit of gossip, "I thought him charming and quite handsome, if a little stiff."

"I think 'charming' is the last word I would use to describe him," Catriona said with somewhat more feeling than necessary. "He seems to enjoy frustrating me. Our interactions have been somewhat antagonistic."

"Perhaps you have mistaken his professional discretion for hostility?" Beth suggested gently. Before Catriona could ignore her sudden pang of doubt and offer a protest, Beth continued. "But in either case, Jessamine mentioned something else you may find interesting. Apparently, Lady Stratton has refused entirely to speak to the police."

This surprised Catriona. Their friend Jessamine, whose father was the vicar at the church of Holy Trinity, was well informed in that people did not often think twice about what they told their religious leaders—or the wives of their religious leaders, for that matter, who might tell their daughters and all and sundry as well.

"Of course," Beth continued, "her ladyship is in a vulnerable position now. Imagine being associated with something as ugly as murder! I've sent her my condolences."

"As have I," Catriona said. "One hopes she's not entirely without supporters."

"It could not hurt to nurture our friendship with her," Beth said. "If she doesn't wish to speak to the police, she might prefer a sympathetic ear."

"I quite agree. I wonder why she refuses them, though. Surely any information she might provide could only help them find her husband's killer."

"Perhaps the shock has been too much for her. I think of how she must have felt upon receiving such awful news, very much alone here." Beth began again to twirl her spoon in her teacup. "It's too distressing to think about. Let us speak of something else."

"Happily," Catriona said. "I hear the lady mayoress will soon send out invitations for her next charity ball."

"Oh? Good. We could all do with a little cheering up, and I do so anticipate a ball. What a fine occasion that would be to show off my new dress!" Beth gave a radiant smile.

They abandoned any discussion of the dreadful events of the previous morning in favour of more suitable topics: the latest fashions on the continent, the recent turn of the weather. Talk of murder could wait. Though they did not know it at the time, after the coming days, their conversations would revolve around little else.

# CHAPTER 4

When Catriona arrived at the *Messenger* offices that afternoon, her papa was nowhere to be found. She had hoped to update him on her progress, or lack thereof, with the inspector, but, assuming he was out on business, she decided she had might as well make herself useful, so she got to work organising the endless papers piled atop his desk.

As she slowly chipped away at the mountain, regretting that her papa had stubbornly refused to hire a book-keeper, she uncovered something unexpected. There, lost amidst bills of sale, old editions, and printing proofs, was a photograph of her mama.

Something about seeing her in dreary grey made her feel like a stranger. The image was such a contrast to what Catriona remembered, the blur of cloudless sky and turquoise sea, the Madras dress fluttering across the sand, the colourful processions of the flower festivals in late summer. A Creole native of St Lucia, her mama had been a captivating beauty, but beneath the surface had lain bleak extremes, highs and lows of emotion, fits of ecstatic joy followed by weeks of interminable weariness.

Catriona sighed, still holding the photograph, and that was how Sir Frederick found her as he returned at last and said, "My dear, what an improvement you have made to the state of my office."

"Papa, good evening," she said without glancing up, too afraid of the emotion he might see in her face. She set the photograph down gently on his desk, and when at last she looked over at him, she saw who had accompanied him and stood there with him in the doorway. "Oh. Nathaniel," she said tonelessly. She felt caught out again, just as she had the night before—and despite herself, her heart fluttered at the sight of him.

"Catriona, hello," he said.

"We two have been out sourcing equipment for a darkroom," Sir Frederick explained with satisfaction. He stepped in to deposit a folder of papers on his desk but did not remove his coat or hat. "The whole process is rather beyond me, I confess, but I'm determined to introduce photographs to the paper as a regular feature. Innovation is key to our continued success!" He turned back to clap Nate on the shoulder. "Now, I must be off again. Nathaniel, will you join your father and me at our club tonight?"

"Another time, thank you," Nate said. "I have promised this evening to my sister."

"Of course you have. No doubt Bethany is thrilled at your

return," Sir Frederick said. "On that note, perhaps I could ask that you escort Catriona home with you. Someone has to force her out of the office, or I suspect she will be here all night."

"That's certainly not necessary," Catriona said. "I'm sure Nathaniel—"

"It would be my privilege," Nate said.

Sir Frederick folded his gloved hands before him and levelled a pleased glance on his daughter. "Most excellent," he said. "You have some catching up to do, I'm sure. I remember when you were only children, chasing one another through the gardens. How time flies!"

After her papa said his good-evenings and swept out of the office, a tense silence descended.

"Shall we?" Nate finally said.

"I meant what I said, you know. I'm perfectly capable of getting myself home."

He crossed his arms. "Let's not argue about it, Kitty. Now, it's a pleasant evening and the train is dreadfully crowded at this hour, so we'll walk."

"If you insist," she said. "Give me a moment to collect my things, please."

She did so, feeling him watching her as she retrieved her reticule. Without a word, he took her overcoat from the stand and held it out for her to slip into, and he followed her as she left the office and descended to the street below.

They walked in silence which was neither awkward nor companionable. In many ways, Nate felt like a stranger to her now, and she could not help but feel guilty, for she suspected deep down that she was responsible for the estrangement.

"So, photography," she said.

"Yes, what of it?"

"Papa has been most interested in getting an edge over the other daily papers. I had thought there were certain limitations to the collodion process which prevented—"

"I'll be applying a new dry-plate method with which the Americans have seen some success," he said. "Have you got any other pressing concerns about the mechanics of photography?"

"Simply making conversation," she said. She felt she was embarrassing herself somehow. "But perhaps your time away from society has deteriorated your manners."

"Yes, perhaps it has."

They continued, and she glanced at him, wishing for him to smile at her as he once did, yet he only stared ahead at the footpath, deliberately disaffected. Things had been so different between them once, when summer had come rushing over the city in a wave of humid heat and flowers bursting into bloom. But she had made her choice, she reminded herself. Dusk had descended, and the air held the promise of snow.

"Here we are," Nate said some time later as they turned the final corner and the square came into view.

"I trust I'll see you at our offices tomorrow, then," she said.

"Yes. Good evening, Kitty."

"Nate, I..." She had not been able to stop herself. She did not know why she had said it or what she had intended to say next. She felt only that something so very important remained unsaid between them, and she could not figure out what.

"Hmm?" He was already half turned from her, his hands in his coat pockets.

"Nothing," she said. "Good evening."

As she lay in bed that night, watching the cloudy moonlight travel across the ceiling, she could not stop thinking of him or the events which had brought about the rift between them. Being with Nate had once felt like standing at the edge of a precipice, leaning over a vast expanse into which, if she had only let herself, she could have fallen forever.

April of that year had been a month of rain punctuated by blissfully sunny days. Just after the opening of the London season, Nate had come home from university for the week-end, and to celebrate her engagement to Bancroft, Beth had held a small dinner party, playing hostess to the notables of society. There had been, of course, much to gossip about.

It had all begun innocently enough, when Catriona and Jessamine Parsons experienced a most unfortunate collision. In the drawing room, where they stood shoulder to shoulder, Jessamine had misstepped and tilted her glass of sherry directly down the pale marigold silk front of Catriona's dress.

"Goodness, Kitty, I am ever so sorry!" she had cried out at once, flushing a becoming shade of rose. "How clumsy of me."

Bethany pressed her handkerchief ineffectually to the spreading crimson stain and said, "Shall I call for our maid to assist you?"

"No, please don't trouble her," Catriona said, stepping back quickly, having resigned herself to the need to change into another dress for the remainder of the evening. The marigold was amongst her favourites, and she was eager to hand it off to Emily to ensure it could be salvaged and the stain treated properly. "I'll head home and return presently."

"Don't be long," Jessamine said, reaching out to clasp her hands. "You'll miss the games, and it'll be my fault."

Catriona turned and made her way through the room, past a group discussing the respective merits of each rowing team, Cambridge versus Oxford. As she descended the stairs and passed the parlour, where the men were gathered over port, she saw Bancroft and several of his business associates, and he acknowledged her with a nod. She did not see Nate with his school friends at the card table across the room. Nor did she notice him rising to follow her until she had reached the foyer and he called out, "Kitty, hold on a minute."

The footman had already pulled open the door to the warm spring night. She turned to Nate. "You will all miss the tableaux if you don't head up soon, you know."

"I never much cared for the theatre," he said, coming to stand with her. His posture was relaxed, his necktie loosened. "Besides, I need some fresh air."

"Do you care to walk me home, then?" she said, stepping out. "I had an incident involving Jessamine Parsons and a glass of sherry."

"A plot to dispatch you as her rival, no doubt."

"Her rival!"

"For the wandering eye of every bachelor inside," Nate said. They had stepped down, crossed the street, and reached the footpath by the gardens. "Sorry. In vino veritas and all that."

"Drunkenness isn't an excuse for you to accuse the poor vicar's daughter of sabotage."

"No, and in fact, perhaps we should thank Miss Parsons for giving you an excuse to escape."

"Perhaps." She closed her eyes and breathed in the smell of roses from the trellises, the fresh green leaves of pines and birches.

"Let's take the path through, shall we?" Nate said, extending his arm, which she took as they stepped past the iron gate between the hedges. "I promise to resist the urge to chase you as once I might have done. Ah, where was that spot where we…?"

"Nate!"

"You're blushing."

"Am I?" she said, very conscious of his arm under her hand, solid and warm. "We were children. Surely you've had better kisses to think about since then."

"Yes, practice does make perfect."

"So they say."

He glanced down at her with a quick flash of his teeth, like a fox. "Why, would you like to confirm it?"

"Oh, whatever has got into you tonight? You are drunk."

"I'm not, really, I promise," he said, and she believed him. She had said it only to change the subject. "So what if I did want to kiss you?"

"One cannot get everything one wants," she said.

"Are you rejecting me?"

"No, we're simply not having this discussion."

He stopped, causing her to stop too. They were halfway across the gardens, far enough that the noise from the party was just a quiet murmur.

"Why-ever not?" he persisted.

"Because you're toying with me."

"I'm not, Kitty. I swear it."

"You are," she said. She pulled her hand from his arm and withdrew it to her chest. "Please don't deny it."

"What, do you think me incapable of genuine affection? I'm not a total rake, you know."

"Oh? You put on a fine act as one."

"It wounds me that you think so poorly of me."

She wanted to turn from him so he could not see her face and the stricken expression she felt she wore. The tone of their conversation had shifted so abruptly and unexpectedly that she was at a loss for words. "Stop," she said, taking a step backwards. "We're friends, are we not? You could have any girl you like, so don't ruin things just because you're bored tonight."

"I don't want anyone else," he said. He stood so near to her, taller than she remembered him, or perhaps she was only now noticing everything about him that she had forced herself to ignore—the perfect lock of ash-blond hair that had fallen across his forehead, or the sensuous curve of his mouth, or his eyes, dark and painfully sincere. "What do you wish me to say? Shall I tell you how fondly I feel for you? Shall I tell you I cannot stop thinking of you?"

"Oh, no, please don't." She felt a sensation akin to panic, as if some eventuality were hurtling towards her, and she must try at all costs to stop it.

"I love you, Kitty. I love you." He had breathed it out in a rush. "There, I've said it. Now don't push me away, because I couldn't bear it, not from you."

His fingers fluttered over her collar and then to the back of her head. She did not push him away. Her heart was pounding so quickly that she felt it through her dress, through the sticky stain where her hand was pressed to her chest. Almost lightheaded, she breathed in, and he leaned towards her, and his mouth closed over hers.

He was insistent, unhesitant. He had crossed the distance between them and was pressed to her, holding her tightly against him. Her thoughts, so accustomed to racing ceaselessly, had been silenced, and there was only the taste of port on his lips, and his strong hand in her hair, and flowers, flowers...

"Turner, are you out here?"

He pulled away at once. Someone had called out from the doorway, and she turned to see Sidney there, hand cupped to his mouth, peering out into the darkness. But they were hidden, shrouded in the shadows of the garden.

"The poker is starting, what?" Sidney continued.

"Just a minute," Nate called out, his voice rough. "Go ahead without me, please."

She closed her eyes as the door swung shut behind Sidney and the party noises quieted again. When she opened them, Nate was still there, a dark silhouette in front of her.

Just like that, the spell had been broken. She had become herself again, herself, the girl who had been reconciled to the knowledge that this could never be.

"Stop," she said. The word burst out of her. "Stop, Nate. We can pretend—yes, pretend this never happened, and everything can be exactly as it was, and we need not worry about it again."

He stepped back as if she had slapped him. "We need not worry about it?" he said, his mouth twisting. "I see. Because my affection is an inconvenience to you. No, I don't accept this. I know you feel as I do."

"I do care for you," she said. "I do."

"Do you not believe me to be sincere? I love you. I love you, damn it!" Something in him recalled their childhood, the remnants of a stubborn insolence, a sense of entitlement he had never outgrown.

"Please don't make this difficult," she said. "You know we would only resent each other. I would ask too much of you, and you would do the same of me."

"I can change, Kitty. I would do anything for you. Believe me, please. You know me." He had reached towards her, his fingers brushing her knuckles, but she flinched away.

"I do know you," she said, hearing herself as if from a distance. "I know you too well."

For the briefest second, his brow furrowed, and something keen and cold as a shard of ice lanced through his expression. Then his face was calm again. "I see. Fine. I won't trouble you any longer."

She immediately regretted all she had said. So what if she knew he would hurt her in the end? She could have him now, all of him, all she had ever wanted. But he was already looking back towards his house.

"Good evening, Kitty," he said, and he turned and walked away, leaving her standing there in the garden, flooded with the smell of roses, pressing her hand against her chest as if she could hold her heart in place.

Afterwards, when Nate had returned from Cambridge that June, they had not spoken of it again. But his confession had remained there between them in each glance, each passing touch. Even now, she despaired at the coldness with which he had regarded her as they parted at her doorstep that evening. In truth, she felt she had no one but herself to blame.

The clatter of a coach in the street shattered the silence, and she sat up and looked out across the square. It had slowed to a stop at the Turner residence, and out stepped Lord Ashford, his white hair glinting in the gaslight. From within the coach, a pale slender hand emerged, and he kissed it before backing away and watching as the coachman spurred on the horses and pulled off. The coach rounded the corner and disappeared at the street.

Catriona remained perched there in bed, looking out her window, until Ashford made his way inside and closed the door behind him, leaving the square below deserted again. Her papa had returned from their club several hours earlier that night, and she had assumed the two would have shared a cab home as they so often did. So what on earth was Ashford up to, returning at that ungodly hour, and who had that woman been?

It was certainly none of her business. But for reasons she could not have explained, the sight drew her interest. Perhaps, on that night, she was not the only one with a secret.

# CHAPTER 5

The next morning, as Catriona made her way to the dining room to join her papa for breakfast, she was thinking of Lord Stratton and his watery fate. Had he felt the cold seeping through his clothes but been powerless to save himself, or had he been unconscious and simply drifted off into that endless darkness?

"Good morning, Papa," she said.

Sir Frederick glanced up at her over his paper, the light from the window reflecting in his blue eyes, so unlike hers. He was still in his housecoat and appeared in no hurry to depart. "Morning, my dear. What dreadful weather we're having."

"Will you promise to take care today?" she said as she sat and poured herself tea. "I dislike the thought of you out and about in this cold."

"I suppose I have correspondence to catch up on, and in front of a fire in the study is as good a place as any," he replied with satisfaction.

"I am relieved to hear it, Papa," she said.

From behind her sounded the flapping of coattails as Hughes, their butler, swept into the room. "A letter for you, miss," he announced, presenting it on a small silver plate.

"Thank you, Hughes," Catriona said, taking it and snapping the seal. Having scanned it, she exclaimed, "Papa, it's from Lady Stratton! She thanks me for writing and asks that I call on her this afternoon at three."

"The poor girl must feel very much on the outs amongst her late husband's ilk," Sir Frederick said. "Will you go to her?"

"Of course. I must." Catriona set the letter down and resumed the preparation of her tea.

"I would certainly be interested to know what Stratton was up to in Limehouse that morning," Sir Frederick said, setting aside his paper. "Though, for all we know, he had been in the water since the night before."

"A shame I wasn't able to pry any information from Inspector Marlowe yesterday," Catriona said, though recalling the man had annoyance fluttering up inside her again. "Just narrowing down the time of death could help immensely in finding potential witnesses."

"Yes, I fear we may not have enough material for a follow-up story at this rate, at least not quickly enough to capitalise on the public's interest in the inquiry." Sir Frederick drummed the stack of papers beside him idly, and Catriona saw the cogs turning in his mind.

"Papa, let me see what I can learn today," she said. "I do not wish to abuse Lady Stratton's confidence, but she might at least point us in the right direction."

Sir Frederick gave the stack of papers a final decisive tap before saying, "I agree. You know, I sense there is some potential scandal here that the police are doing their part to keep under wraps. In fact, Ashford didn't even make an appearance at our club last night. Can you imagine?"

"Oh, indeed? I had thought…" She recalled the event of the previous night, the coach pulling up outside the Turner house, Ashford kissing the slim hand extended from within.

"It is quite unlike him," Sir Frederick said. "He did send a note, claiming he was needed at Scotland Yard until late, but I rather suspect he wanted to avoid the possibility of letting something slip after a few drinks."

Catriona sipped her tea to keep herself from speaking out of turn. Was it possible Ashford had lied to her papa regarding his whereabouts? The hand had been that of a woman, certainly no police colleague.

"Hmm. That is quite possible, Papa," she finally said. "I have wondered how someone so fond of gossip has made such a fine police director."

"Too true!" Sir Frederick gave a booming laugh. "Now, you must let me know what your visit with Lady Stratton reveals. And perhaps you might stop by our offices afterwards to fetch tomorrow's proofs for your dear papa?"

"Of course," Catriona said. "It would be my pleasure."

Like many amongst the peerage, the Strattons lived in the fashionable district of Piccadilly, a short walk from Brompton, notable for its dining establishments and other diversions. The stately houses loomed up from either side of the street, their dark windows reflecting the fog, and Catriona thought of Lady Stratton, in mourning in one such house, entirely alone.

She felt somewhat apprehensive at the idea of calling on her, and in truth, the invitation had surprised her. Following a death, social calls from anyone but intimate friends typically ceased until the funeral. Moreover, the two were hardly friends at all, having met only in passing since the Strattons' marriage the year before. But Lady Stratton's present predicament pulled a cord within Catriona's heart, and she felt sympathy for her, alone and far from home.

She had decided she would allow the conversation to flow naturally, though it was her hope Lady Stratton might reveal something of interest.

"Kitty, is that you?" came a voice from within the fog. A pale grey bonnet emerged, under which was a familiar person whose long blond hair was pulled back in a knot of plaits. "Goodness, what a dismal fog today."

"Beth, I hardly saw you there," she exclaimed. "What are you doing here?"

"Calling on Lady Stratton. Imagine my surprise to receive her invitation this morning. And you?"

The two had stopped on the footpath and stepped away from

the street, where fine carriages clacked past.

"The same," Catriona said. "Papa thinks she finds herself without friends. Shall we go in together?"

"I daresay the conversation will go easier with us both present," Beth said. She offered her arm, and Catriona took it. "If any grimness sets in, we can distract from it by asking after the baby. By all accounts, the new Lord Stratton favours his father."

"Poor little one, so young and already bereft of a parent," Catriona said.

Before long, they had reached the Stratton house. By the gate were stationed two police constables, who tipped their hats as the ladies passed and, Catriona thought, watched them carefully as they proceeded up the path. They were greeted at the door by a tall footman, who admitted them quickly and showed them through to the parlour. A second footman served tea and biscuits, and they waited.

The tea had cooled by the time the parlour door swung open to reveal Margaret Stratton, and Catriona and Beth rose as she entered and sat across from them.

"Thank you for coming," Lady Stratton said.

They lowered themselves back to the settee, and Catriona took a moment to observe the woman. She wore a black mourning veil, which she lifted to reveal her face to them. Catriona did not recall her being so plain in appearance, but then, the dismal parlour was a far cry from the events at which they had previously become acquainted.

"We were so sorry to hear of your loss, my lady," Beth said.

"Thank you, Miss Turner," she replied. She reached for her cup of tea on the low table but did not drink. "I was most touched by your notes of yesterday. You have been amongst the first to extend your sympathies."

"Perhaps some find it difficult to express themselves in the face of such a great tragedy," Catriona said.

Lady Stratton glanced towards the windows, over which the curtains were drawn. The parlour, lit only by gas wall sconces, was dim and stuffy. "No, I understand I am on the outs," she said. "People believe his lordship married below his station with me. It is true that my father made his fortunes on the financial markets, but the Stratton estate was in such dire shape."

She stopped and turned back as if expecting one of them to interrupt her, but they only listened. Catriona wondered whether she had spoken to anyone at all since her husband died.

"It was an advantageous match," her ladyship continued, "and we loved each other. But I suppose people have always been looking for an excuse to cast me aside, and now, with the rumours surrounding the circumstances of my husband's death, perhaps it might be best if I left London and returned to my family."

"My lady, you must not despair," Catriona said. "People take even the smallest and most unfounded hint of a scandal and run wild with it."

Lady Stratton folded her hands in her lap. Her face was pale, her eyes and nose an irritated red. "I know I must be strong, especially for my son. But I simply cannot bear the thought of having to face those who would besmirch my husband's name. Damn Atherton for putting us through this!"

A bolt of anger had struck her expression, and her voice had become shrill, but she withdrew into herself immediately, and her former placid tone returned. "Goodness, I am sorry. It was only the morning before last that this nightmare began, yet it feels as though a lifetime has passed. The police have been hounding me nonstop. What must the neighbours think? But—oh. Miss Turner, your father is… I do see why they must speak with me, of course."

"I understand, Lady Stratton," Beth said. "There's no need to explain. I expect my father has little direct involvement in the inquiry, but I'll speak with him on your behalf."

"I thank you," Lady Stratton said. "It's true what they say: In dark times, your true friends make themselves known."

Bethany sipped her tea delicately and rested the cup in its saucer. "Is there anything we might do for you, my lady? Perhaps you need help with the arrangements."

"You are most kind," Lady Stratton said. "In fact, I—don't quite know how to bring it up. It was something I wished to ask you, Miss Winters."

"Of course, anything," Catriona said.

"I read the papers that evening, all of them," Lady Stratton began. "His lordship never liked my doing so. I suppose he thought there was no use for it. But from the description of the scene where—where his body was found, I know enough to imagine what people must be saying. That he must have been engaging in improper behaviour."

Her hand had risen to the starched collar of her dress, and it trembled as she spoke. "I simply wish to know if… I am aware your father publishes the *Messenger*. Do you know, was there any indication at the scene that my husband had been engaged in something illegal or—or immoral?"

The question had caught Catriona off guard. Her immediate impulse was to deny it and spare Lady Stratton the angst of pondering it any further. But Marlowe had hinted that his lordship had been up to something unbecoming in the hours before his murder. Catriona decided against revealing that she had attended the scene herself, since Lady Stratton might find that distressing, but she felt she had to give her something.

"My lady, I do not wish to trouble you," she said carefully. "I really cannot say what business his lordship may have had in Limehouse. Perhaps he was simply in the wrong place at the wrong time."

Lady Stratton lowered her eyes. For a moment, Catriona was sure she had said exactly the wrong thing, but then her ladyship appeared to steel herself with a deep breath, and she raised her eyes again.

"You are kind to think of my feelings, madam," she said. Her hand had returned to her collar, but she dropped it. "In truth, the reason I ask is because…but I can trust you, can't I? I have a shameful secret, yet I must share it with someone. To say nothing would risk even more. It was only yesterday that I… Hold on a moment. I will show you."

She stood and left the room abruptly.

Bethany turned to Catriona on the settee, neither having had the chance to rise. "Kitty, this is rather thrilling," she whispered.

"Poor Lady Stratton. She is distraught."

"If anything has come from this," Beth said, "I know I must speak with my father about the lack of tact the police have shown. The woman is on the brink."

"Hush," Catriona said quickly, hearing footsteps in the hallway beyond. Lady Stratton returned, and they stood until she was seated again.

"Excuse me," she said. "I stowed this away amidst my personal things. I didn't know where to put it. I burned the others, but..." She handed Catriona a crumpled note. "I entered my husband's study yesterday. I wanted to feel close to him, I suppose. It was then that I saw this in the bin. There were several of them—scattered snippets, like drafts of a letter. But the contents, I don't know what to think."

Catriona smoothed the paper over her knee and lifted it. The hand was heavy, the ink splotched in places. She read aloud: "...And, so that no one should learn of this sordid scheme, I am sure you agree we must come to an arrangement."

Bethany started beside her. "My lady, this sounds like...was your husband being blackmailed?"

"No, that's the thing," Lady Stratton said, a small crease appearing on her brow. "The notes, this is his lordship's hand! I simply cannot imagine what could have spurred him to write such a vile threat. It's as if he were—yes, as if he were planning to blackmail someone."

"My lady, have you shown this note to anyone?" Catriona said.

"No," she replied, and her gloved hand twitched as if to retrieve it, but she stilled at once, and it remained in Catriona's hands. "I found it only yesterday and have kept it hidden since."

"And you burned any others?"

"Yes, there in the hearth," she said and gestured to the grate, though a housemaid had since cleared the ashes.

"The contents of this note may imply blackmail," Catriona said, "but perhaps there is an innocent explanation."

Although her eyes were dry, Lady Stratton delicately raised a handkerchief to each in turn as if on instinct. "I wish I could assume the best, but the truth is that I fear my husband may indeed have resorted to something desperate. Our financial affairs were in ruin. The fortune I brought to our marriage only delayed the inevitable. The estate is haemorrhaging cash, but my husband hesitated to sell it off piecemeal. On top of that, he had a gambling problem. He swore he would stop. He told me our trials would be over soon."

"My lady," Bethany exclaimed, "you aren't saying you believe his lordship could indeed have been blackmailing someone?"

"I am," Lady Stratton said with surprising decisiveness. "So you see, I have much to lose if this were to be made public."

"But is it not possible that his lordship didn't follow through with it?" Catriona said. "Perhaps he considered blackmail, began several drafts, then simply discarded them."

She imagined the scenario: Stratton, having come into possession of compromising information, paced in his study, deliberating how best to use it to his advantage. Admittedly, it was what she herself might have done, though she rather thought she would not have stooped to blackmail.

"My lady," she continued, "there is the question of whether

the police should be made aware of this note."

"No, I couldn't bear it!" Lady Stratton cried out at once. "If it were just my reputation at stake, it would be different, but I have my son to think of. A blackmailer for a father? No, I cannot allow the police to discover this note, even if it could help shed light on whoever killed my husband."

"You could burn it as you burned the others," Bethany said.

"I cannot," Lady Stratton said. Her voice, thin as a reed, had taken on a steely determination. "Although I fear what this note may suggest, I must know the truth. I must. I cannot simply pretend I never saw it."

Catriona folded the note back up and said, "How do you wish to proceed?"

"I wish none of this had happened," Lady Stratton said. "I wish to wash my hands of it and try to move on with my life for our son. So I must ask one of you to take the note until I decide what to do. Please, you must help me."

Bethany stiffened. "My lady, this note is evidence in a murder inquiry."

"I know so!" Lady Stratton said. Her pale brown eyes were vivid. "I know so more than anyone. But I cannot keep it. The police will want to search the house."

"I will take it," Catriona said. The words had burst out before she thought better of them. "I'll take it and—hide it somewhere, I suppose, until you know more."

Bethany laid a careful hand on her arm but said nothing.

"Thank you, Miss Winters," Lady Stratton said. "I cannot thank you enough, both of you. I have felt so alone these past two days."

"You aren't alone, my lady," Beth said. "We are in your corner."

"Yes," Catriona said. "I will do my best to find out more about the events of that morning for you, and I'll keep the note whilst the police are still about."

Lady Stratton rose, and Beth and Catriona followed suit. "Thank you again," she said. "I will see you to the door, and if I uncover anything further, I will reach out."

Upon departing, the two were relieved to emerge from the house, so heavy had been the atmosphere inside. They stopped on the footpath a distance away from the constables, and Beth shielded Catriona from their view as she tucked the note into her diary.

"Blackmail," Catriona whispered. "I can't imagine how Lady Stratton must have felt upon making such a discovery. But to whom might the note have been addressed?"

Bethany levelled her concerned dark eyes on her. "Kitty, perhaps it would be prudent to share this with the police," she said carefully.

"Who knows whether the note is even related to the crime?" Catriona replied very quickly. She knew Beth was right, yet she would not admit it now, having already decided on her course. "We're simply doing a favour for her ladyship, at least until we know more."

She felt Bethany would not push the matter. Unlike her brother, or perhaps because of him, she was a peacemaker by nature and deftly avoided even the slightest hint of interpersonal conflict. So Catriona was surprised when her friend reached out and grasped her firmly by the wrist. She was about to protest when Bethany glanced pointedly into the fog ahead of them, and Catriona immediately understood that the gesture had been a warning to fall silent on the matter of the note.

For out of the fog emerged a male figure whose grey eyes pierced her keenly.

"Miss Winters," Inspector Marlowe said, stopping on the footpath and removing his hat. "And Miss Turner. A remarkable coincidence."

# CHAPTER 6

"Inspector Marlowe," Catriona said. "Yes, remarkable indeed. What brings you to Piccadilly this afternoon? Coming to hound the grieving widow?"

The inspector glanced over to the constables instead of at her as he replied, which only infuriated her further. "No, madam. If you must know, I've come to apologise to her. I've learned some of the constables have been less than tactful in their handling of the inquiry so far."

"Oh," Catriona said—and then, unable to think of a way to soften her earlier sarcasm, "I see."

"I'm sure Lady Stratton will appreciate the gesture, Inspector," Beth said, extending a gracious smile. "In fact, I was going to bring up the matter with my father this evening. I am most relieved to learn it has been addressed."

"You've been visiting with her, then?" he said.

"Yes," Beth replied. "She's quite out of sorts, of course. I imagine she won't be up to speaking with the police for several days yet, at least not until after the funeral."

"I'll instruct the constables as such."

"Your understanding does you credit, Inspector." Beth turned towards Catriona and raised a delicate eyebrow. "But now, if you might both excuse me, I have an appointment with my seamstress for which I simply must not be late."

She was half turned from them already, and Catriona felt she was giving her the opportunity to escape if she wished. In truth, she did wish nothing more than to be away from the inspector as soon as possible, yet she had just promised Lady Stratton she would try to find out more about the inquiry. Perhaps this was her moment to do so.

"Miss Turner," Marlowe said, with the slightest nod, by way of farewell.

Beth grasped Catriona's hands, pressed a quick kiss to her cheek, and then turned to disappear down the street. As soon as she had, Catriona felt an almost irresistible urge to follow. What point was there in trying any further to coax information from such a man?

"Inspector, good evening," she finally said. "I am off to the newspaper offices."

He held a small envelope, and his attention was on the house—or rather, she thought, on the large reflective windows, over which the curtains remained drawn and through which no signs of movement could be observed. "Miss Winters," he said then, quite suddenly, "if you might wait a moment, I'll escort you. It's not far out of my way, as you know."

"Overcome by a fit of chivalry?" She could not help herself.

"You may reject the offer, of course, but let us not dance around the matter: I wish to know what you and Lady Stratton have spoken of."

"It was an obvious ulterior motive, Inspector. But fine. I shall wait."

"Just a minute, then," he said before proceeding up the steps.

The days were getting shorter, and dusk had already begun to descend over the early evening. Had her companion been anyone else, she might have been glad for the company in that oppressive darkening fog. As she waited, she held tight to her diary, which held a blackmail note that should rightly have been turned over to the police.

The inspector returned, having spoken briefly as well to the two constables at their place by the gate, and he and Catriona began down the street in an easterly direction. She expected him to begin questioning her at once, yet he did not. She glanced towards him to find that his gaze was firmly on the footpath ahead. To their right lay the vast dark expanse of Green Park, obscured by the fog.

"So," she said, "how does your inquiry progress?"

His reply was immediate. "I think not, madam. I will ask the questions this evening, so you may put away that diary of yours, curious though I may be as to its contents."

She sighed and tucked it into her reticule, then tensed. A most absurd thought had struck her: The inspector had sensed her deception and knew of the evidence she hid. That was impossible, of course.

"This is not a trap," he said. "I simply wish to hear how Lady Stratton is faring."

"She's distraught, as I'm sure you can imagine."

"Naturally," he said. "So you knew the deceased, as well."

"The deceased!" Her voice had risen an octave. "The man has a name."

"Of course," he replied quickly. "Forgive my insensitivity."

They had reached Leicester Square, a cacophony of coach wheels and nickering horses. Cutting a path through the crowds, they were illuminated as they passed under each lamppost.

His ready apology had taken her aback, even brought her guard down somewhat. Perhaps she could lessen her hostility towards him. After all, were their aims not aligned in that they both wished to see Stratton's killer apprehended?

"You are forgiven," she said finally. "I did indeed know him, and I became acquainted with his wife after she arrived in London last year."

"Miss Turner, as well? I was surprised to come across you both. You know her father is the director of my division."

"I am aware. Lord Ashford has been a dear friend of my papa since they served together in the Crimea. I gather bonds forged in combat are not easily broken."

He did not reply at once, and as the silence stretched out, she thought their conversation had ended. Then he said, "No, not easily."

"Have you served?"

"The navy, seven years."

They had passed through the square and into a narrow street, colder and quieter. Since that morning, a blanket of fog had insulated the city, and she had left her heavy overcoat at home. She drew her arms over one another and suppressed an involuntary chill.

"Did life at sea not suit you after all?"

"On the contrary," he said. "It suited me more than anything. I was invalided out."

"You were wounded?" she exclaimed, then clasped a hand over her mouth. "You must forgive me. I do not mean to pry."

He shot her a sidelong glance. "A bullet to the leg," he said. "At Amoaful. Not fatal, obviously, but it never mended."

A not uncomfortable silence fell upon them. She took the opportunity to observe the inspector somewhat more neutrally than she had before. He was no more than thirty, she thought, with a confident and unaffected bearing. Though his gait was slightly uneven, favouring his left leg, she would not have noticed ordinarily. Everything about him was stern, even in profile: the straight nose, the hard jaw.

Bethany was right. He was handsome—in a way.

She returned her gaze to the street ahead. They were halfway there, and she knew nothing she could share with Lady Stratton yet.

"So you found a role with the Birmingham City Police," she concluded. "And do you feel the same passion for your work now as you did then?"

"Passion?" He was no longer looking at her but ahead, expressionlessly. "I take pride in a case closed. Some might call that passion."

"Perhaps," she said.

"Miss Winters," he said, having turned to face her again, "I must advise you that if your enquiries yield anything of relevance, you are obligated, both legally and morally…"

"You need not apprise me of my obligations," she said, annoyed. "If I uncover anything, you shall be the first to know, I assure you."

It was a lie, of course, the first of many she would find herself telling over the coming weeks. Her enquiries had already yielded something: Stratton had likely been blackmailing someone, or at least planning to, in the days leading up to his death. She rationalised her deception with the excuse that she was simply protecting Lady Stratton until she could learn more. But what Beth had said earlier haunted her. Was it moral to hide such evidence from the police?

"Something the matter?" Marlowe said, and she realised she had stiffened, her hands having unconsciously tightened over her forearms.

"Just a bit chilly," she said.

"Then you must take my coat."

She nearly flinched away from him. "I couldn't possibly."

He had already removed it, wearing a fitted jacket underneath. "I insist," he said.

She regarded him before presenting her back, and he draped the coat over her shoulders. It was heavy and unfamiliar, and it warmed her almost immediately. They continued along the narrow street.

"Your determination to uncover the truth behind this murder is admirable," he began.

"But you intend to warn me off again?"

"Not per se. I must impress upon you the need to exercise caution. It is unlikely Stratton was set upon by an unknown assailant."

"You imply the killer is someone with whom he was familiar?"

"Yes," he said without hesitation. "The idea of a killer on the prowl in the East End may sell papers, but the reality is that murder is almost always a more intimate affair."

"A professional associate, then, or an acquaintance."

"Or a wife."

She bristled. "What a preposterous idea."

"You don't believe women capable of murder?"

"Is that why your constables have been circling poor Lady Stratton like a pack of wolves, because you have no other leads to speak of? You cannot seriously think she had anything to do with the crime."

"And why not? She need not have killed him directly. The two were arguing, he stumbled backwards into the river, and she left him there to drown."

She tried to picture it. In her mind, as she shoved her husband into the dark water, Lady Stratton was still the pale creature she had seen that morning. Had he cried out to her? Had she turned and left him there, unable to swim, weighted down by his fine clothes, until the river filled his lungs?

She recalled the morning at the docks, the wine-dark stain of blood over the planks nearest the water.

"So drowning was the cause of death?" she said. "His entering the river was prefaced by some act of violence, an act of which I believe Lady Stratton to be incapable."

"True, the man was injured before hitting the water. But whether the crime was murder or manslaughter, it does not rule out his wife as a suspect."

"You and I will not see eye to eye on this, Inspector," she said, a stubborn annoyance rearing its head within her yet again. "And if she is your primary suspect, your inquiry is on poor footing indeed."

"I do not suggest she is our primary suspect."

"So why bring the possibility up at all? The idea that she was involved in her husband's death is inconceivable to me."

"Perhaps I simply wish to hear your opinion on the matter," he said.

"You have placed a great deal of trust indeed in my ability to judge her character, in that case."

"You feel my trust is misplaced?"

"No. Only you surprise me, as you have shown no inclination till now to place any value whatsoever in my judgement."

"Then you have misunderstood me," he said.

"You have given me little on which to base my understanding of you, so the blame is yours," she returned.

"Fine," he said immediately. "I accept it. Regardless, something is rotten in Limehouse, and Stratton almost certainly got caught up in it." He turned to her and said gravely, "Hence my warning to you, madam. You must tread carefully."

They had reached Covent Garden, at the centre of which stood the market. Porters carried towering stacks of baskets on their heads holding fruit, vegetables, and flowers in and out of the main structure, a row of buildings over which, earlier in the century, great steel arches had been erected to brace a glass roof. Like the *Messenger*, Covent Garden had reformed itself, having once been known for its wide selection of brothels. Now it served as a hub of commercial activity for the working and middle classes alike.

"Inspector, may I ask what has brought you to London?" Catriona said, stepping aside for a small boy towing a cart of straw. "Lord Ashford implied he had a personal hand in your secondment."

"Did he? I couldn't say."

"Surely you could, but you don't wish to."

"You're right," he said. "The prospect of preserving the mystery is too tempting to pass up."

They proceeded through the square and onto the quieter Southampton Street, heading in the direction of the Strand. She did not have to guide him.

"Do you take pleasure in frustrating my curiosity?" she said.

"Am I the object of your curiosity?" he returned.

An altogether unexpected frisson jolted through her. Aside from his accent, she thought, he had a pleasant voice.

"Don't change the subject, please," she said. "Why London, and why now?"

"Perhaps Lord Ashford wanted some fresh insight. The city is smaller than it appears."

"I should not have asked. Your cryptic answer has merely intensified my interest in the matter."

He glanced down the lane at the corner of which, rising three storeys above the street, was the *Messenger* building. "Here we are."

"Oh. Yes, here we are," she said. She felt put out suddenly and did not know why. "Thank you for the company. And for the use of your coat."

"Think nothing of it," he said as she turned and allowed him to remove it from her, whereupon the cold night suffused her again. "If anything of interest arises, Miss Winters, I trust you know where to find me."

"I do," she said, "and I will."

He draped his coat over his arm and turned to continue down Southampton Street, after which she gathered he would proceed southwest along the Strand towards Scotland Yard. Small flakes of snow had begun to drift down in the lamplight, but instead of heading inside immediately, she remained on the doorstep, watching as Marlowe disappeared into the fog at the end of the street.

Their conversation had left her disconcerted. He had confirmed her suspicion that Stratton had been killed or at least seriously injured before entering the water, but how did that fit with everything else she knew?

The scandalous note remained secreted away in her diary. Had Stratton met with the object of his blackmail that morning or even the night before only for that person to turn on him in a murderous rage? How could she determine when Stratton had written the note? More to the point, she had only the word of his wife, herself apparently a suspect in the killing, that the note was written in his own hand.

At last, she turned to head in, aiming to pick up the proofs for her papa before returning home for the night. The office would likely be empty at that hour, the reporters sharing a few rounds at one of many local public houses. She did not plan to encounter much in the way of distractions.

# CHAPTER 7

As Catriona headed up, still mulling over her walk with the inspector, light spilling into the stairwell alerted her to a presence in the office. She ascended the final step to see him clearly through the long corridor window: Nate, alone in the bullpen, his hair golden in the lamplight, adjusting the lens of a camera. As she entered, his head snapped up, and his lips parted when he saw her.

"Oh," he said. "Good evening."

"Good evening. Sorry to intrude."

"It was your office first, Kitty." He had bent to the camera again, his face obscured by the accordion fabric between the brass-mounted lens and the back panel of wood, which held a glass plate.

"Regardless," she said, "please do continue with whatever it is you were doing."

She proceeded past him into her papa's office, where she found the stack of proofs set neatly at one corner of his desk. She intended to take them and leave immediately.

"And what has you out so late?" Nate said, still adjusting the lens.

"Nothing at all that should concern you."

"I heard about your little investigation, you know."

"Could you sound more patronising?"

"Could I?" He rose to look at her. "I'm actually intrigued, truly. It's not every day someone gets murdered, especially not a fop like Stratton."

"You might speak more respectfully about the dead."

"Yes, well, the man was obviously no saint," he said, focussing on the camera again. "Anyway, I know you're secretly thrilled at the prospect of uncovering whatever scandal lies behind the incident."

"You think you know me so well, hmm?"

"On the contrary," he said. "I don't presume to think I know you at all anymore."

She stopped in spite of herself. Alone in the office, he had removed his jacket, and he had not put it on again when she entered. His sleeves were rolled up to his elbows, his necktie loose around his collar. She looked away.

"As much as I've missed our mutual acerbity," she said, "I have better things to do than linger in the office tonight. Do close up when you leave."

"And here I was," he said, "thinking you might offer to keep a new colleague company as he slaves away."

"I suppose such an offer would depend on how interested I am in whatever you're slaving away on."

"How do you like having your picture taken?"

"As in a portrait?"

"Not quite as dull as that," he said, then gestured to the desk between them. "Here. Sit in front of me."

"Fine, but I hardly think I make a good subject," she said, gathering her skirts to perch on the desk.

He had bent to the camera again. "It's just a test to see whether I need to adjust the emulsion."

"All right, like this?" she asked, folding her hands in her lap.

"Yes, like that," he said, peering into the glass.

Something about facing the camera felt imposing, as if he were appraising her. She straightened her back and raised her chin, looking into the lens, knowing she was looking into his eyes. Her body felt pulled as tight as a bowstring.

"Relax, would you?" he said. He closed the distance between them, and his fingers brushed her neck as he tucked a loose curl of her hair behind her ear. "Perfect." His voice was low even though they were alone in the office. "Now look at me and hold still until I say so."

He stepped back and lifted the covering from the lens, and she tried to keep still despite the slow shock descending throughout her body from the point where he had touched her. What was likely only a few seconds seemed to stretch into an eternity.

"All right, done," he said. "Thanks for that."

She pushed herself off the desk at once. "How do you know

whether it worked?"

"I suppose I'll find out when I develop the plate. I took some others today, as well, when the light was better, though the fog was somewhat of an impediment."

"Coming back to the London particular must be a shock after your time in the country."

"The air was certainly clearer there," he said. "But London has its attractions."

She looked away from him, towards the windows, through which, in the street below, a light dusting of snow had covered the cobblestones. "Well, I am ever so curious to see the finished product."

"I was planning to work in the darkroom for a while this evening," he said. "You may accompany me if you promise to keep distractions to a minimum."

"God forbid I distract an artist from his work." She had meant to tell him no and be off, but instead she heard herself saying, "Lead the way, then."

She followed him to the darkroom, a small annex off the bullpen which had previously been used for storage. With no window, it was perfect for its new purpose, fitted with a long table against each wall, shelves of various chemicals, and a sink with a cold-water tap.

"Light that lamp there, will you?" Nate said. "The one with the red glass."

As she did so, casting the room in a peculiar devilish glow, he closed the door and proceeded to one of the tables. Into three shallow basins, he poured a series of solutions that smelled strongly of vinegar, but not unpleasantly so.

"Shall I explain the process?" he said. He had lowered the glass plate into one of the basins and allowed the liquid to slide over it as he tilted it back and forth. "We submerge the exposed plate in a developing solution, which reduces the silver halide of the coating emulsion, thus revealing the negative image."

She stood near him, watching over his shoulder. "How long does it take?"

"Only a minute or so."

She was silent as he worked. It was strange to her, seeing this side of him—focussed, skilled. Despite the chill outside, the darkroom was warm and close.

"Is that Westminster Bridge?" she said. An image had begun to swim into view on the glass, a series of pale arches.

"Looks like this one turned out all right," he said. Having removed the plate from the solution, he submerged it into the second basin, then into the third. "We cease the development by rinsing the plate in a stop bath. Lastly, we fix it in a solution of sodium thiosulfate to prevent the unexposed silver from fogging the image over time. Then we wash it to remove any remaining chemicals, and the negative is ready for print."

She followed him to the sink and watched as he ran the plate under the water. "May I see?"

He held it out to her and turned back to rinse his hands. "I'll do yours next."

As he returned to the table, she studied the photograph. It was a negative, as he had said, but it was still striking. She had crossed the bridge hundreds of times without stopping to admire it. Yet the image disturbed her too. Perhaps it was the way the structure receded into the fog, or the stillness of the water below, which recalled to her the body of Lord Stratton lying under that tattered sheet at the docks.

She set the plate down on the table as Nate rinsed off the second. When he was finished, he turned it to show her, and she recoiled.

"Oh, is that really me?" she said. "I look like a ghost."

He shot her an intolerable smirk before turning away. It was the starkness of the negative image that had startled her, he must have thought. But it was something else entirely, a resemblance to that dreary photograph of her mama. She forced herself to stop thinking of it at once.

Catriona perched against the opposite table and watched Nate as he began working intently on a third plate. Something about this reminded her of his first few visits home from Harrow, when he had suddenly known all sorts of interesting things about the world and the way it worked. Though they were still children, she had already felt him slipping away from her.

Her knowledge had been limited to the lessons she and Beth shared with a governess, the eldest daughter of an embarrassed earl. But Latin and household arithmetic, even practising the pianoforte and painting watercolours in the afternoons, had not compared to what Catriona suspected Nate was learning away from her. She had resented and envied him for it, all the while yearning to be in his presence whenever he was gone.

"You can send it off to old Hampstead, if you like," Nate continued mildly, shooting a glance at her over his shoulder. He meant the photograph, she realised. "He'll make good use of it, I'm sure. How is he, anyway?"

"Splendid," she said. "Enjoying life in Boston very much, he tells me."

"But not so much that the engagement is off?"

"There was no engagement, as you well know. Anyway, his work takes up the vast majority of his time. He has ambition, unlike some."

"Yes, ambition—that greatest of aphrodisiacs." He had gone to the sink, still turned from her. She wished she could see his face. "Do you love him?"

"I don't see what business that is of yours. Besides, we make a fine match."

"Since when did you care about a fine match?"

"Forgive me for having practical concerns about my future," she said. "We can't all aspire to traipse around taking pictures."

"Now you're just trying to change the subject by riling me up," he said, and it was true.

"Because I don't want to argue about Sidney," she said. "You were right before, when you admitted you don't know me."

As he turned the tap off and faced her, the red lamplight flickered strangely in his eyes. "I know you're not going to be content as an industrialist's wife," he said. "I know you want a little more than that."

She said nothing in reply, but he moved closer, so close that she could have reached out to touch him, so close that she could feel the heat radiating off him in the dim confines of the room—so close that if she simply stepped forwards…

"If this interrogation is over, I'm leaving," she said, then pushed herself away from the table and away from him. "Good evening. I have my little investigation to get back to."

"Fine," he said, and as she left the room, she imagined the corners of his lips curling as he remarked from behind her, "Good evening, Inspector."

Catriona sat in bed in her nightdress, her legs tucked up under her as she leaned towards the lamp and read the letter that had arrived for her that evening. It was as if Sidney had heard her and Nate talking about him, she thought. But as much as she loved hearing about his escapades, she was distracted. Her thoughts kept returning to the scene at the docks and to the blackmail note tucked into her diary, about which she had not told Marlowe.

She felt it most probable that the victim of the blackmail had been involved in killing Lord Stratton, either directly or by enlisting someone else to carry out the deed. But whilst she now had information about the case that the police did not, it was not useful to her, at least not until she knew more. And the possibility that Lady Stratton had been involved in the murder, as the inspector suggested, had shaken her.

She doubted very much that her ladyship had killed her husband. Surely one could detect a murderous inclination from certain mannerisms—a glint in the eye, a sinister turn of the features? When she thought of the frail woman she had seen that day, made small by her great black mourning veil, she thought she did not have it in her. Yet Lady Stratton was reluctant to speak with the police, a reluctance which, Catriona conceded, could perhaps stem from deep guilt. Could she have known about the blackmail beforehand or even encouraged her husband in it?

She turned away from Sidney's letter, the last sentence of which she had read several times without absorbing any of the words, and glanced to the window. Her papa was at his club that night, and across the square, the Turner house was dark. A thought was nagging at her. That Monday morning, she had seen Lord Ashford questioning a woman outside the boarding house by the docks. They had been deep in conversation—about something she had seen with relation to the crime?

Catriona acknowledged that she must return to Limehouse. She had known as much for some time. She wished to speak with the boarders who had been present that morning, and she regretted not going earlier. Sailors must come and go from such places frequently, she thought, and perhaps any witnesses had already set sail for their next port of call. She could not waste any more time, yet as she recalled that cold river lapping wetly against the docks, and the shrouded narrow laneways in which one could disappear without a sound, she understood she would be unwise to venture into the East End alone.

Outside the gardens were dark and quiet, blanketed in a thin white snowfall, and the lamplight of the square ascended into the bare branches. She was not cold, but she drew her blanket closer. She felt a profound sense of loneliness. How unfair it was! Sidney was off having adventures in America whilst she was too cautious to chance another visit to the docks. She was intensely jealous of him, knowing that were he in her place, he would have gone to Limehouse without hesitation. In fact, were he still in London, she would have solicited his help.

# CHAPTER 8

The following morning, Catriona sat poised at her writing desk, pen in hand. She had awoken filled with an almost electric certainty as to her proper course of action. First, after their visit with Lady Stratton, she hoped Beth might be willing to participate in her enquiries. It was to her dearest friend Catriona would turn to accompany her on her visit to Limehouse.

Second, she dutifully wrote back to Sidney, and what interesting news she finally had to share. There was more to her letter than her journalistic ambitions, of course: She wrote about the unseasonable cold and the antics of their garden foxes, and what did he think of the latest instalment of *The Trumpet Major*? Nothing at all of consequence, but it was only polite to touch on such pleasantries.

Having signed the letter with a flourish, she sealed it in an envelope and headed quickly to the post office to mail it off. The day had dawned bright and clear, the snowfall of the night before having driven away the persistent fog. As she trekked along the footpath, she tried to avoid submerging her boots in the filthy slush that accumulated with the passing of carriages on the road. So focused on her next step was she that she did not see Lord Ashford until she nearly collided with him, also heading towards the street from the opposite side of the square.

"Catriona, good morning!" he exclaimed, reaching out to steady her. She took his assistance gratefully, resting a hand in the crook of his arm, and they proceeded along the footpath together. Ashford cut a tall, striking figure, and he weaved them around morning passers-by easily as they reached Pelham Street.

"Are you in to town today?" she asked him.

"Yes. This is an awful business with Lord Stratton." His mouth curled in distaste. "We hope to make some progress in the case soon, or so I hear."

"Indeed?" she said. "I had occasion yesterday to converse at some length on the subject with Inspector Marlowe."

"Oh? I am glad to hear it. He is new to the city, as you know, and likely in need of pleasant company."

"Whether he finds my company pleasant is debatable," she said. "Nonetheless, he is a competent conversationalist."

If Ashford perceived the strange turn in her voice as she spoke of the inspector, he did not mention it. "I hope we have made a good impression on him so far," he said. "He comes highly recommended by an old colleague in the Midlands, and these days, the

Yard needs every detective it can muster."

"To investigate the murder, you mean?"

"Not only that."

"You are being very secretive, my lord."

"You know I quite like a bit of intrigue every now and then," he said. "Rest assured, it's nothing with which you need concern yourself."

"Of course not," Catriona said, thinking she very much would concern herself with it. "Then I shall simply congratulate you on your acquisition of him and keep my questions to myself."

They had rounded the corner to the main thoroughfare, where shopkeepers were setting out their signs and newspaper boys were hawking the morning editions.

"There are detectives whose minds are less inquisitive than yours," Lord Ashford said, patting her arm affectionately. "As a man, you might have done well in the police. But I know your papa would never have traded you for a son."

"I should rather hope not," Catriona said. "I daresay I will find a way to put my mind to use nonetheless."

"I do not doubt it." Lord Ashford chuckled, then fell into an uncharacteristic silence. "I suppose life takes us in directions we do not anticipate. I had high hopes for my own son, and now here we are."

Catriona looked up at him. His face was stony, his dark eyes inscrutable. Privately, she often wondered whether the idea that Nate should leave London that past summer had come from him or his father. Of Bethany, Ashford was endlessly proud, even indulgent, but ever since Nate had returned from Cambridge, his father's demeanour towards him had been marked by a distinct and determined coldness. Was that how all fathers eventually treated their sons? Catriona had no way of knowing.

"Perhaps you are too hard on him," she ventured gently.

His expression relaxed as he glanced at her. "Darling Catriona, you wouldn't say that if you…" He gave his head an almost imperceptible shake, and she felt he had been on the verge of revealing something. He again patted her arm before continuing: "You always have been a good friend to my son. Might I ask that you continue to exert your good influence? He will not always have me here to look out for him, you understand."

"Come now," she said. "I don't wish for us to speak of such things."

"No, of course not," he said. They had reached the train station, and their parting was imminent. "But thank you for indulging my sentimentality."

Catriona knocked at the Turner house and was admitted by Arthur to wait in the foyer beside a bouquet of freshly cut pink cabbage roses and cedar leaves. A gift from Bancroft to his fiancée, she suspected—and flowers were the perfect gift, irreproachable and chaste. What might it be like to receive flowers, she wondered? A sensation akin to envy pierced her keenly at the realisation that there existed a realm of experiences about which Beth perhaps knew and she did not.

She pushed the feeling down at once. Arthur had yet to re-emerge from the back stairs, which, as in her own home, descended to a basement which held a kitchen, pantry, scullery, laundry, and servants' hall. She suspected Beth was still abed, although it was not so early in the morning, and the footman was most likely seeking out a maid to enquire. But no sooner had she resigned herself to leaving a note than Beth emerged in her wrapper at the top of the staircase, her pale hair still curling loose to her waist.

"Kitty, I thought that was you I heard," she said. "Come and join me in the drawing room, and I shall have some tea brought up."

Catriona did so, sitting beside her on the long settee facing the window. Unlike her home, which she felt was distinctly masculine in decor, Sir Frederick having acquired the property after they returned from St Lucia and spent very little time furnishing and decorating it, the Turner house was styled per the preferences of Beth and Nate's mother. Lady Ashford had died of consumption four years prior, but the withdrawing room, with its pale yellow wallpaper and framed watercolour paintings, would ever remind Catriona of the dear lady she had respected and loved.

"Forgive me for barging in on you," she said as one of the maids came in with the tea and set it on the low table in front of them, "but I have a matter of some urgency to discuss."

"Thank you, Anna," Beth said, then waited until the maid had left the room. She poured two cups, handed one to Catriona, and toed her slippers off so she could tuck her legs up under her on the cushion.

"No need at all to apologise," she said. "I was tempted to accompany Nate to your office this morning, so curious was I to hear what happened yesterday after I abandoned you in Piccadilly with that dashing inspector."

Catriona did not precisely agree with this use of the word 'dashing', but she withheld her protest, and Beth continued with a little sigh.

"But you know how unbearable I find it to rise from bed so early," she said, "so to have you delivered to my doorstep is good fortune indeed. Now, go on and tell me everything."

"Sorry to say, but there is precious little to tell," Catriona replied. "The main thing, which I found most disconcerting, was that Inspector Marlowe wished to know whether I thought Lady Stratton capable of murder. Can you imagine?

"I suppose they have to exhaust all avenues," Beth said. "But, what, does he think she threw him into the river herself?"

"He as much as confirmed Lord Stratton met some act of violence on the docks, then was left to drown. I wonder if his attacker did not have the heart to finish him off?"

"Surely they have other leads, in that case," Beth said with a wave of her hand. "The docks are rarely deserted, from what I hear. A little shove into the water is one thing, but to be struck, or stabbed? How grim—but someone must have seen or heard something."

"Those are my thoughts also," Catriona said. "In fact, that is the matter I have come to discuss. I wish to return to investigate the scene more fully. There was a boarding house nearby, and I feel I might seek out potential witnesses there. I wondered if you might come with me."

As she spoke, Beth's expression had alternated in rapid succession between concerned, incredulous, and scandalised.

"To Limehouse?" she cried out, then glanced quickly to the doorway behind her. But Anna had already descended the stairs, and they were alone. She swung her feet back to the floor decisively and lowered her voice to a whisper as she said, "I certainly cannot let you go alone. But we must be discreet about it. If Henry found out, not to mention Papa, I would never hear the end of it."

Not having expected her to say yes without a great deal of coaxing, Catriona had not thought any further ahead and had no plan as to how they might proceed.

"We must go during daytime," Beth continued quickly, as if she had already given the matter some thought, "and you are in luck, because my afternoon is marvellously free."

The docks felt much different without the oppressive fog which had greeted her on her last visit, Catriona thought as she and Bethany picked their way through a throng of horse-drawn carts and stevedores unloading cargo from the wharfs to the south. White sunlight pierced icily through the sparse clouds overhead, and the cold had already numbed the tips of her fingers through her gloves.

Through Regent's Canal, a steady stream of barges made their way into the Limehouse Basin. Unlike on the morning the body had been discovered, the district was bustling. To blend in with the crowds, both ladies wore walking dresses in muted colours, and Beth had concealed her distinctive hair with a substantial bonnet. Catriona felt the risk of being recognised was low, but Beth had assured her that whilst Bancroft typically kept to his offices on the Strand, he did occasionally oversee practical business at the docks, and her vise-like grip on Catriona's arm betrayed her misgivings.

"Stay close, Kitty," she said as the two approached the boarding house, which overlooked the basin to the west and the Limehouse Cut to the south. "I keep thinking back to what Henry said about criminals in the district."

"I have the impression people here are simply doing their best to get by," Catriona remarked.

She had said it because she felt it was the charitable thing to say, but the district was indeed scarred by poverty. In the Middle Ages, Limehouse had taken its name from local kilns which processed limestone into quicklime. But with the rising importance of maritime transport over the previous century and the construction of the Regent's Canal dockyards, the place had quickly become home to communities of foreign sailors, the Lascar and Chinese crews of merchant ships. Catriona could not help but feel as if she were an intruder, peering in upon the lives of others less fortunate than she, all the while knowing she had the privilege to leave whenever she wished.

"I cannot believe Lord Stratton was so irresponsible," Beth said quietly. "A married man loitering about the docks? If not his own reputation, he might at least have thought of his wife."

"Is his behaviour so unusual?" Catriona remarked. "Husbands get into mischief and their saintly wives pretend they do not see it."

"Does that thought not bother you?" Beth said. "If you found out Sidney had been getting up to that sort of thing…"

"We hardly know what sort of thing Lord Stratton was getting up to," Catriona said quickly. "Anyway, Sidney would never."

"You seem quite sure of that."

"I am. Predictability is a virtue he possesses in spades."

"Ah, would that someone might one day think so highly of my brother as you do of Sidney," Bethany said.

"Perhaps you need not worry so much about Nate," Catriona said. "He seems to be settling in fine at the paper."

"You know how he was before he left, Kitty," Beth said. "I suppose I simply suspect he might fall back into old habits."

An uncharacteristic expression had come over her, and Catriona felt the same odd apprehension she had felt whilst conversing with Ashford that morning. She sensed Beth wished to say something further, but she did not want to push, so they lapsed into silence, re-tracing her steps down the laneway to the arch where she had seen Ashford speaking with a woman the morning of the murder. Despite the bustle they had just left behind, the courtyard beyond the stone arch was deserted, and the cloudy windows of the boarding house revealed no movement within. But then, she suspected such places provided little more than a meal and a bed at the end of the day.

"Through here," she said.

Bethany suddenly grasped her arm and whirled towards the laneway from which they had come. "Shh, did you hear that? Footsteps."

Catriona peered into the shadowed brick laneway. Beyond its

mouth were the crowded docks, but the street on which they stood was still deserted.

"Come," she said, nudging Beth to precede her through the archway. "If someone is trailing us, he can't be so bold as to follow us inside."

The door of the boarding house swung open easily to a dimly lit room. Thick smoke assaulted her, not altogether unpleasant but heavy, like incense. An opium den! She could scarcely believe it. Marlowe had been hinting at something after all with his mention of vice. Stratton had been murdered mere steps from a den of iniquity.

The figures within barely glanced up at their entrance, so accustomed must they have been to the comings and goings at the place. Those Catriona could make out in the light had the appearance of sailors and dockworkers—all except one, a distinguished older woman perched just beyond the entryway, the very woman Ashford had questioned.

"Good day, ladies," she said, her voice pleasant, lightly accented, but wary.

"Good day," Catriona said, stepping forwards, "and please forgive our intrusion. I am a journalist with the *Messenger*, and I have some questions about the events of Monday morning. I believe you know to what I refer."

"I do," the woman said without expression. "A journalist, you say? Please wait here."

She disappeared at once behind a mass of sheer curtains which fluttered in her wake. As the two waited for her to return, Catriona stepped further into the close heat of the den.

"Kitty, no," Bethany said, reaching out towards her, but Catriona slipped her grasp.

"Just for a second," she said.

Away from the door, the air was still, and the sweet stickiness of it lingered in her throat. The further she advanced, the more oppressive became the silence and the heat, and the more grotesque seemed the figures sprawled out about the room, their mouths slack, faces gaunt, eyes bleary. From cushions in the far corner, a lone Malay looked up and through her. Did his dreams transcend the misery of the East End, she wondered, and return him to a faraway home?

She wished to turn back, but something possessed her to continue, passing one silk curtain after another until she was surrounded, and her vision swam with a strange lightness. Gone was the den. She had been transported back to St Lucia, to the innocence of her childhood. The sun shone over her face once more, heat tickling the springy curls at the back of her neck, thousands of cicadas droning from the trees. The stuccoed house of her memory overlooked Castries and the yawning mouth of the bay below, and even the cries of the birds welcomed her home.

But behind it all was the opium smoke, and behind that was the smell of rain and wet earth, a looming tropical storm, the ugly eventuality of that night on the ridge, when her mother had stood beside her, her dark curls loose and streaming in the wind. The steady lapping of the Thames had transformed into waves thrashing against the face of a cliff—a cliff over which she must never look.

She could not go back there. She could not bear it.

Catriona reached out to hold on to something but found only empty air. Smoke filled her lungs. Strong arms encircled her then, but it was too late. Her feet had found the infinite height at the edge of the ridge, and the storm rushed through her ears as she tumbled endlessly towards the jagged rocks, the white seafoam, the fathomless deep blue below.

# CHAPTER 9

"Kitty, wake up."

Someone had grasped her firmly by the shoulders and was shaking her, and the fog which had descended over her lifted altogether, leaving her awake and shivering as though dredged up from deep water. She had forgot where she was, but it came back to her quickly: an opium den in Limehouse, trying to track down witnesses to the murder of Lord Stratton.

Lamplight illuminated Beth in a halo, perched on the divan beside where Catriona lay. Behind her, like a panther, someone emerged from the shadows.

"If I may interject," he said.

Catriona shot up, and black spots immediately flooded her vision. He had stepped forwards into the lamplight. He was Chinese, she thought, fashionably dressed and exceedingly handsome, his hair tied up in a knot.

"Apologies," he said. "I didn't mean to startle you. Victor Tsang, proprietor of this establishment, at your service."

"Then I have some questions for you," Catriona said.

"Now, now," Tsang said. "I know not who you are, and we have no one to introduce us."

"My name is Catriona Winters," she said, "with the *Messenger*, and this is—my colleague."

Bethany shot her a look. Catriona had luckily thought better of introducing her, but her creative wits had momentarily deserted her.

"Colleagues? How charming," Tsang said flatly. "In that case, what business has brought you to the docks?"

"The business of murder, sir," Bethany said.

"Namely," Catriona added quickly, "the murder of Lord Stratton, which took place on your doorstep Monday morning."

"Ah." His mouth twisted. "That unfortunate affair."

"Quite so," she said. "I have reason to believe someone at this establishment, or several someones, may have witnessed something pertaining to the crime."

"My associate has already spoken with the police about this," he said. It was a dismissal, but he did not turn to leave.

"I am not the police," she replied.

"No, you are not," he said, surveying her intensely. "And let it not be said that I play favourites, so I shall repeat the information for your sake. A confrontation was overheard late Sunday night, perhaps early Monday morning, out by the docks, between his lordship and someone else."

"And?"

"And that was that. No one saw or heard anything else. I gather he shuffled off this mortal coil sometime afterwards."

"The other party to the confrontation, was that person male or female?" she said. "And—hold on. How could you be sure it was Lord Stratton you overheard?"

"I don't recall saying it was I who overheard him. Stratton is known generally to those at this establishment. His voice was recognisable."

"And the subject of the argument?"

"I could not say."

"But you confirm Lord Stratton visited this place regularly."

"Madam, do read between the lines. You cannot expect me to say so."

"I see," Catriona replied. She was acutely disappointed, as though he were a lock and she could not find the right key to open him up.

"Now, as pleasant as it has been to find myself in your company, you must excuse me," Tsang said. "I have further business to attend to this evening. Please feel free to stay and continue your investigation, however. On the house."

He turned to leave, and a sensation akin to panic prompted her to rise and pursue him.

"Mr Tsang, wait," she said. As he stilled in the doorway, she closed the distance to him and reached into her reticule. "Please take my card. If you think of anything you wish to share, I should be most grateful."

He took it, and his eyes raked over her. "Madam, I can think of several things I should wish to share with you if given the opportunity."

A fierce heat flooded her face.

He continued: "But perhaps you could answer a question for me first. In the smoke, what did you see?"

She searched for the hint of a trap in his eyes, as dark as ink, but she could discern nothing. In truth, it was a question she was unwilling to answer even to herself. For in the depths of the opium smoke, she had come face to face with the darkness she had been fleeing since her earliest memories, the darkness she and her papa had crossed an ocean to outrun.

She stepped back. "I shall answer your question when you truly answer mine."

"Ha!" He had laughed as if surprised, and she felt the reaction was genuine. "I expect we'll meet again, madam. Good evening."

He departed through the curtains, and she felt Beth draw near behind her. She had not got any answers at all. In fact, she had more questions now than upon arriving at the den. But, like a dowsing rod tipping towards the earth, the necessary direction of her inquiry had been made clear.

"Such an intriguing man," Bethany said. "Do you get the sense he was hiding something?"

"I do, but what?"

"Perhaps he does know who killed Lord Stratton."

"Perhaps," Catriona said. "He knows more than he lets on.

That much is certain."

Her wits returned, she took in her surroundings. The pale rose divan on which she had lain was threadbare but clean. She and Beth were in a private rear alcove curtained off from the other patrons, lit by a lone paraffin wall sconce, but the sounds of the den carried through: quiet murmurs in foreign languages, floorboards creaking under shifting bodies, long crackling inhales through slender ceramic pipes.

"We ought to leave," Bethany said. "This place gives me an awful feeling. You were lucky, earlier. Mr Tsang caught you before you fell."

"Oh, I wish you hadn't told me that. How embarrassing."

"He was quite gallant about it, actually. Most brusque, but gallant nonetheless."

"Then let's leave before I cause any further harm," Catriona said, "to our persons or dignity."

The docks were dark when they emerged into the damp air. Recalling Beth's suspicion that they had been followed, they moved quickly to leave Limehouse behind, but even in the chill evening, Catriona could not shake the heaviness of the opium smoke. It had nestled into her clothes, her hair, and the deepest recesses of her mind.

"Kitty, are you all right?" Beth said. "You look as though you've seen a ghost."

"Oh," Catriona said. "I'm terribly sorry to have frightened you earlier. I had no idea the smoke would have such an effect."

"Mr Tsang mentioned it can cause visions."

"I did see—or I thought I heard…"

"Yes?"

"My mama," she said, and immediately regretted it. It was not until that moment that she had allowed herself to acknowledge it.

"I dream of my mother too sometimes," Beth said.

The two continued in silence till they passed the small chapel at the turn onto Commercial Road, across which lay the comfortable style of terraced houses with which they were familiar. Having emerged into society once again, Catriona felt as if her time in the opium den had been a dream.

Yet a slow shiver crept up her spine.

Her papa had taken her from St Lucia so quickly after her mama died. They had not been able to hold a proper funeral, having never found her body despite the search parties and all the days her papa had spent trawling the bay. After coming to England, they had moved on as if none of it had happened. It had been an accident, standing too close to the edge of the ridge during a storm. That was the story they would tell, because no one could know the shameful truth of what Catriona had seen that night.

"I'm sorry, Kitty," Beth said. It was the first either of them had spoken in some time, and Catriona had thought their conversation was over, but perhaps in their shared silence, Beth had been thinking of her mother as well.

"I barely remember her anymore," Catriona said. "But I remember her voice. She had the most beautiful voice. I wish…"

She did not know what she wished. She grasped for the words. Aside from her papa, she had never told anyone what had happened on the ridge, but she felt that if only her dearest friend could be made to understand her, the ugliness of what she remembered might somehow be blunted. She could not tell her. The sin was too great to speak of.

Bethany laid a gentle hand on her arm. Her eyes were dark and sincere, the eyes of a doe, but Catriona could not meet them. The guilt of her secrets was almost suffocating. She said nothing at all, and the two continued westwards.

The rest of their walk and the following train ride passed mostly in amiable silence. Beth disembarked to call on Bancroft at his offices on the Strand, whereas Catriona continued home to South Kensington, where she trudged off the platform, looking forward to a bath and some tea. That was likely how her evening would have unfolded had she not spotted a familiar figure amidst the bare trellises of the gardens.

"Staring is often considered rude," Nate said, rising from the bench on which he had sat.

"So is continuing to smoke in the presence of a lady," she returned, glancing pointedly at the cigarette clasped loosely between his fingers.

"Do you want me to put it out?" he said.

"I suppose not."

"Come and join me, then."

She lowered herself to the bench, and he sat a careful distance beside her. The branches above them were bare but for a few stubborn brown leaves clinging precariously, yet in the north end of the gardens, a strand of Scots pine, trees they had clambered up as children, remained evergreen.

She folded her hands in her lap. "Smoking is a filthy and ungentlemanly habit, you know. Whenever did you pick that up?"

"About the same time I picked up all my other filthy and ungentlemanly habits," he said. "You sound like my father."

"Perhaps because we both care for you."

"For me?" He flicked the ash off his cigarette but did not raise it again, and after a moment he put it out after all, grinding it beneath the heel of his shoe. "He is concerned only with preserving his reputation."

A sharp needle of annoyance pierced her. "You could be a little grateful for that, you know," she said. "His reputation is the reason you get to swan about without a thought for your future."

"Yes, my poor father, saddled with a wayward heir. I daresay he is happy to have replaced me with Bancroft in my absence," he said.

She rose, intending to leave him to his poor mood, but he rose as well, the instinct of politeness engrained in him. They walked in silence. Her breath fogged in the cold, but still she remembered them running as children, sticky in the heat amidst the heady smell of flowers. She had once thought he was a perfect little prince, the boy she would one day marry.

"Why did you come back to London, Nate?" she finally said. "I see you and your father are not reconciled as we all had hoped, so why?"

He stiffened and stopped. "Can you not spare my pride?" he

said. There was venom in his voice, but underneath was something keener, like begging. "Must you make me say it?"

She felt it again, the sense that something inevitable was hurtling towards her. She did not wish to turn and face him as she said, "Perhaps I should go."

"I came back for you," he said. "Damn it, you know I came back for you."

She said nothing. Her heart was racing, and she felt as she had in the opium den, as if she could not get enough air.

"You know that I love you," he said. "You know it. And I have tried, I swear I have tried, to quell my affection for you." He had reached out to take hold of her wrist, and she wanted to break free and run.

"Yes, all right, we need not—"

"No, we must have this out." His expression twisted between pain and anger. "Do you deny your feelings for me? I can take your honesty, but I must know. And if you want to pretend afterwards, then fine, but this isn't all in my head."

"What's the point, Nate?" she said, wrenching her arm away from him. "I could tell you what you want to hear, and it wouldn't change anything. You know we would make each other miserable."

"Do you really think so ill of me?" he said. "I can be better for you, Kitty. I can give up all my bad habits, and—and everything, anything you want. Can you not see how I have tried?" He stepped towards her again, but she raised both hands, her fingers splayed across his chest as if she could stop him.

"Nate, I do love you," she said. "Is that not enough, to have my love as…as a dear cousin?"

"Stop, Kitty." He looked away from her. "It makes me sick if you say it like that."

"I mean—"

"I know what you mean," he said. "You strut about the city as if nothing can hurt you, but at the end of it, you're afraid, so afraid that you would choose Hampstead, a man fathoms beneath you, rather than risk me breaking your heart."

She felt as if he had struck her. "Sidney is a good man. A good man! How dare you?"

"You don't love him, Kitty. No matter what you tell yourself, you know it," he said. "You threw me over once, and I would keep coming back to you again and again, but perhaps you could leave me with a little dignity. So tell me now. Tell me you've got even the faintest feeling for me."

No longer the cold, dispassionate creature of the previous day, this was the Nate she remembered. She would rather have his anger than nothing at all. The words were on her lips. It had hurt so much to be the sensible one, to protect her heart, to tamp her feelings down into something as cold and hard as iron. She had grown around her defences like ivy, clinging so desperately that she knew without them, she would collapse.

"Why must you force it out of me?" Her voice had gone high and thin, as if she were pleading. "What does it matter?"

"It matters to me," he said. "Of course it matters." He had almost snarled it at her. He closed the space between them in one stride and drew her towards him.

The kiss was a collision. He had entwined one strong hand around the back of her neck, the other at her waist, pressing her against the wall of his body. She could not have fought him had she tried. But she did not try. Tormented for months by the memory of him, she had wanted this.

It was all wrong, and she knew none of it could be real. But they could pretend. She could pretend he was the kind of man she could have a future with, because he knew her flaws and she knew his, and he already had her heart.

All too suddenly, he pushed himself away.

"You'll drive me mad," he said roughly.

She breathed in to speak, but he had already stepped back.

"No." He cut her off although she had not known what she would say, as if he sensed she would try to take it back, make it small and meaningless, if he let her.

In the night, his eyes were infinitely dark. She felt hot and cold, fevered, shaking. Something electric, something much more biting than fear, had seized her entire body.

"Good evening, Kitty," he said finally, and turned and left her in the gardens.

Her confrontation with Nate had so unsettled her that she very nearly barrelled back into the house, directly into the path of poor Hughes.

"Good evening, miss," he said, stepping aside without missing a beat. "Everything all right?

"Yes, Hughes, fine, sorry." She forced herself to become calm—

which, in the presence of their unflappable butler, was not so difficult. "Is Papa in yet?"

"I believe he is at his club this evening." Hughes surveyed her with a kindly eye, but he had far too much discretion to pry, and if he had noticed her state of heightened emotion, he did not comment on it. "You did receive a letter, though. Here you are."

He held out the silver plate, on which sat a pristine white envelope addressed with her name.

"Oh!" she exclaimed. None of her correspondence was outstanding, and she had not expected anything that evening. "Thank you. Could you please have tea sent up?"

"Right away, miss," he said, giving her a short bow as she passed him and ascended the stairs.

In her bedroom, she stared at the envelope. It was a little game she played idly with herself, trying to identify the handwriting. She had just mailed her letter to Sidney and would not receive a reply until early the week after next, so it could not be him.

She flipped it over to find that it had come from an even more unexpected source, sealed with the Stratton crest.

# CHAPTER 10

Catriona rose to find the midday sun streaming across her bed. She had finally fallen asleep early that morning, having spent much of the night tossing and turning over her confrontation with Nate. The attraction between them was undeniable, as it always had been—a glowing ember that had occasionally flared into flame only to be extinguished over and over again.

But Nate promised very little in the way of stability, and they could go barely two minutes without bickering over something, both too stubborn and hot-headed to concede. Could he really give her the future she wanted for herself? The alternative was what she feared most, each of them wearing the other down over the years until whatever affection they felt was eroded to nothing.

She had to put her thoughts on the matter aside for now. Given the shamefully late hour, she had only a short window of time in which to dress and make haste to Piccadilly. The letter of the previous evening had been from Lady Stratton, a request that she call on her that afternoon to discuss what she had referred to only as a matter of mutual interest.

By the time she reached the house, she was nearly aflame with curiosity about what her ladyship wished to discuss. Catriona suspected she regretted handing away the blackmail note which was at that very moment tucked into her diary. Marlowe had suggested the widow could perhaps have been involved in her husband's murder, so if indeed she wished the note returned, could that be a sign of guilt?

She was admitted and shown through to the parlour, where Lady Stratton was seated.

"I thank you for coming," she said as Catriona lowered herself to the settee across from her.

"It's no trouble," Catriona said. "Your letter suggested some urgency."

The second footman entered with tea, and Lady Stratton waited until he had set the tray down and left before speaking. Her colour was brighter now, Catriona thought, and her demeanour less frantic, though she still wore the black veil without which she would not leave the house for one year, the duration of full mourning for a widow.

"Forgive me," she said, "but perhaps it's best I get straight to it. After our conversation on Wednesday, I had the thought that if my husband did engage in some sort of—unsavoury…I am referring to the blackmail, of course."

"Of course," Catriona said.

"I had our banker call on me under the pretence of reviewing the state of our financial affairs. The police have yet to seize his records, but I suspect it will be only a matter of time after the funeral on Monday. I thought this might be my only chance."

Lady Stratton paused to take a sip of tea, then continued with a clever expression. "I requested a log of any transactions over the past few months, as any irregular deposits might indeed suggest some impropriety. To my great relief, there were no indications that my husband had received any unusual payments in the weeks preceding his murder. However, one sum stood out to me, a withdrawal early on the morning of November first."

"One week before his death," Catriona said.

"Precisely. His lordship often withdrew cash for gambling," Lady Stratton explained with a little wave of her hand. "However, the amount on the morning in question was significant: fifty pounds."

"No small sum."

"No. I found it odd that he would have made such a substantial withdrawal, given our reduced circumstances preceding his death," she said. "I checked his personal calendar—and on that same day was a note for two o'clock, a meeting with one Alan Randall, an antiquities dealer. Are you familiar?"

"No, I cannot say I am," Catriona said.

"Nor can I, but the note said his office is in Holborn. I cannot imagine what the meeting would have been about. My husband was careless with our finances, but the timing of this outlay is especially curious."

"Do you wish me to look into the matter?"

"I thought it best to confide in you," Lady Stratton said. "I was tempted to seek the fellow out myself, but the past few days have made me realise I wish to preserve a certain naivety when it comes to my husband. It must seem silly, but if he was involved in anything, I would rather not know."

"I quite understand," Catriona said. "My lady, I must ask, have you given any further thought to speaking with the police?"

Lady Stratton regarded her frankly. "I know it would be the right thing to do, to simply turn over everything—the blackmail letter, all his personal records… My husband was murdered, yet I feel as though I am covering for his guilt somehow. Until I know the reason he was killed, until I know he was blameless, I cannot bear for his actions to be scrutinised. You would feel the same, wouldn't you?"

Catriona sipped her tea to give herself a moment to think. Her immediate feeling was one of pity that the woman would choose to be ignorant of her husband's improprieties. But the more she thought on it, the more she wondered. She knew very little of what secrets might often exist between men and women, especially in a marriage. Perhaps a degree of ignorance was vital to maintaining a relationship, particularly on the part of the wife. But privately, Catriona thought she could never stand it, knowing her husband was keeping secrets without extending her the same lenience.

"The impulse to protect someone you love is entirely understandable," she replied finally, lowering her cup to its saucer with a light clink. "You must do what you feel is right. I might do the same in your position."

"Miss Winters, you have been a godsend to me these past few days," Lady Stratton said. She turned briefly to glance out the window towards the gardens, which, in the clear light of day, without that ominous shroud of fog, were revealed to be unkempt and overgrown. "Knowing I have someone on my side has made all the difference. Thank you."

"Please don't thank me yet," Catriona said. "Let us see what my visit to this Randall character turns up. If the meeting was unrelated to the tragic event the following week, I will not trouble you with the knowledge."

Lady Stratton reached out to the low table to retrieve a handwritten card and an envelope, which she extended to Catriona. "Here is the address of the office along with a letter sealed with our crest, granting permission for him to disclose any information you request. Hopefully, that will be enough."

Catriona took the materials and tucked them into her reticule. "If not," she said, "I can be quite persuasive."

She planned to visit the antiquities dealer immediately, but as Holborn was only a short walk from the paper in Covent Garden, she thought it best to drop in first and keep her papa apprised. Perhaps, if she was lucky, he would know of this Randall fellow from any of the great number of professional associations gentlemen in London used as excuses to socialise.

"My dear! Impeccable timing," Sir Frederick crowed as Catriona entered his office. "I was about to head off to a meeting," he continued, in fact having already risen from his chair and retrieved his coat from the stand, "but I was hoping you might swing by so I would have the chance to deliver this personally."

He held out a note to her. "From one Detective Inspector Marlowe, of the Metropolitan Police. He waited a short time in hopes of catching you, but I gather he could not be pulled away overly long."

She took it from him and unfolded it:

*Miss W., — I must speak with you at your earliest convenience.*
*Marlowe*

"Not one to beat around the bush, I gather," Sir Frederick said, peering over her shoulder at the missive. "This is the fellow leading the murder inquiry, correct?"

"Yes," she replied, tucking the note into her diary. "I wonder what he could possibly want."

"I tried to weasel it out of him, trust me, but he insisted on speaking with you personally. I must say, my curiosity is piqued."

"As is mine," Catriona said. "However, I'm afraid Inspector Marlowe may have to wait. I've just had the most interesting meeting with Lady Stratton."

The office was tucked away on a quiet street off Chancery Lane. Unfortunately, her papa had been of little help, having no familiarity with the name Alan Randall whatsoever. She was thus going in blind, and as she tugged the door handle and entered, her expectations were let down. She had expected to see busts and frescoes, perhaps even a few mummies, but instead she found the establishment plain and unassuming.

A small bell above the door had sounded her arrival, though a clerk was already present at the front desk.

"Can I help you, ma'am?" he said, looking up from his work.

"Yes, good day," she said. "I was hoping to retrieve some information on behalf of Lady Stratton. I have here a letter permitting the disclosure."

He took it and scanned over the text. "A moment. Please have a seat whilst I see whether Mr Randall might accommodate you," he said, then rose and disappeared down a narrow corridor that led to an inner office.

She waited in that stiflingly dusty foyer for what felt like ages, growing increasingly disconcerted by the utter silence beyond the corridor. When the door re-opened, she found herself confronted by an unfamiliar gentleman in perhaps his early thirties, with slick black hair, sharply dressed. Something in his features called to mind a rodent, a certain weakness of the chin, disguised by his neatly trimmed dark beard, yet the effect was not entirely offensive.

"Good day, madam," the man said. "Do come through, please."

He had motioned for her to precede him towards his office, so she did so. "My name is Catriona Winters," she began, "and I come to make enquiries on behalf of Lady Stratton."

"Alan Randall. A pleasure," he said, pulling out the chair across from his desk for her. "I understand her ladyship is reconciling her late husband's expenditures, is she? I heard about the unpleasantness at the docks, of course."

"It should be there in the letter," Catriona said, "but she wishes to know the reason for a sizeable payment on Monday of last week. A purchase?"

He gestured towards the waiting chair. "Please do sit, madam."

"Thank you," she said, "but this should not take long. I appreciate your making time for me on short notice."

She had chosen to remain standing in case she needed to make a quick getaway, unlikely though that scenario might be in a seemingly respectable office. She felt that in doing so, she had thrown the man off somewhat. He had no choice but to remain standing also, facing her from across the desk.

"I do wish I could be of assistance," he said, "but I am afraid my arrangement with Lord Stratton was of a confidential nature."

"Is Lady Stratton not assumed to be party to that confidentiality?" Catriona said. "She is his wife, and the funds were hers as well."

He raised a hand to stroke his beard. "From a moral standpoint, I do not disagree. However, I am nonetheless not at liberty to disclose the reason for the payment."

From the corridor behind came the chime of the front bell, then murmured voices. Randall seemed poised to seize upon the interruption as a reason to end the meeting, so she pressed on.

"Even a vague explanation would be of great assistance to a grieving widow attempting to piece her financial affairs together in the wake of such a very great tragedy," she said. "Had his lordship commissioned you to retrieve a new piece for his estate, perhaps?"

"You make this difficult, madam. I—"

A light knock interrupted him. The door swung open, and the clerk appeared and said, "Mr Randall?"

Randall nodded to him. "Excuse me for a moment, please."

"Certainly," Catriona replied.

As he stepped out, she took stock of the office: shelves of records, scattered correspondence, the customary carafe of spirits—and a ledger lying open on the desk.

She was seized by an undeniable impulse. This was her chance.

She hurried behind the desk and began to flip through the book, running her finger downwards over the clients and associated payments on each page. There, marked on November 1, was indeed a record of the payment, and her hand stilled over the nondescript notation.

*November 1*

*Stratton £50 o.b.o. Tsang*

Her heart ricocheted through her chest. She flipped back further. There were other payments too, all from Tsang directly now, once every fortnight. He had indeed known more than he was letting on, but she could not make sense of it. Stratton had paid the antiquities dealer more than most men earned in several months—on behalf of the opium den proprietor?

Beyond the office door, the bell chimed again. Footsteps sounded in the corridor.

She had only a second to think. She tore the page from the spine before she could convince herself against it, then tucked it into her diary, turned the pages of the ledger as they had been, and went to stand before the window, where she forced herself to take a deep, calming breath in hopes of appearing composed.

The door swung open.

"My apologies for the interruption," Randall said, "but a client is waiting outside. I believe we were nearly finished here—unless there's something further with which I might assist you?"

"No, thank you," Catriona said, turning to face him. "I believe our business is concluded. Though, may I ask how one might select a piece to purchase? I confess I expected to see your wares on display."

"Looking to begin a collection?" he said. His tone was patronising, but she kept a polite smile pasted firmly to her lips as he continued. "I keep my pieces in a more controlled environment—to protect from degradation, you see. But it is nothing that should interest Lady Stratton."

"I shall have to take your word for that," she said.

They exited his office, she holding her diary tightly to her chest, keenly aware of her deception, feeling him following half a pace behind her in the narrow corridor. But she was in for another shock—for as they neared the foyer, she caught a glimpse through the window of the supposed client pacing in the street outside.

With that white hair, that commanding stature, there was no mistaking Lord Ashford. Catriona could not leave, she realised, as she would have to walk right past him. In fact, at any moment, he could turn and spot her through the window.

She turned abruptly, nearly colliding with Randall. "Apologies," she said quickly. "Might I ask for a receipt of the payment, at least? I understand your discretion, but perhaps it might be reconciled as a consultation fee."

Randall gave her barely a glance, his attention already elsewhere. "That can be arranged," he said, then barked out, "Anderson! My clerk will assist you."

He passed beyond her to the front door, and she perched as close to the reception desk as she could, hoping that and the angle of her bonnet would be sufficient to shield her from Ashford as he passed.

"Just a moment, ma'am," the clerk, Anderson, said as he filled out the receipt.

The bell chimed again behind her, bringing with it a gust of wintry air, then footsteps.

"Good afternoon, my lord," Randall said. "Please come through to my office."

"Thank you," Ashford said. "I trust this is not an inconvenience."

Then they disappeared down the corridor, and she was unable to make out anything further of their conversation.

She had not been discovered.

The clerk looked up and extended a short receipt to her. "Here you are. Fifty pounds for a consultation on November first."

She grasped the receipt, stowed it away in her diary alongside the torn ledger page, and thanked the clerk before fairly hightailing it out of the office, again left with more questions than answers.

If Ashford was also looking into the antiquities dealer, she was on the right track. She briefly considered returning to Piccadilly to ask Lady Stratton whether she knew of any deeper association between her late husband and Victor Tsang. However, late afternoon was fast slipping into evening. A sharp chill had pierced the air, and the lamplighter was making his way down Chancery Lane.

Catriona returned to the *Messenger* offices to find the bullpen empty enough. A few reporters were still in, but the main hub of activity was now the lower floor, where the press whirred away and ranks of newspaper boys filed in and out, retrieving stacks to hawk all over the city. It was as good enough a place as any, she thought, to make notes in her diary regarding all the evidence she had collected. She set herself up at her desk.

About the murder victim, she had one key clue: Lady Stratton had admitted the family were facing severe hardship as a result of his gambling and careless management of the estate, and, perhaps because of that hardship, Stratton had been attempting to blackmail someone before his death. But whom?

He was apparently known to those at the opium den, so was it possible he had been a patron for some time and perhaps come to owe Tsang money? That would explain the payment to the antiquities dealer on his behalf, but it would not explain why Tsang had been making fortnightly payments to Randall in the first place. A fondness for antiquities was one thing, but so many payments over such a span of time?

It was inexplicable, Catriona thought, unless Randall were in fact somehow also involved in the operation of the opium den. If he were, had Stratton, having made that payment to him, put two and two together and tried to blackmail him over his association with an illegal enterprise?

She looked up from her diary some time later to find the office deserted. Even the lower floor was now quiet, and the clock in her papa's office read almost half past eight. Several hours had passed without her notice, so caught up had she been in her theories.

It was only then, as she flipped idly to his note tucked into her diary, that she recalled Marlowe wished to speak with her. Her inclination was to ignore the missive; if whatever it was he wished to say to her were so important, he could put in a little more effort and call on her himself. But perhaps it was related to the murder inquiry, she could not help but hope, in which case she would be irresponsible to pass up such an opportunity.

It could not hurt to stop in at Scotland Yard and see whether he was in his office. After all, it was only a short walk.

She headed out, and before long, the headquarters of the Metropolitan Police loomed before her as she passed under the brick arch which opened into Great Scotland Yard. A mass of dark clouds had gathered above the city, and she looked forward to again getting out of the cold, which had begun to sting her nose and cheeks as the first flakes of snow drifted down.

She pulled open the door to the back hall to find the place deserted, as the police constables were often out patrolling at that hour. At the reception desk, the freckled young detective constable she had encountered previously, Whitby, was dozing lightly, leaning back in his chair, feet up and arms crossed. She decided against waking him. She remembered the way.

As Catriona proceeded down the corridor, soft lamplight spilled out from Marlowe's office, and she saw his shadow across the floor before she saw him. He was filing something away, half turned from the door. In his ignorance of her presence, he seemed unguarded, somehow younger. But the illusion was broken as she rapped on the door frame and his gaze snapped to her.

"Miss Winters," he said. He had turned abruptly, but his expression betrayed no surprise. "You received my note."

"I did, vague as it was," she said. "Will you ask me to sit?"

"This should not take long."

"Here I thought this would be a social call," she said. "Pity."

Something flickered across his face. She felt inexplicably as if she had stepped into a trap. He said, "Like the social call you paid to an opium den in Limehouse yesterday afternoon?"

She inhaled sharply.

"Close the door," he said.

She turned from him and, for the briefest moment, entertained the idea of simply leaving. She did not owe him an explanation. But something inside her thrilled at the idea of their impending confrontation. She and the inspector had so far been like two hawks circling the same prey. At some point, either would have to dive for it.

She closed the door.

"Did you think I would leave the scene at the docks unattended?" Marlowe began. "Whilst waiting for the killer to return, Detective

Whitby had the unexpected pleasure of spotting you and whomever you were with entering the very establishment outside which the murder took place."

She bit her lip to keep from speaking.

Bethany had been right about their being followed. But Detective Whitby obviously had not recognised Ashford's daughter, if he knew her at all, so at least Catriona could keep her name out of this unfortunate turn of events.

"Have you nothing to say for yourself?" Marlowe said.

Her hands, still holding her diary, had clenched into fists around it. "If I went looking for witnesses to the murder," she said, "I uncovered nothing you did not already know. So is that all, Inspector, or do you wish to have me followed home as well?"

"You think I—?" He cut himself off. For a second, she thought he was about to dismiss her, but just as she had decided to leave after all, he continued. "You once suggested I might experience an attack of conscience where you were concerned."

"I recall the conversation," she said. "You seemed rather set on its being an impossibility."

"That was before I realised you are incapable of seeing the risk in your actions."

She raised a brow. "Have you summoned me here to warn me off yet again? I fail to see how my actions are any of your business."

"Perhaps a wiser man than I would leave well enough alone," he said, "but I cannot stand idly by whilst you wade deeper into dangerous waters."

"If you wish me to back off," she said, "you might answer my questions about your inquiry."

His expression was indecipherable, but she understood she would get nothing from him even before he said, "You know I'm not at liberty to disclose such information."

"Then let me be frank," she said. "I have yet to write another article on the murder despite the evidence I have collected, some of which would indeed be of interest to the public. I have given you no reason to doubt my motives, so why do you do so?"

As she spoke, he had rounded the desk and stood facing her. If what she had said unsettled him, he did not show it. "Have you no remorse for my position?" he said.

She was indignant, colour rising in her face. "You must say whatever it is you wish to say."

His knuckles were white on the edge of the desk, his jaw clenched tight, and she realised it then. Triumph surged through her. She set her diary on the desk with finality.

"Does it frustrate you," she said, "that I may be one step ahead of you?"

His steely gaze had sharpened to a lance. "What frustrates me is wasting my time advising you against misadventure when you clearly could not care less about your own well-being."

"Then why not simply wash your hands of the matter and ignore me, come what may?" she said.

Exhilarated by her brazenness, she had stepped closer to him. She did not know why she had done it, only that in doing so, she had taken the upper hand. The space between them felt like a cord pulled taut, and the office was remarkably small, each mote of dust travelling infinitely slowly in the lamplight.

"Because, Miss Winters," he finally said, "you make yourself quite impossible to ignore."

It was not what she had expected him to say. In fact, she knew not what she had expected, only that his answer had thrown her entirely off balance. Perhaps because of the memory of their first encounter at the docks, or because she knew he had been a navy man, his eyes reminded her of the sea—fathomless and stormy. She forced herself to step back. A retreat, she acknowledged.

"I thank you for your concern, but it is unnecessary," she said at last. "If there is nothing else?"

He regarded her for a long moment, his eyes narrowing. "No, nothing else," he said, then motioned to the door. "Allow me to walk you out."

She was barely conscious of her feet carrying her into the corridor. He walked beside her, but they did not speak. A fluttering sort of sensation, a kind of nervousness, had arisen within her, but she did not wish to dignify the feeling with further contemplation.

Somewhere in the building, a clock chimed nine.

Catriona had visited Ashford in his office enough that the sound was familiar, that of the old grandfather clock set against the wall opposite his desk. As she pictured him sitting there, snow falling in the window behind him, the realisation went through her with a jolt.

How could Ashford have known to visit the antiquities dealer at all? Lady Stratton had not spoken with the police, so he must have learned of the connection from someone else. The morning of the murder, when she had come upon Ashford speaking in hushed tones with that woman, the den madam, what had they discussed?

She had stopped in the corridor. Marlowe regarded her oddly.

"Are you quite all right?" he said.

She could not speak. Her heart was beating so quickly she feared she might faint. If Ashford had known since the morning of the killing that Randall could be responsible, why had the man not yet been arrested? She knew Ashford was a person of character, so some circumstances must exist, more than met the eye, to justify his actions. She simply had to ask him to explain, and all would be set right.

"Inspector," she said, "do you know if Lord Ashford is in?"

"At this hour? Perhaps."

"I would be remiss in leaving without so much as a good-night to him," she said.

They emerged into the back hall, and the inspector exhaled quickly before barking, "Detective Constable Whitby!"

The young constable started awake, shooting up in his chair and swinging his feet off the desk. "Sir!" he cried out. He rose to attention at once. "And Miss Winters! What brings you to—"

"Detective," Marlowe said, "is Lord Ashford still in?"

Whitby collected himself. "Yes, sir. I believe so, sir. In fact, his son went up to see him some time ago. Might still be up there. They were having the most incredible row. Not that I was eavesdropping, mind!"

Catriona glanced up the back stairs, and a curiously guilty shiver ran through her. Nate had been there?

If he still was, her plan to speak with his father would have to wait. Yet she had heard nothing upon entering the back hall earlier, and the building was still quiet.

Before she could reply, from somewhere upstairs, the crack of a shot rent the air.

Her breath left her in a rush. The sound was familiar. Ears ringing, her first illogical thought was of the afternoons she had spent at the Turners' country home, watching from the window as her papa and Ashford trekked off into the misty countryside to hunt, rifles slung across their backs, laughing…

Sound rushed back into the silence. Marlowe had grasped her forcefully by the shoulders and pulled her behind him.

Footsteps pounded upstairs. Then, from the front of the building, a door slammed shut.

Marlowe turned to her, and Catriona could only nod at him before he set off in pursuit and disappeared to the front hall, whereas Whitby was headed towards the nearest stairwell, trying to determine whence the shot had come.

She raced up the steps after him. At the end of the upstairs corridor was an open office door through which lamplight streamed. She rushed past the detective towards it and burst into the room.

"Lord Ashford!" she cried.

For a moment, she expected him to look up at her with that magnanimous smile. But he was sprawled back in his chair, a bloody hand splayed over his chest, his expression caught in disbelief.

She was at his side in an instant, pressing her hands over his. Hot blood pumped out between her fingers, soaking through her gloves at once. He did not seem to see her. He was looking somewhere over her shoulder, his face drained of colour.

"Sir, please," she shouted, turning back to Whitby in the doorway, "fetch a physician, for God's sake!"

"Yes, I..." the young man stammered, then stumbled back, gave his head a shake, and disappeared down the corridor.

Catriona pressed down with all her strength, but her hands were slick, coppery. She could not find purchase. It would not be enough. Ashford had been shot through the heart, and his strength was fading.

"Please stay with me," she said. But her voice was the voice of a child, the voice of the little girl before whom he had knelt on that day at the train station so long ago, when she and her papa stepped off, to welcome her to a cold, unfamiliar grey land. "You must try to stay calm," she said, "and everything will be all right."

"Darling..." he gasped out. "Darling...you must..." Bright blood bubbled on his lips. He swallowed. "Bethany..."

There was no pain in his expression, only a stricken sense of regret in the deep lines around his eyes, the furrowed white brow. His fingers had gone limp between hers.

His breath left him in a long exhale.

Catriona held to him tightly, a painful expectation suspended in her chest. But she was waiting for something that would never come.

A scream tore from her throat. She fell upon him.

She would not remember the following moments. The world had closed in on her. Everything she held dear of him, every beautiful memory, had spiralled into an infinite unknown streaked with blood and the smell of gunpowder.

His dark eyes had closed forever. He was dead.

# CHAPTER 11

The city had always felt quieter in the snow, as if the firmament had descended over the towers and bridges, the clattering trains, even the Thames lapping endlessly at its banks, and hushed it all.

Catriona stood before the window in Ashford's office, staring down numbly at the snow falling on Whitehall Place, her dress drenched in blood, as the body was carried away on a stretcher behind her.

Marlowe was saying something, but it was as though he had spoken from a great distance. She did not hear him. Black spots swam before her eyes, and when she blinked back to awareness, she had been seated in a chair along the wall.

He was knelt in front of her. "Madam, look at me," he said.

"Oh..." Her hands shook where they lay in her lap, bare. She supposed someone had taken away her gloves and brought her a kerchief to clean herself, but she did not remember it. "I am quite all right. I do apologise," she said in a voice that was not her own, and he glanced away and rose with a little difficulty, bracing himself against the chair.

The past minutes had unfolded as if in a dream, with time bending strangely around her. She had knelt there with that impossibly still body, gasping past the suffocating pain in her chest. At some point, Marlowe had re-appeared and, with hands still cold from the outdoors, pulled her away to make space for the arriving physician, though it had been too late for anyone to save Ashford then.

"Forgive me," Marlowe said. "I should have caught him, damn it."

"You cannot blame yourself," she said. "He had a head start."

"I had barely a glimpse of him," he said. "The darkness obscured him. His cap hid his colouring." He had turned from her and was speaking as if to file it away. "He was able bodied, anywhere from twenty to forty years of age. He stowed something in his jacket as he ran."

Steady with determination now, she rose and forced herself to focus on the room around her. The killer must have left something behind, some clue—yet the thing that drew her focus was the chair in which Ashford had died. It was stained with blood, the back and arms and the carpet below it.

On the desk was a glass of whiskey. It was not unlike Ashford to enjoy a whiskey of an evening, yet he usually did so at the Flag. Had something driven him to drink at the office that night? It was nearing half past nine now. Why had he been there so late, and who had been the last to see him? The chair across the desk was pulled out slightly, as if by a visitor, someone he knew. Had the killer sat in that very spot and, at the right moment, risen, levelled the pistol…?

She approached the desk and stood where the killer must have, and as she followed the direction of his gaze, she noticed a most peculiar detail. The desk was in disarray, yet where one might have expected to see whatever Ashford had been working on, there was only a curiously bare space, bare even of the blood spattered over the rest of the desk. She ran her hand over it.

"Madam, I must insist you not disturb—"

"You mentioned the killer stowed something in his jacket as he ran," she said.

He had come to join her by the desk. "Yes, what of it?"

"Lord Ashford was here late. He must have been working on something, yet his desk is empty."

Marlowe was silent for a long moment, and she felt he was inclined to dismiss her suspicions. "Miss Winters," he finally said, "do you know of anyone who might have wanted Ashford dead?"

"Certainly not."

"You recall what Detective Whitby overheard, a row between his lordship and his son."

Tension gripped her. "Inspector, I do not mean to cast stones, for I know you all have been working round the clock this past week, but Detective Whitby was asleep when I arrived, just as he was when we left your office."

He said nothing in response, surveying her with that unreadable expression she felt might always put her on the defensive. Perhaps this was how policemen compelled their suspects to confess.

She felt she must continue. "I heard nothing upon entering the back hall, and do you expect he could have fallen asleep amidst a row such as he described? No, whatever confrontation occurred between Lord Ashford and his son must have concluded long before then."

"I know your families are close," he said carefully, "and personal attachments can cloud our ability to see—"

"Do not presume to judge my abilities," she replied quickly. "The suggestion that Mr Turner could kill his father in cold blood is unthinkable to me for many reasons."

"I was wrong to bring it up," Marlowe said. "Forgive me."

That he had dropped the subject so easily only aggravated her further, for she knew he had not abandoned his suspicions and would in fact now pursue his inquiry without her input, having decided she was not to be trusted. She felt backed into a corner, certain she must defend Nate but uncertain how.

"If there is nothing more to be done here," she finally said. She had been breathing rapidly, and blackness lurked in her peripheral vision again. She sighed and closed her eyes, then opened them just as quickly when she heard Marlowe stepping forwards. "I am quite all right, Inspector," she said. "I should simply like to go home."

"Then I insist on escorting you and will brook no argument," he said. He offered his arm. She took it.

"Very well," she said. "I will not try to dissuade you."

. . .

As they travelled by police coach through the dense fog that blanketed the gaslit streets of London, neither spoke. Marlowe sat across from her, watching out the window as the grand edifices of the city centre shrank into row houses.

Catriona had found herself overcome by exhaustion, her dress stained with blood, her throat tense from crying. She leaned against the wall of the coach, the vibration of the wheels over the cobblestones lulling her into a restless stupor until it came to a stop and she struggled back to consciousness.

Thurloe Square was quiet, the windows of the neighbouring houses spilling light out into the street. Just the night before, Catriona had stood with Nate in the gardens as they spoke of his father, amongst other things. She had not yet thought about how she might break the tragic news to anyone, not Nate or Beth or her own papa. She simply hoped she could proceed inside without impediment.

"Thank you, Inspector," she said as she descended from the coach. He had taken her bare hand but released it as soon as her shoe touched the footpath. "Will you return to the Yard tonight?"

"I intend to see you safely inside first," he said.

She glanced up the front steps, hoping none of the staff were at the door. One look at her dress and the house would be in an uproar.

Behind them, gravel crunched underfoot. The iron gate of the gardens had creaked open.

A feeling like vertigo surged inside her as she turned to see

Bethany, who had emerged with Bancroft, her hand over the crook of his arm. She surveyed Catriona and the inspector with a mildly curious expression.

"Good evening, you two," she called out. "Do you care to join us? We were taking a turn around the gardens…" Her hand flew to her mouth. She had caught sight of the bloodstained dress. "Good Lord, Kitty, are you injured?"

"No, I…" Catriona felt as though she were gasping for breath. "Beth, something terrible has happened."

Bancroft had stepped in front of Bethany ever so slightly, and his brows drew together. He gestured towards Marlowe and said, "You, sir, what is the meaning of this?"

"Miss Turner," Marlowe said. His voice had gone toneless. "I regret to inform you there has been an incident at Scotland Yard. Your father…"

"My father?" Bethany said with an odd little laugh, but her face had lost all its colour. "No!" she cried. "I do not believe it. I…" She reached out blindly. Her legs buckled beneath her, and she fainted away into Bancroft's arms.

A fire blazed in the hearth. On the settee, Catriona sat beside Bethany, who was still holding the restorative glass of brandy Hughes had fetched for her, having immediately grasped the situation upon their entrance.

Bancroft stood impassively before the fire, arms crossed, his shadow cast back across the parlour ceiling, while Marlowe stood by the doorway to the foyer, surveying the group, Catriona thought, carefully.

"I had the most inexplicable anxiety," Beth said, so quietly that Catriona thought she was the only one who had heard her. "I was so relieved when I saw the police coach. I thought it was Papa."

"Marlowe, is it?" Bancroft said, turning to face the room. "How could this have happened—for his lordship to be shot in his own office…?"

"I cannot begin to speculate," Marlowe replied.

"Oh, Papa," Bethany said. She had withdrawn into herself.

"His last thought was of you," Catriona said. "In the end. It happened so quickly."

Bancroft looked down at them with a pained expression. "What possible motive could there have been?" he said. "Is a suspect in custody, at least?"

"The killer remains at large," Marlowe said. "Miss Turner, I must ask you, are you aware of any enemies your father had, any acquaintances which ended badly?"

"He did have enemies, of course," Beth said, looking not at the inspector but down at the nearly empty glass. "His position made that inevitable. But to be murdered? This is an unbearable loss for our family. Oh, how will I tell my brother?"

Catriona took the glass and set it on the low table, replacing it with her own hand, which Beth grasped weakly.

"Is he at home tonight?" Marlowe said.

"No," Beth replied. "I mean—yes. But he is indisposed." Her grip had tightened as she spoke.

"Indisposed?" Marlowe said. His mouth quirked downwards

briefly and almost imperceptibly. "I see."

Catriona was surprised he had the grace to drop the subject. Bethany had been lying, and they both knew it. Yet Nate must have left Scotland Yard well before his father was shot. He must have, of course.

"Inspector, where is my father?" Beth said. "His body."

"He has been taken to the police surgeon," Marlowe said. "Because the death was unnatural…"

"Must he undergo a post-mortem?" she said weakly. "No. I shall go to—to retrieve him immediately."

"No, Bethany," Bancroft said. "I will go and make the arrangements. You should not have to see your father in such a place."

"Yes," Bethany said quietly. "Thank you, Henry."

Catriona faced the windows, looking out at the street. Ever circumspect, Hughes had not interrupted their conference to draw the curtains. In the gardens across the road, the skeletal branches of trees rose into the night, and snow drifted in the warm cone of light around each streetlamp.

"Inspector," Catriona finally said, regarding him frankly, "can anything further be done tonight?"

"I'll return to the Yard at once to commence the inquiry," he said. His hands were folded, holding his hat. "Please accept my condolences, Miss Turner. Your father was an honourable man. I will do all I can to apprehend his killer."

"Thank you, Inspector," Bethany said. She did not look up, her eyes glassed over with tears.

Bancroft stepped forwards. "I'll accompany you into town now then, sir," he said. "Bethany, I shall call on you tomorrow morning. Please try to rest."

She nodded but did not speak, and Catriona remained seated beside her as the two men proceeded out.

For a long moment, neither she nor Bethany said a word. Catriona thought back to all the things she wished someone might have said to her after the death of her mama. But the circumstances had been entirely different. So she simply sat there with her friend, their hands clasped together, listening to the crackling of the fire.

"I knew something terrible had happened," Beth finally said. "I cannot explain how. It was as if a cold hand had constricted my heart." She looked towards the parlour doorway as if to ensure they were alone. "Papa would be so ashamed," she continued. "I was not truthful when the inspector asked whether Nate was home."

"Beth, is he not?"

"No, but does it matter?"

"At Scotland Yard, someone overheard him and your father arguing," Catriona said. She felt as though she must brace herself. A strange fear was building within her. "Beth, I think Marlowe might suspect… Why lie to him?"

Bethany withdrew her hands and clenched them to her chest. "Because I heard the accusation in his question, and I panicked! It's no secret Nate and Papa haven't been getting on well recently. So I thought if I said he was home…"

"Then where is he really?"

"Do you think me my brother's keeper?" Beth snapped. Her voice had gone shrill. She closed her eyes for a long moment before continuing. "I rarely know what he gets up to in the evenings. You know how he is."

"Yes, I… I apologise."

"No," Beth said. "No, Kitty, forgive me. Such questions must be asked. If I were the inspector, I would suspect my brother, as well."

"He will not let it go, not until Nate has accounted for his time tonight," Catriona said, and neither would she, though she could not say so.

"Oh, what a mess," Bethany said. She glanced out across the street corner, where, just visible through the gardens, was her home. "Papa would have known what to do. Papa…!" She gave a hitching gasp. Her hands fluttered up to cover her eyes.

Catriona said nothing. There was nothing to say.

Sleep did not come easily that night. Waiting in the darkness were her memories of the events at Scotland Yard. She woke more than once from a feverish dream, her heart thrashing against her ribs, unable to shake her guilt. If only she had somehow staunched the bleeding, could she have saved him?

Soft footsteps sounded in the hallway, and the door opened with a thin shaft of light. She had not heard her papa come home.

"My dear, may I enter?" he said.

"Papa…?"

"Shh." He was still wearing his coat and his gloves, which he removed and set on her bureau. "I came home as soon as—as soon as I heard what has happened."

She sat up, pulling her knees to her chest and drawing the blanket to her chin. "I tried to save him, Papa. I'm so sorry."

"No, my dear. You've nothing to apologise for." He had come to sit at the edge of the bed, the way he had done when she was a child with nightmares. "To know you were there with Ashford when he passed is my only comfort tonight."

"But you heard of it at your club?" she exclaimed. "Oh, Papa!"

"No, the knowledge is not public. Inspector Marlowe tracked me down and told me, for which I owe him a debt of gratitude."

"Marlowe did?" she said.

She knew not what to think. Upon his departure earlier, she had gathered the inspector was keen to return to Scotland Yard and formally begin the inquiry. Yet he had first taken the time to find her papa at his club and tell him the tragic news, sparing her the pain of doing so.

Perhaps it was because of her very great relief at this that she now found herself unable to hold back the tears she had quelled since arriving home.

"I see," she said quietly.

"There, there," Sir Frederick said as he patted her hand. He never displayed an excess of emotion, but the gesture was enough.

"I simply need—to collect myself for a moment," she said.

"Of course, my dear. How frightened you must have been." He removed his hand from hers and looked into her tear-streaked face. "But how did you come to be at Scotland Yard in the first place?"

Her heart gave an odd little jump. It was a feeling she had come to recognise, the feeling of a lie forming. She could not tell her papa why Marlowe had summoned her, which was to chastise her about her visit to the opium den. Nor could she tell him that as of that moment, the main suspect in the murder of Lord Ashford was his son and heir. But of course Nate had not been involved. He was not a killer, or so she told herself then.

"I was discussing some particulars of the Stratton case with the inspector," she began.

# CHAPTER 12

When Catriona woke, the grey light of morning filtered through the curtains, and a soft knocking sounded at her bedroom door. For one blissful moment, she had completely forgot the events of the previous evening.

"My dear, are you awake?" Sir Frederick said from the hallway.

"Yes, come in," she called out. Her head felt heavy, her eyes tired and sore, and even though she had scrubbed herself raw in the bath the night before, she still felt the ghosts of bloodstains on her hands. "What time is it, Papa?"

Sir Frederick sat to face her. "Nearly nine," he said. "I found myself rising at first light and decided to head into town to find out what I could about the progress of the inquiry."

"Have you learned anything?"

"I was in luck to find the inspector still at Scotland Yard," he said. "The man was practically asleep on his feet, mind."

"Marlowe was there?" Catriona said, sitting up straighter. "I suspect he cannot forgive himself for allowing the killer to make his escape last night. But it all happened so quickly."

"I insisted he get some rest and return to the task with a fresher mind," Sir Frederick said. "Whether he will take my advice is another matter. Regardless, it seems they have made very little progress. He was loath to part with any information—especially since he knows my profession, of course. But from what I surmised, the killer disappeared into the night without a trace."

She recalled the sequence of events: the shot, the pounding of footsteps, the seldom used door on Whitehall Place thrown open to the snow as the unseen killer fled.

"Papa, Marlowe asked yesterday whether Lord Ashford had any enemies," she said. "Perhaps he mentioned something to you?"

"Hmm." Sir Frederick glanced away from her towards the window, over which the curtains were still drawn. "Despite his fondness for gossip, Ashford held his cards close to his chest. But it may be that…"

"What is it?"

"Many of our acquaintances were mutual. However, he did mention… But that cannot have had any relation to the events of last night."

"He did mention someone?"

"Not an enemy." A curious expression had dawned upon him, and he determinedly avoided meeting her eyes. "The person he mentioned was a… He intimated she was a rather close personal friend."

"Oh. I see."

"He has been a widower for nearly four years now," Sir Frederick said, as if to excuse it, though no excuse was necessary.

As her papa spoke, Catriona had been struck by a memory of the previous Tuesday night. Had she not witnessed Ashford returning home at a late hour, accompanied by a woman, perhaps the close friend in question?

"Do you know this woman, Papa?" she said.

"No, and I suspected she was not from within our circle," he said. "Otherwise, I would surely have known of their acquaintance."

"Could she have been someone he met through his work, through a colleague? I wonder if this could be relevant to the inquiry."

Sir Frederick seemed to collect himself and rose. "I do wish I knew who she was, if only to break the news of his passing in a sympathetic manner. As it stands, she will likely read of it in the papers, and I cannot imagine what a shock that will be."

"Perhaps I should speak with Marlowe about it," Catriona said. "If anyone can be relied upon to exercise discretion…"

"Yes, I gather they are trying to keep the scene tightly under wraps, but it's only a matter of time before the news gets out. You could go to his office tomorrow, and we can hold off on printing a story until Monday," Sir Frederick said.

She sensed the cogs turning in his head, and she wondered briefly whether he was considering which reporter he should entrust with the assignment. She was certain she should be the one to write the story, being that she had been present during the events in question, but she knew her papa would disagree. Perhaps he even regretted encouraging her to meet with the inspector the following day, as that would only deepen her interest and involvement in the matter. But she never could tell exactly what her papa was thinking.

"One hopes the circumstances of the killing will have become clearer before then," he finally said.

Later that morning, Catriona wandered through Covent Garden, which was bustling with the Saturday crowd, in the vague direction of the *Messenger* offices. Vendors hawked flowers, round wheels of hard cheese, stacks of dried fish, soaps and pomades, and tins of sweets, all of which combined to form the familiar characteristic aroma of the market hall.

She walked as if in a trance, as if part of her were still in the office at Scotland Yard, staring at that bloodstained chair.

She was unable to stop thinking about the two murders. There must be a link between them, she thought. Was it any coincidence that Stratton had been killed soon after meeting with the antiquities dealer, Alan Randall, and the same had happened to Ashford? But she would keep her thoughts to herself for the moment, at least until she knew more.

In fact, that morning, she was faced with a rather more immediate problem: Her diary was nowhere to be found. The previous day had become such a blur. She was sure she must have left it at her desk at the *Messenger* offices. With any luck, she could slip in and out without drawing undue attention from the skeleton crew of week-end reporters. She was not sure she could maintain her composure otherwise.

She pulled open the door of the office and proceeded through the bullpen. The few men present rose as she entered, of course, but, after an exchange of pleasantries, quickly returned to their work, allowing her to head directly to her desk and begin rifling through it. Yet the diary was not there.

A clatter of glass interrupted her search. The sound had come from within the newly appointed darkroom, and she stood in a sort of paralysis, hands buried halfway in a drawer of documents. Was it possible Nate had not heard the tragic news yet? Why else could he have been at the office?

She composed herself and waited a moment outside the dark-room before knocking lightly. He opened the door almost at once.

"Yes?" he said, and saw it was her. "Oh. Come in."

The room was warm, lit in dim red, and she entered after him, feeling somehow as if she were stepping into the cave of a wild animal, which smelled of developing solutions, alcohol, and sweat.

"Trust you to find me here, licking my wounds," he said, leaning back against one of the long side tables, on which were laid out a series of glass photography plates. His eyes were bleary, his pupils pinpricks even in the darkness.

"When did you hear?" Catriona said.

"When I got in last night." He glanced away. "Beth told me what happened, that our father is—gone."

"You must know how sorry I am."

"Oh, not you too, Kitty." He pushed himself off the table and turned back to his work. "Everyone tiptoeing around me as if I might lash out at the wrong word. My father and I never got on. And now we never will."

He spoke without emotion, as if it were a matter of fact, and Catriona felt inexplicably nervous, struck with the same sensation of helplessness she had felt four years earlier, the bitter winter his mother had died. Lord Ashford had sent a telegram instructing Nate to return home from Cambridge at once, but his coach had been delayed by the snow, and when at last he arrived, it had been too late for him to say good-bye.

"He loved you," she finally said.

"I know." He turned to face her again. "He was still my father, even after everything."

"Have you any idea, any suspicion…?"

"About who shot him?" he said. "I rather thought I might ask you. You were there, after all."

"I was too late to save him."

"There was nothing you could have done, Kitty," he said. "Bancroft stopped by before I left this morning, and the police surgeon apparently told him there would have been no saving my father, even if a physician had been present. The shot was too true. Point blank."

"The surgeon said so?"

"Yes. So I forbid your feeling guilty about it," he said with finality. "Anyway, I figured I would spare myself the spectacle of Bancroft trying to comfort my sister, so here I am."

She glanced pointedly towards the flask on the tabletop. "Taking comfort of a different kind?"

"Yes. Care to join me?"

"No, thank you. I don't drink before noon," she said.

"Lucky I have no such compunctions," he replied before raising the flask to her and then to his lips.

"Then where were you last night?" she asked. She had tried for a mildly curious tone, but his eyes narrowed immediately when she said it.

"Nowhere out of the ordinary."

"Oh? You were overheard arguing with your father at the Yard."

"By whom?" he said quickly. "Never mind. He was very much alive at the time, I assure you."

"But this means you were the last person to see him before—the tragic event."

Nate set the flask down hard on the table. "What, you think I shot him?"

"Of course not," she said.

"But the police think so?"

"They will need to rule you out as a suspect."

"I was in my father's office for barely a quarter of an hour. It could have been no later than eight o'clock when I left."

A little thrill of relief shot through her. But she had not really suspected him, had she?

"The shot was fired about nine," she said.

"Then I was nowhere near it."

"Will you be able to prove that?"

His mouth twisted with something like pain. "Kitty, you really think I killed my father?"

"This isn't about what I think, Nate. You were never heard leaving his office."

"Should I have announced my departure?"

"I wish you had. Could anyone vouch for your whereabouts, at least?"

"If it comes to it. So are you quite finished? I came here to work and drown my sorrows, not be accused of patricide."

She could not tell him what she wanted to, which was that she was only trying to protect him. "Perhaps I should take you up on that drink, after all," she said instead.

"Perhaps you should," he replied, and handed the flask to her.

Unable to stand his dark eyes watching her, she turned and faced away from him, towards the opposite wall, along which a series of photographs hung. Amongst them was her portrait. It had come out better than she expected, but she felt conscious of her own expression, the hesitancy of it, the question she saw in her eyes.

"Your photographs turned out well," she said with deliberate mildness.

"You doubted they would?"

"No," she said. "I suppose you've got a fine eye."

"I had a fine subject," he said.

He was standing close behind her, radiating heat, and despite everything, she could not help but remember their meeting in the gardens the evening before last. His fingers brushed across her neck.

When she turned to face him, his body was blocking the red lamplight, and she could barely make him out. His throat tensed as he swallowed. She laid her hand against his chest.

His lips brushed hers once, softly.

It was disappointment she felt, a dull understanding that of course, he thought of her as a distraction, as a convenience. Nate was so used to getting his way that her initial resistance had been a novelty. But now he knew he had her, and the challenge in it would soon be gone, and she would not hold his attention any longer. She had seen it before.

This was his nature, and part of her acknowledged that it was the reason she was so certain he had not killed his father. Whilst Nate succumbed often to fits of passion frowned upon by society, he was not a murderer. His transgressions were the transgressions of a child, committed out of selfishness rather than malice.

"I should go," she said.

"Please wait." His hand caught hers, but he quickly released it and stepped back. "No, never mind. I wanted to ask whether he suffered. But perhaps I would rather not know."

"It happened quickly," she finally said, because she knew it was what he wanted to hear, and she carefully set her feelings back in their box and locked it tight. "I think there would have been very little pain."

"Henry says the body should be returned to us soon," Bethany said. She sat in an armchair in the drawing room, a needlepoint canvas lying in her lap, its threads hanging loose.

Catriona sat on the settee across from her, watching the snow fall through the window over her shoulder. After leaving the darkroom, she had searched her desk, retraced her steps, even questioned the staff as to whether anyone had seen her diary lying about. But no one had noticed anything amiss.

So she had resigned herself to returning home to Thurloe Square and calling on Beth in an attempt to alleviate the relative social isolation in which her friend would find herself until the funeral.

"He is so good to me, you know," Bethany continued. A peculiar expression had crossed her face, a tightness about the eyes and mouth, but it was so brief that Catriona thought she must have imagined it. "Yet the wedding will have to be pushed back until the summer now after all."

"Poor Mr Bancroft," Catriona replied. "But he certainly cannot argue with it, eager though he must be to make you his wife."

Beth gave a few futile stabs of the needle through the cloth. "Life is so odd," she said. "Just a few days ago I was looking for reasons not to rush into the institution, but now I would be married at once if only it meant Papa would be there to give me away." She finally abandoned the needlepoint, setting it on the low table between them. "I feel so out of sorts, you know. But it will pass, and in the meantime, I suppose I must keep my mind occupied. A task with which I shall entrust you."

"How fortunate that I am practised at it," Catriona replied.

As Beth called down for some tea, Catriona forced herself to relax. Her thoughts kept flitting back to her missing diary, and a vaguely nauseous realisation was creeping up on her, one she did not entirely wish to confront.

Her diary, which contained all her information on the case, all the little pieces of evidence she had gathered, could not have been at the *Messenger* offices after all, because what had she done but taken it with her to Scotland Yard, into the office of a person who had expressed a keen interest in its contents? She had set it on his desk and carelessly left it lying there, an irresistible temptation to which he must since have succumbed.

Marlowe, damn him!

# CHAPTER 13

Under the pretence of speaking with the inspector about the mystery woman Lord Ashford had been seeing, as her papa had suggested, Catriona rose at first light the next morning and was on the train into town within an hour. However, upon arriving at Scotland Yard to find Detective Whitby again manning the reception desk, she was to be disappointed: Marlowe would apparently not be in that day.

Luckily, in what she considered a coup of persuasion, she managed to convince Whitby to part with the inspector's personal address. So it was that she exited King's Cross station and headed east onto Collier Street, lined with tenements, until she reached the number the young detective had jotted down.

The environment inside was an assault on the senses: laughter from behind one door, the heavy smell of tobacco from the next. It was not entirely unpleasant, although an altogether different sort of accommodation than she was used to. Determined though she was to confront the inspector and retrieve her diary, she did find herself slightly ill at ease at the prospect of doing so on his territory.

She waited outside his flat and listened for a moment, but from behind the door of No. 9 came only silence. Distantly, she heard the rattle of passing trains and voices from the street. She knocked, waited, and knocked again.

"Yes, hold on!" came the hoarse reply from inside. A thump, footsteps, and then the door swung open to reveal him.

A flame of heat engulfed her face. He was straight from bed, wearing linen trousers but no shirt, and she caught the briefest glimpse of well-formed torso before whirling at once to face the opposite direction.

"Good heavens, Inspector," she exclaimed breathlessly.

When at last she glanced back over her shoulder, he was looking out into the hallway as if to ensure none of the other tenants had seen her there.

"Do come in, then," he said with impressive sangfroid.

She followed him inside, looking in vain at the door frame, the floorboards, anywhere but the bare expanse of his back. It was nothing to get flustered over, she reasoned. She had seen entirely nude male statues before—though those had produced decidedly less of an effect.

"A moment," he said, turning towards the bureau to pull on a shirt. "I assumed you were a messenger from the Yard."

"Naturally," she said, and distracted herself by determinedly studying the flat. The room was small and tidy, with the faint scent of shaving soap, the bed sheets rumpled and thrown back. An open window overlooked the street below, admitting the cold air. Catriona was suddenly, mortifyingly aware of herself as an unexpected feminine presence.

"Not a social call, I take it," Marlowe said.

"May I turn around?"

"Yes."

She faced him. "No, it is certainly not a social call. I suspect you know why I am here, so shall we skip playing coy?"

"You are direct as ever," he said, crossing his arms.

"The diary I so carelessly left in your office Friday night," she said. "I wish it returned to me at once."

He levelled his peculiar grey eyes on her. "Perhaps I intend to keep it as evidence."

"Do you?"

"Your decision to withhold information from me was not well made, madam. All you have uncovered, that blackmail note, the financial trail connecting Stratton to the opium den proprietor..."

"As gratified as I am that you have enjoyed your reading—"

"Listen to me," he said, his voice so commanding that she stopped in spite of herself. "You have concealed evidence in a murder inquiry. This is a criminal act, not to mention a total dereliction of your moral duty."

A strange sensation akin to indignation had arisen within her. Indignation and embarrassment, and even a defensive sort of shame.

She had been caught out, yet she knew he would not arrest her, so why should she feel so out of sorts? There was only the obvious conclusion, which was that she cared what he thought of her. The realisation repulsed her.

"Are you quite finished scolding me?" she said. It had come out shrilly, her nails digging into her palms through her pale blue silk gloves.

"Nowhere near so," he said. "Is this a game to you?"

"You know it is not. Several times have I approached you in good faith to propose a quid pro quo—"

"A quid pro quo! You have approached me with the intention of coaxing information out of me, information you know I cannot give you."

"At least I had the courtesy to coax," she said. "I ought to have distracted you and taken your police notebook."

"Madam, it was you who set the thing on my desk and left it there," he said matter of factly. "I saw an opportunity and capitalised upon it. Do you expect me to believe you would not have done so?"

"I would not betray the trust of a friend," she said, "and you know so, because is that not why we have found ourselves here? Because I did not divulge information Lady Stratton disclosed to me in confidence?" She glanced away. "But then, I see we are not friends, Inspector, and I was foolish to think we ever could be."

Something in him relaxed, a loosening of the shoulders and jaw. When faced with female emotion, men often made excuses to flee, as if anything other than a placid expression on the face of a woman were unsettling, even obscene. But he regarded her with no disgust or pity, and he showed no sign of retreating.

"Did you not once say you thought us on the same side?" he said. "Our aims are aligned, yet your good opinion of me is so quickly lost?"

"My opinion of you was middling at best, and it has plummeted considerably," she said, but with little feeling.

"Come down from your horse, Miss Winters," he said. "If you mean to try to convince me the only reason you withheld this information was because of a sense of loyalty towards Lady Stratton, I will not believe it."

"Believe whatever you like," she said.

His eyes narrowed, and she breathed in to speak, to protest whatever he might have been about to say, only to find that hesitation had lodged itself in her throat. If it was not loyalty towards Lady Stratton, it was at least a compulsive sense of obligation, a way for Catriona to make right the fact that the ghastly spectacle of his lordship lying dead at the docks had served as fodder for her first story.

But she could not tell the inspector that.

Coming to confront him had been a mistake. She realised so now. She had underestimated him, and she knew she must remove herself from his flat immediately, get out from under his perceptive gaze before he could compel her to reveal anything further. The diary could be abandoned. She could start another and be more careful this time.

"If you are so intent on not returning my property, I suppose you may keep it," she said at last, then turned from him and took a step towards the door.

Something like disbelief flickered across his expression. He had stepped forwards and held a hand out towards her. "You wished to know why the late Lord Ashford put in for my secondment from Birmingham," he said. He watched her warily, as if she were a horse on the verge of bolting. "Perhaps it is time we discuss your quid pro quo."

At the small table by the window, Catriona watched the street below. Earlier in the century, Islington had been home to a fashionable set, but with the influx of poor families pushed to the outskirts of London by the construction of the railway, the district had become rundown. Yet it was far from the utter destitution of the rookeries, and something about the crowded tenement even felt homey.

From over her shoulder, Marlowe set a cup of tea on the table in front of her. "I hope you take it plain," he said. "I have no sugar."

She observed him as he sat across from her. There was something strange about seeing him so disarmed. His hair was still out of place from sleeping, he was unshaven, and by the dark shadows under his eyes, she suspected he had spent much of the past two nights at Scotland Yard. Had she not been so incensed at the compromising situation in which she found herself, she might have felt bad for interrupting his morning.

After some silence, she staring down at her tea, he out the window, she said, "I think it only fair you lay your cards out first."

He turned back to her. "I mentioned the late Lord Ashford was the reason for my presence in London," he said. "He was pursuing an inquiry at the docks into the illegal sale of opium."

She did not react, though this confirmed her suspicion that in some capacity, Randall was involved in the operation of the opium den.

Marlowe continued. "Ashford reached out to a colleague in the Midlands for advice," he said. "My governor, as we uncovered a similar operation in the Fens last year."

"So he brought you here to look into the criminal enterprises of the East End," Catriona said.

"Yes," he replied. "Do you understand why you must step back from your enquiries? These people are dangerous."

"Are you saying you believe the two killings to be connected?"

"Do you think it unlikely? His lordship was investigating the very opium den outside which Stratton was killed," he said. "Ashford left me with very little information about the status of his inquiry. I gather he meant to brief me this past week, but the Stratton murder derailed his plans."

As he spoke, a conflict had arisen within her. It was quickly becoming clear that Ashford may not have known about the connection between Randall and Stratton. His visit to the antiquities dealer had had nothing to do with the murder at the docks; it had simply been part of his ongoing inquiry into the illegal sale of opium, with which Randall was somehow involved. Aside from Randall himself, and his clerk, Catriona believed she was the only person who knew Ashford had visited his office that afternoon—and she was thus the only person capable of linking the two murders.

She could not have explained her hesitation to share this information with the inspector. She knew it would be right to do so, yet regardless of her personal opinion of him, which she acknowledged had evolved over the past few days, something in her railed against it. It was a reluctant acceptance that once she had told him, her upper hand would disappear, and she would be forced to step back from her enquiries completely.

"Inspector, I must tell you something," she finally said—and then, because she could not help herself, "something that is not in my diary, so I have you at a disadvantage."

"Exactly where you like me, I gather," he replied drily, but he leaned forwards in his chair and steepled his fingers on the table to listen.

"On Friday, as I left my meeting with Randall, someone else arrived to see him. It was the late Lord Ashford."

"What?" The word was a sharp exhale. She had surprised him after all.

"He did not see me there. Randall seemed taken aback at his arrival. I assumed his lordship was following the same trail I was, though I later wondered how he could have uncovered the connection."

"He must have suspected Randall was involved with the opium den," Marlowe said, quickly reaching the same conclusion she had.

"Regardless of why Lord Ashford met with Randall that day, I agree it is surely no coincidence that he was killed so shortly after, just as Stratton was."

"Rest assured, Randall will be questioned," he said.

She felt this indicated a dismissal of sorts, as if now that he had his information, he would usher her out. So, with a sense of desperation, she pressed on. "I think Stratton was trying to blackmail Randall, having gained knowledge of his possible involvement with the opium den, which could have ruined his professional reputation. Could Randall have killed Stratton to silence him?"

"You suggest it follows that Randall would have been willing to silence Ashford, as well, if he thought he was close to being discovered," he said. "But I struggle with the idea that Randall met Ashford and then ventured into Scotland Yard itself hours later to kill him."

She exhaled. He was taking her seriously after all. She sipped her tea, glanced out the window, and then turned back to him. "In the interest of coming clean, there is one other thing you ought to know."

"Only one?" he said.

"It concerns the late Lord Ashford and his personal life."

His eyes narrowed. "Yes?"

"My papa told me that—he may have been seeing someone."

"To be clear, you mean romantically?"

"Yes," she said, quashing her natural embarrassment at the topic. "You know his lordship was a widower, I presume. My papa suspected that the woman he was seeing, whomever she might be, was from outside our circle."

"I see," Marlowe said.

"Will you make enquiries? My papa wishes to reach out to her before we publish a story on the tragedy tomorrow."

"I'll try to track her down, but I think it unlikely we should find her before then. I must speak with her as well, of course—amongst others," he said. "You know to whom I refer."

"You cannot mean Nathaniel Turner," she said.

"He was heard arguing with his father," Marlowe said. "And I know you will defend her, but I really doubt Miss Turner was being truthful when she told me her brother was at home that evening."

"I cannot speak to that," Catriona said a little too quickly. "All I know is that he did not kill his father, so you are better off not wasting your time on that dead end."

"I will take that under advisement."

"Infuriating," she muttered. It had come out involuntarily.

"What?" he said, the corners of his mouth quirking almost imperceptibly, though she was certain he had heard her.

She drew herself up. "I said you infuriate me, Inspector."

"The feeling is mutual, I assure you," he said.

"But," she ventured, "I suppose friendships have been based on less."

"Then I have it, your friendship?"

"If you extend me the same trust I have extended you. I believe I have well demonstrated my capacity for discretion."

"You know I cannot tell you everything," he said, but he had not rejected the proposal outright.

"Then tell me what you can. Whatever you say off the record, I promise not to publish it."

He stood abruptly. "I agree to your terms," he said. "In the meantime, I suppose you want this back." He turned towards the bedside table, where her diary lay. She had not seen it there.

"Are you sure you wish to part with it?" she said archly. "I should hate to deprive you of your bedtime reading."

"Very droll, madam." He extended the diary towards her.

She rose and hesitated only a moment before reaching to grasp it. "In truth, I doubted you would return it," she said, "so you have surpassed my expectations."

"Let this not be the last time I do so," he said.

She tucked the diary into her reticule. "Then I wish you good morning," she said with a nod, and turned to leave.

"One thing more," he said.

She glanced back to him. "Yes?"

"I know you will wish to confirm their connection, but you must not contact Randall or the opium den proprietor again."

"You think me very reckless indeed," she said. When he did not deny it, she continued, a little offended: "I will not contact either of them. Now, unless you've any further demands?"

Had he known her better, he might have found her lack of protest suspicious. As he did not, he said only, "None, thank you," and escorted her to the door.

By the time Catriona descended to the platform at South Kensington, she had come to entirely regret what she had agreed to. Tsang would indeed have been the next target of her inquiry. She needed to know, was Randall involved with the opium den to the extent that Stratton could have blackmailed him over it? She could not help but consider going back on her word. It would be a simple thing to return to the opium den—alone this time.

But for now, she had other matters to attend to. The first, she thought as she passed the Turners' house, was to write her report on the tragedy at Scotland Yard, though the circumstances behind the killing of Lord Ashford were as murky as ever. The second was to extend her condolences to Lady Stratton on the occasion of her husband's funeral the following day. If her ladyship wished to discover what her visit to the antiquities dealer had revealed, she would reach out in reply. The third and final matter was to look into the identity of the woman Ashford had been seeing, though where she might begin on that front, Catriona had no idea.

She felt some relief at returning home, whereupon Hughes took her heavy overcoat and bonnet. Before she could disappear to the withdrawing room, he presented a note on the familiar silver tray, and she took it. There was no return address, and she did not recognise the hand. A strange little thrill shot up her spine. She had to restrain herself from tearing open the seal right there, instead waiting until she was upstairs, safely away from prying eyes.

As she scanned its contents, the tension which had lodged itself between her shoulders lifted. She had in fact resigned herself to keeping her word to the inspector. Left to her own devices, she told herself, she would not have tried to contact Tsang. How fortunate it was, therefore, that the attempt at contact had come not from her but from the opium den proprietor himself.

# CHAPTER 14

"Catriona, good morning," Sir Frederick said as she joined him at the breakfast table the following day. "I hope you know I do not expect you at the office. Your papa can manage alone, I promise." He was thumbing through a stack of the competition and had barely glanced up at her.

"I know you can," she said. "But in fact, I wished to show you something."

She went to stand beside his chair, producing a neatly penned page, which she handed to him. She had risen with some trepidation that morning, having spent the remainder of the previous day perched at her desk, attempting to write her report on the tragic slaying at Scotland Yard. She did not want her papa to pass the assignment to someone else. Catriona felt personally connected to the event and saw it as her duty to convey the information to the public. She could trust no one else to do so.

"My dear, this is…" Sir Frederick began, then fell silent as he read.

She stood beside him, trying to focus on the sound of a coach passing in the street rather than her nervously beating heart. Over the years, she had become adept at anticipating how her papa might react based on the slightest clues—the flare of the nostrils, the quirk of the brow, the twitch of the mouth. But, angled as she was now over his shoulder, she was unable to judge his expression. There was only his impassive back and the steady hand which held the page.

Finally, he set it down.

"I see," he said. He glanced up at her. "My dear, you know I dislike the thought of you slaving away, reliving such a frightening experience. One of the reporters could have produced a satisfactory summary of the event."

"But that would not do at all!" she exclaimed. "I cannot stand the idea of someone else writing about something I witnessed. That is, unless the piece is not adequate?"

He tapped the page. "More than adequate."

She waited for more, a dismissal, an explanation for why he must nonetheless choose another reporter for the story.

But instead he leaned back in his chair and said, "Does the inspector know we plan to publish today?"

"Yes, I told him so," she said.

"Good. I do not wish to jeopardise the inquiry, but better us than another paper," he replied with finality, apparently having settled the matter to his satisfaction, and hers.

"I agree," she said. "Shall I accompany you to town today?"

"Please take the day off, my dear," he said, beginning again to flip through the stack of papers to his right. "You have done more than enough."

She proceeded to her seat at the other end of the long table. "I cannot bear to sit around when there is so much to be done," she said. "We still have to track down the woman Lord Ashford was seeing."

He sipped his tea. "I do hate to think of a loved one hearing the news this way. But there is nothing for it. We do not know where to begin."

"I asked Marlowe about it yesterday, as you suggested," she said, absently spreading marmalade over her toast, "but he knew nothing about it."

"Ashford has always been very secretive about his personal affairs. Ah, my old friend," Sir Frederick said, then sighed. He held up a hand at her look of concern and gave his head a shake. "No, my dear. I am quite all right. The office will be a needed distraction today."

"Then perhaps I ought to call on the Turners," she said. "I expect I shall find some way to make myself of service."

"I spoke with Nathaniel—to get his permission, I suppose, to publish today," Sir Frederick said. "I advised him to take a few days away from the office, at least until the funeral, but I gather he might prefer to keep himself occupied, under the circumstances."

He had spoken without looking at her, still idly thumbing through his papers. Catriona was used to his habit of speaking without necessarily expecting a reply. Sometimes she felt it was his way of working through ideas.

"I should be off," he said at last. "Thank you for your work, my dear. I confess you have taken a weight off my shoulders. Do let Mrs Travers know I should not be home for supper tonight, will you?"

As he rose and departed, her page tucked under his arm, Catriona decided to neglect to mention that she would not be home that night either. The missive from Tsang, an invitation to dine with him that evening at the Café Royal in Piccadilly, had caught her by surprise, but she had no intention of passing up the opportunity to question him, and at a more suitable venue than that dreary boarding house by the docks.

After breakfast, she dressed and called on Bethany at home. She had been seated by the fire in the drawing room with a book, which she set down immediately, glad for the company.

"Henry promised to visit today," she said as Catriona joined her on the settee, "but he had some meeting or other this morning. I rather dreaded the thought of being here alone meanwhile."

"I shall be here as long as you need me," Catriona said. "Is Nate not home?"

Bethany gave a little sigh. "No, he is home but…unfit for company."

"I see," Catriona said.

"You know I dislike speaking ill of my brother."

"Of course."

"But he does make it so difficult to avoid, behaving as he does, stumbling home at all hours, blind drunk."

"We grieve in different ways, I suppose."

"His way embarrasses me, and it should embarrass him, too," Beth said. "Perhaps you could talk some sense into him."

"I could certainly try."

"Papa would not have stood for it," Beth said. She had spoken with such conviction, but now her voice wavered. She looked into the fire, blinking rapidly. "As a girl, I used to watch him leave and wish I could follow. He lived an entire life outside the walls of this house, a life I never knew."

Through the window, the square below was quiet in the pale midmorning. It was the sort of day one might prefer to stay indoors, watching by a fire as puffy flakes of snow drifted softly onto the gardens.

"Then Nate went away for school, too," Beth continued, "and I was jealous beyond anything. I wanted to go off to Harrow right behind him. But it was not my place. I thought one day, marriage would be my adventure instead, yet now I think of the future, and Henry, and babies and dinners and correspondence, and it all stretches out endlessly. I feel myself being chipped away at, disappearing piece by piece until nothing is left."

Catriona knew not what to say. That past spring, Beth had treated her engagement as a triumph. And it had been. Bancroft was a man of industry, and industry was the future. But perhaps the reality of her upcoming marriage was altogether different than what Beth had expected. Or perhaps, Catriona thought, she had been pretending at enthusiasm from the outset, even to herself.

The idea of marriage had always given rise within Catriona to a strange, desperate sort of panic, the same she imagined a fox might feel upon finding itself caught in a trap, realising that a parched, painful end was all that awaited it. She could not have explained her feelings, not without being judged, not in a way that conveyed herself adequately. It was not that she lacked the capacity for love. It was not love she feared but the ceaseless routine of everything that came along with it.

"Perhaps you cannot understand," Beth finally said, each having been caught up in her own thoughts. "You care too little about what others think, and I care too much. I cannot do otherwise."

"You need not marry Mr Bancroft," Catriona said at once. It had burst out of her. She expected Beth to scoff, but in her dark eyes there was only a quiet resignation. "You need not marry anyone at all. If your father expected you to, Nate certainly does not."

"No," Bethany said. "In fact, he might feel infinitely vindicated if I decided against it. God help us both." She gave a little smile and reached over to take Catriona's hands in hers, which were soft and warm. "I am sorry for going on, Kitty, and for saying you cannot understand. I know you do."

"I wish I could help you, Beth. I started at the newspaper offices because of Papa and his heart, but maybe I enjoy it too much, feeling occupied somehow, and I have neglected our friendship because of it."

"No, my dearest friend," Bethany said. "Our duties have simply pulled us in different directions for now."

They sat in silence for a moment, hands still clasped, the way they had sat as children. The fire in the hearth crackled and sparked brightly.

"My duty today is to none but you," Catriona said at last.

"I am sorry indeed to hear Miss Turner is indisposed," said Vera Parsons, who sat on the settee beside her daughter, Jessamine, across from Catriona in the parlour. "The vicar will keep her in his prayers."

"Thank you," Catriona said. "Your kind offer to pray with her was most appreciated."

Mrs Parsons had a stern and imposing countenance. In some ways, Catriona liked her because she did not allow herself to be spoken down to or dismissed. Indeed, her husband's position as vicar of Holy Trinity made dismissing her impossible. One could not very well dismiss God, no matter how tiresome one might find his company over tea.

Having heard from her husband the tragic news, Mrs Parsons had written Beth that morning regarding her intention to call. Though visits from anyone but close friends before the funeral were atypical, Mrs Parsons was not one to let social norms stand in the way of what she saw as doing the Lord's work, administering charity to a bereaved young woman in her parish.

"Her absence was felt keenly yesterday," Mrs Parsons said. "As was the profound absence of the late Lord Ashford, God rest his soul."

"Of course," Catriona said simply. She did not excuse her own absence at church, and she expected Mrs Parsons might soon comment on it, but the Turners' maid, Anna, provided a welcome interruption before she could, entering with a tray of tea and small light sandwiches, which she set on the low table.

Sometimes Catriona did not mind church. She liked the quietness of it. But other times, she felt only that it made her feel annoyed and hypocritical. She fought the sudden perverse twitch of amusement that threatened her expression. She could hardly explain that she had spent the mass hour in the private flat of Inspector Marlowe, a man she had met only a week prior.

"It can be so difficult after a death, being restricted from the usual social activities," Mrs Parsons said with the tone of one about to begin a sermon. "But prayer is a salve for the soul, not a social obligation, so the Lord calls on us to administer it."

"Hmm, quite," Catriona said.

Jessamine sat forwards on the settee but did not reach for her tea. "We were so devastated to hear it," she said. "The late Lord Ashford was always…"

"He was a fine man taken too soon," Mrs Parsons said.

Catriona could only nod.

"Miss Turner is fortunate to have a friend such as yourself to care for her, Miss Winters," Mrs Parsons continued, then looked pointedly at her daughter as she said, "It is a duty her sister in law might have undertaken for her, had she one."

"Oh," Jessamine said, and her expression was very strange, almost self-conscious. "Yes, you must pass along our condolences to—to his lordship, as well."

Catriona had been gripping the arm of the settee, but she made herself relax. Poor Jessamine, she thought. She had pleasing features and pretty blue eyes, with an even rosy complexion that made every colour of dress suit her. She would have no trouble finding a husband, perhaps a banker or a draftsman. But her mother was evidently angling higher than that. She certainly would have her work cut out for her with Nate—or rather, with the new Viscount Ashford.

"I shall," Catriona finally replied. Then, sensing the visit was nearing its natural end, Mrs Parsons' objectives having been accomplished, she said, "Your kindness does you credit. Please do convey my well wishes to the vicar."

Once the two had departed, Catriona remained in the parlour. Glad of the solitude, she sighed and closed her eyes, listening to their footsteps crunching in the snow until they turned a corner and the sound faded. For a moment, although she had spent as much time in the Turners' parlour as in her own over the years, she felt that peculiar sensation of being in the home of a stranger, where the sounds carried differently and the air was a little too cold.

"Morning, Kitty."

She blinked to find Nate waiting in the doorway of the adjoining library, having approached in inexplicable silence.

"It is afternoon," she said, "and by no small margin. Do you find yourself quite recovered?"

"Depends. Care to play Miss Nightingale?" he said, leaning against the frame with an insufferable smirk.

"Certainly not."

"No, I see Beth has you occupied fending off callers instead," he said. "How are the Parsons?"

"Delightful, as always," she replied. "Mrs Parsons is of the opinion Beth needs a sister in law, and I daresay she has her daughter in mind for the role."

"How quickly the vultures descend," he said. He had gone to stand in front of the fire, extending his hands idly towards it as if having come in from out of doors.

Catriona knew she should tell Beth her unwelcome guests had gone, but something held her to the spot, watching his back.

"I should enlist Beth to play matchmaker on her behalf," she said, wanting a reaction. "She does not dislike Jessamine, you know."

"Nor do I."

"No?"

"No," he said. "So what do you think of that?"

"I think nothing of it," she forced herself to say. "You may like or dislike her as you wish."

"Perhaps I shall," he said. "Like her as I wish, that is."

"Then I should be the first to congratulate you on your fine match. I imagine you might do well under her influence."

"Do you, or do you simply wish to be contrary?" he said. His tone was light, but she could not see his expression. "I think you know under whose influence I imagine myself."

Before Catriona could reply, footsteps sounded in the hallway beyond, and Beth came fluttering into the room.

"Oh," she said. "Good afternoon, Nate. Nice to see you up." She threw herself down onto the settee beside Catriona. "Have they gone? I heard a little quiet and thought it was safe to come down.

I was in Papa's study, you know, going through his papers. I thought I might find something to help the police."

"Try not to think about it, Beth," Nate said. "They'll come by to comb through his things eventually, I expect."

"Yes, I suppose so, but I would rather be doing something than lying about," she said. She had flung a hand across her eyes, but she lowered it and glanced at the door. "Henry should be here soon. Shall I call down for more tea?"

"Not for me," Nate said, then finally turned from the fire to face them. "Give my best to Bancroft, will you? See you both."

And with that, he was gone. A moment later, the front door clicked open and closed, and Catriona resisted the urge to turn and watch him through the window behind her.

"Off to do something terribly important, I'm sure," Bethany said. "Will you stay, please, Kitty?"

"Until Mr Bancroft arrives, of course," Catriona said. "Then I have some errands to run in town this evening."

Beth's mouth twisted in a pout. "Oh, I do so wish I could go into town," she said. "I don't know how I'm meant to sit around the house until the funeral. Of course, Nate is permitted to do whatever he pleases."

Catriona sensed her friend was descending into the same discontented melancholy which had afflicted her that morning. She moved quickly to change the subject. "Beth, you said you were in your father's study?"

"Yes. I can't help but think I might notice something, some clue he left behind." Her expression had changed at once, becoming pensive, almost determined, though she said, "I know it sounds silly."

"Not at all," Catriona said. "Few people knew him as you did."

"I thought to enquire about having his personal effects brought home from Scotland Yard, as well. I loved visiting him at work. I hate to think of his office there now, so empty."

The sound of heavy new footsteps over the snow outside signalled the arrival of Bancroft, and Beth rose from the sofa.

Catriona was seized by an unexpected panic. Why had she not told Beth she would be meeting Tsang in Piccadilly that evening? Surely it would be prudent for someone to know her whereabouts—and she could not very well leave a note for her papa!

But it was too late now.

A cold gust preceded Bancroft through the front door, and Bethany was rushing to relieve him of his hat and gloves, saying, "Henry, darling, come in near the fire. How dreadfully chilly it is!"

# CHAPTER 15

The prospect of that evening rattled her conscience. She could not help but recall the unpleasantness of that den in Limehouse, the figures sprawled about with hollow, bleary eyes. She was going to dine with the sort of man who profited off the misery of others, even encouraged them in it. And her own misery? She had fallen into such a startling trance upon breathing in the smoke, transported through time back to that high ridge in St Lucia, with the dark sea below her. She had heard her mother as if from a memory.

"How is that, miss?" Emily said from behind her, having just lowered the comb from her hair, which was piled in becoming curls atop her head.

Catriona forced herself to focus on the mirror. "Very good," she said. "I should not be home until late. Please take the rest of the evening off. I shall fend for myself when I return."

"Thank you, miss," Emily said. "Enjoy your outing."

Catriona, still looking carefully at her candlelit reflection, did not turn as Emily departed. She felt that because her papa had raised her, it was him she took after in her mannerisms. But her mama was there in her appearance, in her colouring, the timbre of her voice, and perhaps her vague yearning for something more than she had yet found from a conventional life.

The chime of the clock from the drawing room below roused her from her musings. It was time to depart. Given the snow and the late hour, she tasked Hughes with flagging down a hansom to take her to Piccadilly. After a journey of no more than ten minutes, she alighted before the Café Royal and proceeded through its marble and mahogany entrance, whereupon a waiter took her overcoat and then showed her through to the impressive dining room.

She had never been before, but she knew it was a popular destination with the Piccadilly set, ornate almost to the point of ostentatiousness. The high ceilings were done in the French style, with gilded frescoes and descending gas chandeliers, and the floors were a varnished warm parquet, over which her shoes clicked pleasingly as she followed the waiter between crowded round tables.

Tsang sat near the window, as distinguished in appearance as she recalled. Watching him unobserved, protected by the veneer of society, she hoped to glean something more of him than she had perceived in the den. But as she approached, his black eyes met hers at once, and he remained a mystery.

He rose, revealing a sharp and well-fitted suit, and pulled out her chair. "Madam, good evening," he said, then sat across from her and gestured towards the uncorked bottle of red wine. "Do you drink? The best cellar in London, they say."

"Thank you," she said, and watched whilst he poured.

As she swirled her glass and sipped, she glanced at him over the rim. He had turned to look out the window at the drifting snow and the passers-by in the street. Something in his posture had a Byronic quality, she thought, languid and relaxed.

"I find life in the city to be exceedingly predictable at times," he began. "How refreshing it was to sit here, entirely undecided as to whether you would be joining me this evening."

She set down her wine. "I would have been remiss indeed in forgoing the opportunity to have my questions answered, Mr Tsang."

"How to the point you are," he said.

"Do I shock you?"

"On the contrary. You act exactly as I imagined you might." He leaned one elbow on the table. "Ask away, madam."

"The antiquities dealer, Alan Randall," she said. "Is he involved closely in the operation of your establishment?"

"You mean to throw me off, asking that first."

"The tactic has failed?"

"Not entirely," he said, "but you might ask yourself what prompted my invitation to you in the first place."

"I would rather you told me outright," she said.

"Perhaps I aim to ascertain what you know. Information can be dangerous in my line of work—to those who discover it and those who seek to hide it."

His words implied a threat, but his expression was only mildly inquisitive. A vague sense of discomfort descended over her as she considered, perhaps for the first time, that Tsang might be the murderer. The possibility had not occurred to her till then. His genteel exterior had been enough to fool her.

Yet if he were the killer, his motive remained a mystery. He was a criminal by profession; he had no reputation to preserve, so surely Stratton had not seen him as a reasonable target for blackmail?

From across the room, a man laughed loudly, and the sound broke her from her musings.

"I pose no threat to your business, if that is your concern," she said, "but a man was murdered just outside its doors, and I wish to know why."

"Have you considered that his lordship might simply have come across a ruffian who tried to rob him and killed him in the process?"

"I have reason to believe the murder was premeditated," she said.

"So why ask about my antiquities dealer?"

"You said you wished to ascertain what I know," she said. "If you expect me to be forthcoming, you might extend me the same courtesy. I have no wish to expose your business to any risk, I assure you. My aims are strictly professional."

"Are they?" he said. As he did, his teeth glinted in the light like those of a predator. "For my part, where you are concerned, I cannot say the same."

Catriona knew she had betrayed her shock. Her gloved hand flew to her lips, which had parted involuntarily in a gasp. How incredibly forward he was, his black eyes almost clinical, watching for her reaction. She forced herself to relax.

"Now who means to throw off whom?" she said.

"Have I succeeded?"

"No," she said, though it was a lie, and she knew that he knew so. "I wish to know what role Alan Randall plays in your enterprise. Does he do anything illegal? I imagine so, given what I have seen of your dealings in Limehouse."

"Smoking opium is not illegal."

"Selling it is."

"Have you got a moral objection to the sale of opium, Miss Winters?" he said. "Perhaps you have—but only when it is sold in the East End."

The statement was a challenge. In Britain, following spates of infant deaths and a perceived threat of public moral decay, the sale of opium had been restricted to licensed pharmacists. Yet in China, agents of the British government peddled Indian opium to an addicted populace in vast quantities. Many of the merchant sailing crews who came ashore in Limehouse, and who made up the majority of his clientele, she had seen, were victims of that ruthless policy.

So determined were they to preserve their trade that when the Qing emperor, grasping the extent of the crisis, attempted to restrict imports, the British had gone to war over the issue not once but twice. The first opium war had ended in the forties, concluding with the ceding of Hong Kong to the British, and the second had ended nearly twenty years later, shortly after Catriona was born.

She felt a keen sympathy for the Chinese, caught as they were in the shadow of a colonial leviathan. The same conquest had occurred in her native St Lucia, by the French and the British in turns, and left its own scars on the island and its people. Perhaps that was why Tsang had made his comment, because he had perceived the many ways in which, like his own, the course of her life had been set by the expansion of the empire.

"Regardless," he continued, "what if I were to tell you Randall plays no role in my business whatsoever?"

"I would not believe you," she said, relieved they had moved on from a topic that had made her acutely uncomfortable. "I know about your payments to him every two weeks."

"Perhaps I have a fondness for antiquities."

"One might think you were purchasing the Acropolis piece by piece, at that rate," she said. "No, I believe you and Mr Randall have a financial arrangement unrelated to his usual profession."

"Do you? Then I have every confidence you will figure out the nature of that arrangement on your own," he said, moving to refill their glasses.

"I plan to," she said. "For all you know, he has invited me out to dinner next."

"Ha!" His laugh was clear and unselfconscious. "Unlikely, as he has left town. But I think you knew that."

She sat very still. He had finished pouring the wine, and he swirled his glass, watching it intently, before his eyes flicked to her.

"No," he said, "you did not know after all."

"Leaving town is not the act of an innocent man," she said.

"What do you imagine Randall to be guilty of?" His tone was

amused, almost incredulous. "You say you pose no threat to my business, but your disruption of my financial affairs leads me to believe otherwise."

"Sir, you have been very reluctant indeed to part with any information that might be of use to me, so why should I answer that?"

"You wish to know why I invited you here tonight?" he said. "Because Randall has cut off contact with me, and when I stopped in to question his clerk yesterday, the man told me Randall had received a visitor Friday afternoon. None other than yourself, of course. Apparently, he experienced a sudden shift in demeanour afterwards, so what about your meeting prompted him to leave the city that very evening?"

She felt put on the spot. Had the clerk not told him about the other visitor of Friday afternoon, the head of the Criminal Investigation Department himself?

"When I visited Mr Randall," she said, "it was because I knew Lord Stratton had paid him fifty pounds prior to his death. I wished to know what the payment was for and whether it could have been connected to his murder."

Tsang simply watched her, waiting for her to continue, which she felt she must, somehow straddling the line between maintaining his interest and giving herself away entirely. For all his civility, she sensed an icy undercurrent in their conversation. As if she were Oedipus and he were the Sphinx, she knew that at her first wrong word, he would devour her.

"One must be so careful not to leave sensitive information lying about where anyone might see it," she said. "Randall left his records unattended for a moment, and that was how I learned the payment in question, the one from Lord Stratton, had been made on your behalf. Sir, I see a web connecting Stratton, Randall, and you. The first has died. The second has apparently fled the city. You alone remain here, unscathed. So what should I make of that?"

He sat back in his chair. "If your only aim is to discover why Stratton was killed, I will tell you what I believe happened, and we can put this to bed." A strange expression crossed his face, almost a sneer, as he said, "Stratton was a fool with only a little more money than sense. Even for as regular a patron as he, my willingness to extend credit goes only so far."

"He owed you," she said.

"He did. A week before his death, he came to the docks with a stack of notes in hand. I told him to put it out of sight and sent him to Randall. To kill two birds with one stone, so to speak."

"In covering your payment to Randall, he covered his debt to you."

"Yes," he said. "So do you see now why I believe Stratton was killed by chance? Most who visit my establishment have the sense not to flaunt their wealth. There are those in the East End who would slit your throat for a shilling. Stratton had no real instinct for self-preservation."

"Perhaps few of your patrons do," she said. She had not liked Stratton, not particularly, but her feeling of protectiveness for his widow prompted her to soften the blow against him. "For they come to you in search of oblivion, do they not? I suppose Stratton found it after all."

"Is that what you saw in the smoke, oblivion?"

Her heart skipped strangely. The change in subject had been abrupt, almost accusatory, but in his voice was only a determined inquisitiveness. That she had opened herself to such a question made her feel defensive, as if she must guard against what she saw in the inky darkness of his eyes. It was a restlessness she recognised, the same she had seen in her mother, the same she felt within herself.

"You asked me that day, too," she said, feeling as if everyone in the dining room were watching her. "But why does it matter? None of it was real."

"If men come to me in search of oblivion, the smoke gives them only as much as they will accept. I know where you went, and I wish to know what you saw there."

"I went nowhere," she said, her mouth having gone dry. She had to look away from him. "I saw nothing."

"I had a brother, or someone who was like a brother to me," he said. Nothing in his voice had changed, but she recognised the grief in him, the same that gnawed away inside her, a feral animal she had reined in and reined in.

"Is that who you see—in the smoke?" she said.

"Sometimes."

She said nothing. Behind him, there in the window, was her reflection, but it was not herself she saw. It was her mama, just as she remembered her, barely older than she was now.

At the sight of it, as if the whole world were rushing around her, Catriona rose, nearly knocking back her chair. Tsang rose as well, but she knew not how to explain herself. If she did not leave immediately, he would recognise the grief in her, too, and that would have been more than she could withstand.

"I regret I cannot stay," she said.

"Miss Winters—"

"No. We have nothing more to speak of, would you not agree?" She was turning already, glancing desperately for the route that would take her through the dining room and out into the street. "I shall not interfere in your affairs any further. What you do in Limehouse does not concern me."

"If you change your mind," he started. He had reached out to take her hand, an impertinence, but his expression held only concern, concern and a strange sort of triumph, and she could not bring herself to wrench her arm away. "You know where to find me."

She wanted to say something, anything at all, to tell him she never wanted to see him or go back to that place again. But it would have been a lie, and he would have known it.

She turned and fled.

When at last out of doors, having stopped only to retrieve her overcoat, she gasped in the cold air until it hurt her lungs. Pressing her hand to her chest, she forced herself to regain her composure, blinking back the burning sensation in her eyes and throat.

She walked aimlessly through Piccadilly, past grand houses and darkened snowy gardens. A coach clacked by, its horses nickering a hot mist, and across the street, a father lifted his child over a puddle of slush. Catriona felt separate from everything in a way she could not have explained, as if she were watching herself from afar, as if part of her had remained forever on that ridge, and at any moment she might snap back across the vast distance that separated her from herself.

By the time she reached Leicester Square, she realised her feet had been carrying her subconsciously towards Covent Garden. She needed to distract herself somehow, to stop herself from asking the questions she had avoided for so many years, questions about her mother and the darkness inside her, the ugly despair that had driven her to the ridge, and the question she feared most of all—whether, after that night, the darkness might have made a home inside her, too.

The city held nothing else for her. But the *Messenger* offices would be empty at that hour. Like a wounded animal, she was seeking refuge in familiar places. There, at least, she would be alone.

# CHAPTER 16

Upon arriving at the office and spotting the thin line of red lamplight spilling from the darkroom, Catriona realised an encounter with Nate was inevitable. She felt numb and thought she must simply turn around and go home. But part of her knew he had already heard her enter.

Occupied with something on the far table, moving with an agitated sort of energy, he did not turn to face her as she stood at the threshold of the darkroom.

"You can come in, you know," he finally said, then did turn to look her up and down. "Had a good evening?"

She ignored his comment. In her rush to leave the Café Royal, she had not fastened her overcoat over her pale green evening gown. "I wondered where you were off to this afternoon," she said. "Are you working on something interesting?"

He wore no jacket, his sleeves rolled up. "Etching a copper plate," he said. "Your father wishes to experiment with a photogravure process that would allow us to print at full speed."

"May I see?" she said, stepping towards him.

"The plate is submerged in ferric chloride now," he said, his gloved hands tilting it back and forth in a basin of dark liquid. The subject of photography was, to her, mundane and grounding. "After the etching is complete, it can be inked and printed."

"How did you learn all of this, the chemistry and everything?" Catriona said. "I've never known you to be so…"

"Competent?"

"No," she said. "I know you can be competent in whatever you wish, but you've never cared to apply yourself."

"My years at Cambridge were not entirely wasted, whatever my father might have suspected," he said. For a moment, there was only the sound of the liquid lapping in the basin. "And I had time enough on my hands in the country."

"Not time enough to write, of course," she said.

"You say that as if you would have read my letters."

"I would have."

He withdrew his hands from the basin and turned to face her, his dark eyes fathomless in the red glow of the lamp. "What more was there to say?" he said. "I suppose you wanted me to beg for a scrap of your affection."

She took a step back from him, suddenly utterly conscious of the closeness of the room. "Perhaps we shouldn't talk about it," she said, "if you wish to turn it into a quarrel."

"Are you going to be cold to me forever? I know it was my fault, trying to force your—your decision…" His mouth twisted with something like regret, but before she could interrupt him, he cut himself off, swallowed hard, and grasped the table, his posture flagging all at once. "Sorry," he said then. "I feel unlike myself."

Her anger faded immediately. "Are you all right?" she said. "Let me fetch you some water, or I could open a window."

"No, just give me a minute," he said. "I haven't been sleeping well."

"You're very pale," she said.

"I'm fine." He straightened. The strength had returned to his voice. "Really, I'm fine now."

"Come home, then, won't you?" she said. "It's late."

He had already turned, refocussing on the plate. "No, you go on ahead, please," he said. "Sorry for worrying you, truly. I'm all right."

Her hand fluttered in the air between them, caught halfway in the instinct to reach for him. She withdrew it but did not turn to leave. She felt as if she were standing precariously on a frozen river in which swirled every unsaid thing, and with one wrong word the ice would crack beneath her. She was too afraid, always too afraid.

"Good night, Kitty," he said, facing determinedly away from her. "It's late, as you said."

She sighed, stinging from the dismissal, then took one step back, then two, then three, until she was clear of him at last, and neither said anything further.

. . .

The following morning, Hughes greeted her with a letter at the bottom of the stairs. The parlour doors across the foyer were closed, which she took to mean that her papa had visitors, early though the hour was. Instead of going in for breakfast alone, she thought she might wait him out, so she perched on a step and tore open the wax seal on the envelope.

It was from Lady Stratton, thanking her for her condolences and extending her own, she having heard of the death of the late Lord Ashford. She had invited her to tea that afternoon, but with no obligation to attend if her grief prevented it.

Catriona refolded the letter and laid it in her lap. Her dramas of the previous day had pushed all thoughts of Lady Stratton from her mind, as she had not expected to hear back from her so soon after the funeral. Her ladyship would no doubt wish to discuss what Catriona had discovered Friday at the office of the antiquities dealer, but she had learned so much more since then, chiefly that there had been an ongoing inquiry into the illegal sale of opium centred around the very den at which Stratton had been a patron. How much could she tell his widow without being indiscreet?

The opening of the parlour doors interrupted her thoughts, and Sir Frederick emerged with a familiar person, Colonel Samuel Isaacs, one of their neighbours from across the square. He was sharply dressed, with a stethoscope around his neck, his features distinguished but kindly.

"Catriona," Sir Frederick said, showing no surprise at having spotted his daughter on the stairs, "good morning, my dear."

She rose at once. "Good morning, Papa. And Colonel Isaacs, what a pleasant surprise. How fares our patient?"

"Fit as a fiddle, madam," he said. "I trust my advice has not gone unfollowed."

Colonel Isaacs had served in the military with Sir Frederick in their youth, then had gone on to rise within the ranks of the medical corps, stationed most recently as part of the Afghan campaign of the previous summer. Since his present retirement, he had taken on the occasional private patient, one of whom was her very stubborn papa.

"A brisk walk each day," Sir Frederick said, "wine instead of whiskey, and my daughter has insisted on taking on some of my duties at the office, as well."

"I am glad and gratified to hear it," Colonel Isaacs said.

"Colonel, will you join us for breakfast or some tea?" Catriona offered.

"Thank you, but no," he replied. "I must be off. I am lecturing the nursing cohort at St Thomas today." He removed the stethoscope from his neck and folded it into the leather medical bag at his feet. When he straightened and regarded her again, his expression was sombre. "My sincere condolences on the loss of Lord Ashford, madam. When I read the dreadful news yesterday, I thought I should stop in to check up on my old friend."

Sir Frederick clapped him on the back. "Sometimes it feels like just yesterday we were young men on that wretched battlefield." His eyes had always been a most piercing blue, but they had faded lately, turning glacial in the morning light. "But time flows ever on," he said. "Will you attend the funeral? It has been set for Thursday, I understand."

"Of course," the colonel said. "My wife and I will be there. Now, good day to you both, and see you tomorrow."

That said, he turned and departed.

"Some good news, then," Catriona said, descending the few steps to the foyer. "We must keep you on the mend, Papa."

"Hmph," Sir Frederick said with a petulant expression. "One rather prefers to enjoy what time he has left! To deprive a man of his whiskey should be a capital crime."

"Are you quite finished?" Catriona said affectionately, patting the arm he had offered. "I shall call down for breakfast."

"Please do, my dear," Sir Frederick said, but stopped before the doors to the dining room. "One thing first. Your papa has done some investigating into the matter we discussed Saturday."

"The woman Lord Ashford was seeing?"

"The very same. I asked Hughes to speak with Jones about it, you know, butler to butler."

"I cannot imagine Jones parting easily with household gossip," Catriona said, picturing the dignified man who had been with the Turners for many years.

"Ordinarily, no. But under the circumstances..." He had lowered his voice, although, of course, the only people who might overhear him were their own staff, none of whom, Catriona thought, would breathe a word to anyone. "Apparently," he continued, "he overheard Ashford speaking to a coachman, having to pay the man extra to take his companion on to her destination."

"But why?" Catriona said.

"I gather she may live in an undesirable area of the city, somewhere cabs do not go. One wonders how Ashford met her." He cleared his throat, evidently having realised he was straying into an inappropriate topic of conversation. "But it does not do to speculate," he said with finality. "He associated with all sorts in the police, after all."

"Should I pass this along to Inspector Marlowe?" Catriona asked. "It could help in the inquiry."

"I think so, my dear, and I do hope something comes of it," Sir Frederick said, then sighed. "To think how many lives I have pried into as part of my work. But prying into the personal life of my oldest friend is an altogether different matter. It feels rather a dirty business."

"Your intentions are good, Papa. This woman may know something important."

"Perhaps," he said. "Yes, tell the inspector, and then we can wash our hands of it. Now do let us go in for breakfast."

At the Turner residence, a black mourning wreath had been mounted on the door. Catriona raised the knocker and was admitted at once by Arthur. She did plan to visit Scotland Yard that day. It could hardly be avoided, now she had her papa counting on her to relay information, and afterwards, she had decided she would indeed join Lady Stratton for tea.

But she thought first to check in on Beth, hoping to make

herself of service somehow, starved for amusement as her friend was. Yet when Arthur ushered her through to the parlour, Catriona found Bethany already entertaining a visitor.

Bancroft rose at her entrance. "Miss Winters, good morning," he said with a precise bow.

"Kitty, your arrival is most fortuitous," Beth said, "as Henry says he must leave me again."

"I am relieved to hear I have not interrupted your visit overly much, Mr Bancroft," Catriona said.

Beth rose from the settee. "You must see what Henry has brought me today." She extended her arm to reveal a delicate string of pearls around her slim wrist. "Directly from the Persian Gulf. Is it not the loveliest thing?"

"Oh, what a splendid present," Catriona exclaimed. It was such an intimate gift, worn directly against the skin, but it was the sort of gift a fiancé was permitted to give, she supposed, especially after a death, as pearls were often said to symbolise tears.

"One does try," Bancroft said brusquely, though not without a hint of pride. "I must be off. Bethany, I'll arrange with Jones to have those boxes moved upstairs before I depart, shall I?"

"Thank you, darling," Beth said, then set a hand on Catriona's arm and explained, "Henry has had Papa's personal effects brought home from Scotland Yard."

"It was nothing," Bancroft said. "Now, good morning to you both."

Bethany kissed him on the cheek, and Bancroft nodded to his fiancée, then to Catriona, before he turned and strode purposefully from the room. At the sound of the door closing behind him, Bethany returned to the settee and gestured for her friend to join her.

"Sit with me awhile, Kitty," she said whilst ringing the bell for refreshments. "I am to be all alone again today."

"Nate is at the office?"

"He left early this morning, I think. And he looked dreadfully sober when he came home yesterday, so that was an improvement." She gave a satisfied little smirk.

Sitting there in the airy parlour, its curtains parted to the white morning light, Catriona felt far from the darkroom of the evening before. But, recalling the strange turn in his demeanour, the suddenness with which the colour had drained from his face, her concern for Nate resurfaced.

"I spoke with him last night," she said, on the verge of bringing it up. "He was working on some kind of photographic experiment for Papa."

Beth had turned to look out the windows, where snow had gathered against the sills, creating patterns on the glass. "I shall be forever grateful to your papa for giving my brother an opportunity to keep occupied these days," she said.

"Perhaps he aims to prove himself."

"His timing could use some work, could it not, now our father is no longer here to see him do it?" Beth returned, then sighed and softened her tone. "Henry has arranged the funeral for Thursday. I gather there will be a procession beforehand, but I should be glad to have it all over with. Papa would have found all this pomp and circumstance somewhat ridiculous."

"He would be impressed at how well Mr Bancroft has acquitted himself, though. The man is entirely devoted to you."

"Yes," Beth said, "and in six months, when the wedding can go ahead, I shall be out of this house forever."

"You'll miss it?"

"I think I will, you know. Not the house but the stage of my life that it represents: the innocence of childhood, when one feels every opportunity in the world is hers for the taking."

"But you have done so well for yourself, Beth."

"Yes, Henry is a fine man. I suppose I simply wished…" She looked down, fingering the clasp of her bracelet. "It is such a silly thing. But I cannot help but wish, for all his fine qualities, that I might feel something more profound for him."

"That may come with time," Catriona said, but she did not know whether she believed it. Really, it had come out like a question.

"And if it does not?" Beth regarded her with a pained, earnest expression. "No, I know this is what it is to marry. A fulfilment of duty."

Catriona said nothing in reply. Beth had reached across to take her hands, and she held them tightly, graspingly, as if awaiting reassurance. But the words were caught on her tongue. Catriona was afraid somehow—afraid that if she spoke, she might encourage doubts her friend should later come to regret, and afraid that Beth had perceived a secret inside her, one she would not willingly have acknowledged.

How could she tell Beth that she understood her entirely, that she too felt it keenly, the suffocating fear of finding herself trapped in a narrow life?

She knew what would happen next. As she always did, Beth would find a delicate way to redirect the conversation. The moment would pass as though it had never happened, the fear relegated to the realm of unsaid things. They would speak instead of the weather, of mourning dresses, each studiously avoiding those topics which truly occupied her thoughts.

Beth withdrew her hands and shook her head softly. "Not to worry, Kitty," she finally said. "I have survived worse than a little ennui."

# CHAPTER 17

That afternoon, as the snowy edifice of Scotland Yard rose from the fog before her, Catriona deliberated over what to tell Marlowe. Her papa had discovered that the mystery woman the late Lord Ashford had been seeing lived in an undesirable area of the city, though exactly where remained unknown.

Yet she had another piece of information that might be of interest to the police. According to Tsang, Alan Randall had apparently fled town since Friday. To Catriona, that cemented his involvement in Ashford's murder. He had committed the killing and then, she imagined, gunpowder still coating his hands, fled to avoid apprehension.

But perhaps Marlowe already knew as much. He had said he would question the man, after all. Better for him to have made the discovery on his own. Then she would not have to admit her betrayal.

She entered Scotland Yard to find the place busy and the familiar Detective Whitby manning the reception desk in the back hall.

"Good afternoon, ma'am," he said, sitting up in his chair. "Here to see the inspector?"

"I am, thank you. Is he in today?

"Afraid you've just missed him," Whitby said. "Off to an incident in Old Nichol. Arson or something of the sort."

"Oh," she replied.

Was it disappointment she felt? For reasons she could not have explained, Marlowe's absence unsettled her. But he had other crimes to attend to, naturally. Had she expected him to wait around Scotland Yard to hear from her?

How silly.

"Shall I take a message?" the detective prompted.

"Yes, please. I'll leave a note, if you could pass it along."

"Of course."

He handed her paper and a fountain pen, and she scrawled a message quickly:

*Inspector,*

*New information. Please call on me at your convenience.*

*C. Winters*

"Thank you, Detective. I am most obliged," she said upon folding the note and handing it to him, then turned and headed back to the street.

Perhaps it was for the best that the inspector was away, she rationalised as she set off for Piccadilly, where she would join Lady Stratton for tea. After all, his absence would give her more time to think over her course of action, even to confirm what Tsang had told her about Randall having left town. What harm could there be in her stopping in at his office to speak with his clerk herself?

At the Stratton house, she was admitted and shown through to the parlour, where her ladyship awaited. For some minutes, the conversation flowed as it often did between acquaintances, the topics inconsequential, rehearsed, each playing her role. But after a time, her ladyship fell silent midsentence, staring down into her tea, which she stirred without purpose.

"I think my husband would have been pleased with it," she said, and Catriona knew she was speaking of the funeral. "Many of his friends were there, and a few even deigned to speak with me. But it is difficult to have a burial in the cold, the ground being so brittle with frost..." Her lips had gone white, a thin line. "I think you know why I have invited you here today, aside from my enjoyment of your company."

Feeling a certain relief at the dropping of pretences, Catriona replied, "You wish to hear what I discovered during my visit with Alan Randall on Friday."

"I do."

"My lady, you were correct about the fifty pounds your husband withdrew. He paid the sum to Randall a week before his death."

"And did this fellow give a satisfactory explanation for the expense?" Lady Stratton said with a fierce expression, then again looked down to her tea. "Or perhaps I do not wish to know. Ever since my husband died, I have struggled with the idea that he may not have been the man I thought he was."

Catriona watched her in silence, thinking of what Marlowe had implied—that her ladyship was as good a suspect as any in the murder of her husband. Seeing the woman before her, she still could not believe it.

"No," Lady Stratton finally said, looking up at her. "I must know. I think I must know."

"If you're sure, I shall tell you," Catriona said. "His lordship owed money to the proprietor of an opium den in the East End. I am unclear on the precise nature of the arrangement, but the money paid to Randall was meant to settle that debt."

"An opium den?" Lady Stratton said quietly. As if a weight had lifted from her shoulders, she straightened, and when again she spoke, her tone was relieved. "I see. I so often agonised over the suspicion that my husband had succumbed to the baser sort of temptations to which men often do. He would come home very late some nights, and sometimes not at all." She spoke matter of factly now. "But whilst he may have had a weak character, I see his lordship was faithful to me in the end. It is a far greater comfort than I might have hoped for."

Catriona said nothing. In their previous conversations, she had sensed a certain degree of delusion in Lady Stratton where his lordship was concerned, perhaps a wilful ignorance of his lesser qualities. But now she saw her for who she was: someone grasping desperately to hold on to her memories of her husband as she had known him.

"There remains the matter of the blackmail note," Lady Stratton continued. "I don't suppose it might also be connected to the opium den?"

"You wish me to continue looking into the matter?"

"I do. Whatever grace the police have shown me will subside now that the funeral is done with. I know they will descend on this house in the coming days, and I must be prepared for anything they find."

"There is one avenue of enquiry I might still pursue," Catriona said, thinking of the possibility that it had been Randall whom Lord Stratton was blackmailing. "I shall let you know what I uncover."

"I know my hope in you is not misplaced," Lady Stratton said, then rose and lowered her veil over her face again as she accompanied Catriona to the door.

Catriona had once thought her ladyship to have a very plain appearance, but now she acknowledged something pleasing in her countenance. Her expression was gentle and unpretentious. Perhaps this was what had drawn Lord Stratton to her, Catriona thought with some surprise. Yet it must also have made her an easy target, in the battlefield of society, for the sorts of petty snipes which were hurled like javelins and landed just as sharply. It was why Lady Stratton found herself so alone now, because her sincerity of character, rather than inspiring empathy in others, instead caused them to feel ashamed and withdraw from her company.

Standing across the street from the office of Alan Randall, Catriona observed the door surreptitiously.

If indeed a business arrangement existed between Randall and the opium den, and Stratton had discovered it and blackmailed the man over it, Randall would have had a motive to commit the killing at the docks. Now Tsang was under the impression that the antiquities dealer had left town. Not the act of an innocent man, surely.

But Catriona hesitated before crossing the street, seized by a strange regret for what she knew she must do. She was on the verge of breaking her word to Marlowe for a second time. He had specifically asked that she not try to contact Randall. Yet there had been no activity at the office, no one coming or going, so she did not anticipate speaking to Randall so much as confirming his absence for herself.

She drew her overcoat closer, stepped out into the road, weaved between coaches and other passers-by, and approached the door of the office to find it unlocked. The bell chimed her entry, and the clerk looked up from his desk and recognised her at once.

"Oh, good grief," he said. It was not the sort of greeting to which she was accustomed. Recovering quickly, he said, "Mr Randall is not in today, and with all due respect, ma'am, I think it best you leave right away."

"Mr Anderson, was it?" she replied. "I know a man came to speak with you, enquiring after Mr Randall, and you told him I was here Friday afternoon," she said.

His face had drained of colour. He had risen but remained behind the desk, and for an almost imperceptible moment, his hand twitched as though to reach down for something.

It was enough for her to realise she must stay close to the door.

Evidently, his visit from Tsang had shaken him, and for all she knew, he had a weapon stashed under the desk and would not hesitate to use it if he felt threatened.

"Yes," he finally said, "a man came looking after Mr Randall, and I told him of your visit. What of it?"

"Why only mine?" she said. "Why not tell him Mr Randall entertained another visitor directly afterwards?"

"I don't know what you're talking about," the clerk said.

"You do," she replied. "As I was leaving this office, Mr Randall received a visit from someone else. But you knew that, of course, so why lie about it?"

The clerk regarded her carefully. Then, like a sail deflating, he sank back into his chair. "I figured out who he was, the man who came to see Mr Randall after you," he said. The words had come out in a rush, as though he were eager to be rid of them. "Mr Randall was hiding several aspects of his business from me. I saw that much. Then that other man came in on Sunday, that Chinese mobster, demanding to know who had spoken to Mr Randall and when. He as much as threatened me to get me to talk, you know! He believed Mr Randall must have informed on him to the police."

She tried to imagine it. How differently might Victor Tsang go about retrieving information when no one was watching? Seeing the clerk was young, no older than she, and somewhat distraught, she softened her tone. "Now Mr Randall has fled the city and left you to deal with whatever consequences he has brought down upon himself," she said. "After his visitor departed on Friday, what happened?"

"Mr Randall told me to fetch some things from his place. He said he needed to meet with someone, and he left immediately. He keeps a townhouse on Kemble Street—for a girl, if you catch my meaning." His face had gone red. "I think it was her he went to see. I met him at the train station after."

For a moment, she thought he would leave it at that. But, as a confessor might address a priest, with relief and resignation in somewhat equal measure, he continued: "Before he boarded his train, he was panicked, completely out of sorts. He gave me the key to his warehouse. The exchange took a minute at most. That was the last I saw of him."

"And what was his destination?" Catriona asked, feeling like a hunter closing in on her prey.

"Dover. I can only imagine he planned to board the next ship to the continent."

Dover was a straight shot across the Channel to Calais. If this were true, Randall would have reached France that very night, and the trail would now be cold.

"The train he caught, it would have left around ten o'clock?" she said.

"No, much earlier than that. I was to meet him at the station at six, and he left immediately."

Catriona had barely managed to contain her surprise. If the clerk were to be believed, Randall had left the city well before Ashford was killed, thus ruling himself out as a suspect. "You're absolutely certain he boarded a train shortly after six o'clock?"

"Yes. I even waited at the station for some time afterwards, half expecting him to turn around at the next stop, but he never did come back," the clerk said. "I must manage the business until he returns, whenever that might be. The police came in yesterday, you know, asking all the same questions you are. I told them only that Mr Randall was away on a personal matter."

"So you know your employer was involved in more than antiquities dealing, but you know not what."

"Look, are you some kind of private detective?" the clerk said. He glanced behind her then as if expecting reinforcements to come bursting in. "Why are you looking for Mr Randall? When you came in on Friday, you had a note from some baroness or something."

"A marchioness, but yes. You may think of me as a private detective if you wish," Catriona said, liking the sound of it—and what would Marlowe think of that? "Mr Anderson, I need you to tell me what Mr Randall and his visitor spoke about on Friday. Did the man take anything from the office, any records?"

"I didn't hear their conversation," the clerk said. "But he did take something with him when he left. A letter or a contract, perhaps? Mr Randall kept all sorts of records I never saw. Good Lord, how will I manage?"

Sensing the moment of potential danger had passed, Catriona approached the desk and set a gentle hand on its surface. "Sir, I must be frank with you. It is highly likely your employer was involved in illegal activity. If the police choose to pursue an inquiry, you may very well be charged as an accomplice."

"But I never knew anything!" he exclaimed, indignant.

"I see that, which is why I recommend you tell the police

everything you have just told me. If you come clean to them, they will see you are innocent of any wrongdoing. But the police are not your only worry. Mr Randall has essentially left you holding the bag, so when his more unsavoury associates come to call, what will you tell them?"

"Are you really not with the police—or that man from Sunday? Is this some kind of trick?"

"No, and you must trust me that it is best you remove yourself from this situation as quickly as possible." She rapped her fingers on the counter as if that settled it. "And you must not object to lending me the warehouse key Mr Randall entrusted to you. There are those who would take it from you by force, so I think we might agree this is the preferable scenario."

He said nothing, only regarded her for a moment, then shook his head and turned to the filing cabinet behind him. Having unlocked the top drawer, he produced from it a heavy brass key, which he extended to her.

She took it and tucked it into her reticule. "And where is the warehouse?"

"Narrow Street, near the entrance to Regent's Canal."

"At the Limehouse docks?" she said without surprise. "You have been most helpful, sir. Now, will you take my advice? Tonight you must think of how you will put your affairs in order here and close up this office, and tomorrow you must go to Scotland Yard and tell your story to the police."

"About the warehouse, what shall I tell them?"

She had not thought that through. She could not very well

instruct him not to mention it, as its existence might prove crucial to the inquiry. Somewhat begrudgingly, she said, "Ask to speak directly with Inspector Thomas Marlowe. You may tell him you gave the key to Miss Winters. He will recognise the name. You see? All above board."

"Yes, I understand," the clerk said.

"Very good." She stepped away from the desk. "I shall leave you to your business now, Mr Anderson. Good day."

He did not answer her. She had not given him the chance to, retreating quickly to the street before he could change his mind. She proceeded with determination to Charing Cross and, upon boarding her train and taking the seat a gentleman offered her by the window, finally had the chance to parse through what she had discovered.

Randall had not killed Ashford, but it was still possible he had killed Stratton, was it not? Perhaps he had thought the arrival of Ashford at his office meant the police were on to him for the murder, so he fled before he could be apprehended. Meaning whoever killed Ashford had done so for a different reason.

She did not like it. This again opened the door to questions about Nate and his presence at Scotland Yard that night, given the row Detective Whitby had overheard. But Nate had told her he left the Yard well before the fatal shot, and she wanted to believe him.

Randall was involved with the opium den, but in what capacity she could not guess. She also had a new avenue of enquiry, his warehouse, yet it struck her that the docks were a strange place to store antiquities. She had no knowledge of conservation, but surely the damp air would do more damage than good. So what was Randall hiding there?

# CHAPTER 18

A snowy mist had settled over the Limehouse docks when Catriona arrived the following morning, having set out before dawn, before she could think better of her plan. She had taken the train to its last eastwards stop and, after a walk of no less than an hour, neared the place just as the sun began its dreary ascent.

The docks were already awake, with barges crowding along the canal, cargo carts rattling across the planks nearest the basin, and stevedores porting crates to and fro. But Catriona passed unnoticed towards the warehouse on Regent Street, the brass key cold and impossibly heavy in her hand. She had deliberated the previous evening as she waited to hear back from Marlowe, having determined that if indeed he called on her as she had asked, she would relinquish the key and let him handle the matter.

But he had not called on her. He had not even sent a reply.

So her decision had been made, and she felt no guilt. Marlowe would find out about the warehouse that very day if Anderson went to speak with the police, and if he did not, the inspector would find out at a time of her own choosing.

The lock clicked open easily, and with an application of concerted force, she was able to roll the large door on its rusty castors enough that she could slip through the narrow opening. Inside was incredibly dim, so much so that she could make out barely more than shadows. As she adjusted to the darkness, a shock went pinging down her spine. Two eyes stared back at her from within the warehouse. But it was only a painted sarcophagus, whose inhabitant would remain unknown.

She would have no choice but to leave the door open for light whilst she explored. She slipped past musty rolled carpets, stone columns no doubt plundered from ancient temples, a handsome bust of some forgotten Mesopotamian prince, and stacked wood crates. She knew not what she hoped to find, but she knew she had not found it yet, and she pressed on into the depths of the warehouse. The exterior was only thin wood boards, beyond which barges churned up the waters of the canal as they passed.

She inhaled the briny river air, then paused to listen, having become acutely aware of nearing footsteps and the wheels of a cart clacking heavily over the laneway. She stilled in place.

"Oi! One of you lot leave this open?" a man called out.

They must be stevedores, unloading cargo from a ship at the docks. She willed herself to blend into the shadows, hidden behind a group of precariously stacked crates. How long would she have to stay there, hoping none of them ventured into her corner of the warehouse?

"Last shift must have forgot to lock up again, those dullards," one said. "Set it down there. Good lads."

Catriona waited for what felt like ages, their shadows shifting over the crates across from her as they carried the cargo inside. The smell of damp wood suffocated her. Even above the lapping of the river, surely they would hear her heart pounding.

After a time, they retreated into the laneway, and she breathed a sigh of relief.

"Lock up behind us, will you?" one called out to another.

She jolted away from the wall in a panic. The padlock was on the outside! If they locked her in, she would be trapped there for who knew how long.

She needed a distraction, a way to make a break for it. There was no time to think. She flung her hand out into the darkness until it made contact, sending a small crate clattering to the floor.

The wood splintered spectacularly, and out spilled statuettes, engraved coins, cuneiform tablets, wrapped paper packages—and a familiar strange smell, heavy and intoxicating.

"Did you hear that?" one said.

But Catriona was no longer listening to them. She had knelt as if in a trance, loosening the twine until the paper unfolded to reveal its secret: a brick of dark opium.

Randall was not merely a dealer of antiquities after all. No, his business was a front for a far more nefarious import.

"You there, show yourself!" A dark silhouette had appeared between the crates.

Catriona rose at once, threw a hand up to cover her face, and barrelled past the man, through the startled group in the laneway, and down Regent Street.

"Stop, thief!" one of the stevedores yelled.

She ran, blood racing, lungs burning, pinpricks of falling snow stinging her eyes. As she reached the docks, she shoved her way desperately through the crowd. The men were on her tail, shouting, gaining on her.

Ahead were the narrow laneways of Limehouse, a shrouded maze of brick which would serve as her escape.

But it was not to be.

Her ankle twisted dully, her shoe having caught a protruding cobblestone. For one confusing moment, cold air whistled past her ears. Then pain lanced through her palms as the impact sent her clattering to the wet stone, jarring all her bones.

She felt stunned, blinking.

"Hurry, can you stand?"

The voice was familiar. A man had appeared like a ghost from the mist at the mouth of the dark laneway to her left.

"Mr Tsang…?"

"Quickly now," he said, extending his hand to her.

She took it unquestioningly, and he hauled her up, pulled her against him, and whirled them into a nearby doorway, hidden from view of the boardwalk, just seconds before the stevedores raced past.

. . .

In an upper room of the boarding house, its window open to the falling snow, Catriona sat before a roaring fire. The enigmatic den madam had brought her a bowl of warm water and soft rags to tend to her scraped palms, and, now clean and warm, she felt altogether more composed than she had earlier, racing across the docks like a prey animal.

"Thank you for your hospitality," she said. "I owe you both a debt of gratitude."

"Think nothing of it, please," the den madam replied. "A friend of Victor is a friend of mine." Then she bowed and retreated, leaving Catriona under the inquisitive black gaze of the man seated on the settee across from her.

"How fortunate you are that my associate spotted the commotion on the docks," he said lightly. "Now, do you care to explain your presence? When last we parted, you said Limehouse was of no further interest to you."

"I came into new information," Catriona said. "I hope you know my only aim is to determine why Lord Stratton was killed. I do not particularly wish to learn what sort of operation you oversee here, but it appears the trail has led me back again."

He shook his head and glanced away, over to the window, before turning his frank eyes upon her once more. "You know I had no involvement in Stratton's death," he said.

"How could I know it—from your word alone?"

"You think my word has no value?" He sounded more intrigued

than offended. "I could have let those men catch up to you."

She realised she had clenched her fist only when the pain of her nails digging into the raw scrape startled her. "I do thank you for your timely intervention," she said.

"A happy coincidence," he replied, "or perhaps fate has brought us together again."

"Do you believe so?"

"It would surprise you to hear that I do?"

"On our first meeting, I presumed you to be an exceedingly practical man," she said. "A belief in fate would have seemed contrary to your character. But perhaps now it would not surprise me."

"And what do you believe?"

"That we make our own fate. It is nothing but my own foolhardiness that has led us to cross paths today."

"You discredit yourself," he said. "What you call foolhardy some might call bold."

"Boldness is not well valued in a woman," she said.

"I cannot agree," he replied.

His gaze was forthright. He was an attractive man, decisive and even perceptive. Acknowledging as much provoked within her a certain wariness towards him, one that dared to be ignored.

"In truth, it was neither foolhardiness nor boldness," she finally said. "It was curiosity, of the kind that killed the cat. I have discovered the nature of your arrangement with Randall."

"You have done, of course," he said. "I had complete confidence you would. And what will you do now?"

"Nothing. You'll have to find another supplier of opium, as

yours has fled town, but that is of no interest to me," she said. "Am I in danger, knowing what I know?"

"Should I expect to soon find the police on my doorstep?" he said.

"Not through my doing."

"Then I pose you no danger. I suppose you thought I would want to silence you?" He drummed his fingers on the arm of the settee. "No, though sometimes necessary, I find murder to be a most distasteful business."

"Is it not murder that you commit here, selling opium to the poor creatures who seek it?" she said, though she did not know what had possessed her to challenge him so. "A slow murder. Murder nonetheless."

His mouth twitched then, an almost imperceptible flash of amusement or disdain. He stood and said, "Come to the window with me, madam."

She followed him to it. Away from the fire, winter had crept into the room. Unmoved by the cold, he stood in silence for a moment before he began.

"In Hong Kong, my father was a fisherman. He took me out onto the water often as a child, early in the morning, at sunrise. I helped him pull the net in, spill the fish out into the bottom of the boat. I remember looking down on them, their silvery bodies, watching them gasp for breath in the cold air."

He was no longer speaking to her but to himself. She said nothing, caught in a strange anticipation, a dim awareness of a growing danger.

"I have been a British subject all my life," he continued. "The empire cast its net over us, an island of farmers and fishermen, and ever since, we have been caught in that net, yearning to go back to the sea."

He had set his hand on the windowsill. She followed his gaze over the blackened roofs, the smoking chimneys, the hulking ships, out to the pale horizon of the city.

"The world keeps turning," he said. "Perhaps I shall find another supplier, perhaps not. Then my patrons will find another establishment in which to slowly murder themselves. Business is my empire, madam, and one must continue to cast out the net."

A chill descended through her. The white sky had begun to burn her eyes, so she lowered them.

Below ran the Limehouse Cut, at the edge of which, perhaps in contemplation, stood the den madam, her white dress stark against the silty water. As if sensing her presence, the woman glanced up, and their eyes met before Catriona looked away.

"Who is she?" she said without thinking.

"A most intriguing person, is she not?" Tsang had turned from the window to face her. "Jingyi Leung, mother of my dear late friend. I have accompanied her to London as her escort."

"And what thinks Madame Leung of your empire?"

Something rippled across his features before his expression again settled into one of cold satisfaction. He quirked a brow as he said, "Have you given further thought to what we spoke of at the Café Royale?"

"We spoke of several things."

"So you will not tell me what you saw in the smoke that day?"

"No."

"Because you do not wish to admit it to yourself."

"You suppose I am in denial," she said. "But it was only a dream, a delusion."

"Does that matter?"

At once she felt the most panicked sensation, a prickling in the eyes, a closing up of the throat. She glanced away lest he see her discomposure.

"My mother," she said at last, and did not know why. She felt trapped, almost lightheaded with the shame of her secrets, and when she continued, it was as if she were pleading with him. "I was very young when she died. She was out on the ridge. There was a storm. It was—an accident."

"I know that sort of accident," he said. "My friend had one too, with a length of rope and a beam."

She realised she had been holding her breath. Unable to tear herself away from the inky blackness of his eyes, she felt very suddenly as though she might faint.

"Come back into the smoke with me," he said.

"I do not wish it."

"You do," he said, "so much so you feel you must flee to stop yourself going through with it."

He clasped her hand. The gesture was not romantic, but his grip was warm and strong. From the pocket of his jacket he produced a white ceramic pipe, and he pressed it into her palm. She did not allow herself to think. Her hand trembled as she raised the pipe to his lips, and he packed dark opium into it, then lit it with the spark of a match.

Cold winter air swirled in from the window, and with it came the briny smell of the river, the soot of thousands of chimneys, and above it all the familiar smoke. He breathed it in, held it in his mouth, and tilted her face towards his.

She closed her eyes. Her lips parted. When he breathed out, she was flooded with warmth, a strange lightness of the body—a sensation of coming home.

# CHAPTER 19

Catriona awoke on the settee, startlingly cold, shaking from head to toe, filled with a vast, gnawing emptiness. Someone else was with her in the room, standing before the fire, a white figure illuminated in silhouette by the flames.

"Where am I?" she murmured.

Madame Leung turned to face her. "Limehouse," she said. "It is early evening, madam. You should leave before dusk. The streets are not safe after dark."

Catriona sat up. Her limbs felt alien. She was almost painfully alert to her surroundings. "Where is Mr Tsang?" she said.

"Away. He asked me to watch over you." Madame Leung lowered herself to the chair across from her, regarding her carefully.

"I feel very strange," Catriona said.

"Have some oolong, please." Madame Leung pushed the steaming cup into her hands. "Drink it before it cools."

"Thank you," Catriona said.

As she sipped the tea, floral and not unpleasantly bitter, she glanced out the window, through which the sky had turned a mottled purple as the sun set over the masts in the port. All those hours in the smoke, and she had not felt time passing without her.

She turned to face Madame Leung again. This was the woman Ashford had spoken to on the morning Stratton's body was found, and now he was dead too. So many questions swirled in her mind, yet she hesitated to ask. Madame Leung had an aura of such melancholy that it compelled her to silence. She remembered what Tsang had said about her son. It was the greatest pain one could imagine.

"I must go," she said at last, setting her tea on the low table. "I have a long walk ahead."

Madame Leung reached across to place a gentle hand on her arm. "Take care," she said.

"I will," Catriona replied. "Thank you."

Those were all the words the two exchanged before she was led back through the winding grey corridors, down the stairs, and through the curtain which separated the smoking room from the foyer.

Catriona made her way home in a daze, wandering westwards through the darkening streets, sitting numbly on the train as it passed beneath the city. Even a hot bath did little to allay the chill lingering inside her, and as she sat before the fire that evening in the drawing room, she was glad her papa was out. He would have seen her scraped palms, prompting her to lie about where she had been all day.

Perhaps it was best, she thought, having splayed her diary open across her lap, that she had an evening to herself to sort out how everything fit together.

"Miss?" It was Hughes, who had ascended the stairs to find her. "There is a man at the door."

"Take his card and send him away, please," she said, irritated not at the butler but at whichever caller had taken it upon himself to drop by so late.

Hughes hesitated. "He says he is from the police. I have asked him to wait."

She started, irritation transforming into mild panic. She could not very well put the inspector off after specifically asking him to call on her. It would be too suspicious. "Thank you, Hughes, very good," she finally said. "Please send him up."

"Right away, miss," Hughes said, and turned to descend.

With very little time to compose herself before she heard more footsteps on the stairs, she closed her diary, straightened her posture, and clasped her hands calmly in her lap. Then he was there in the doorway of the drawing room.

"Miss Winters, good evening," Marlowe said, nodding to her.

"Inspector." She rose.

"I apologise for the lateness of the hour."

"You received my note?"

"Yes, when I returned to the Yard this morning," he said. "There was a fire yesterday afternoon, and it lasted late into the night."

"I hope no one was injured?"

"I have not come to trouble you with upsetting news."

She didn't know how to reply, so she only returned to her armchair and gestured to the one diagonal to her. "Inspector, you must sit. Will you take some refreshment?"

He lowered himself to the chair but remained at the edge of the seat as if he did not intend to stay long, which annoyed her. "No, thank you," he said. "But I will take the key with which Mr Anderson entrusted you yesterday."

She said nothing. The key was in her pocket.

"Yes, madam," he continued, "Randall's clerk came in to speak with me as you so conscientiously advised him."

"I suppose you feel I did wrong," she said. "But I watched the office to ensure it was only him inside, not Randall."

Marlowe expelled a quick sigh. "A technicality. But perhaps I should have known better than to ask you not to seek him out," he said. "You simply are not capable of letting anything go."

Catriona stifled a wince. Again, she had clenched her fists without realising, and she forced herself to relax as she said, "Lady Stratton has been most troubled by the question of what schemes her late husband was engaged in. She asked me to continue looking into the blackmail angle. Would you have had me deny her? I could not."

"It was your own curiosity you could not deny," Marlowe returned. "Do you think I haven't come to understand as much about you?"

"I think you understand me very little indeed, Inspector," she said, abandoning her attempts at calm. "But yes, I took the key from poor Anderson, and with it I went back to Limehouse today. Perhaps you'll be surprised to learn that Randall plays a far greater role in the operation of the opium den than I originally suspected. He is in fact its supplier, using his antiquities business as a front to import quantities of opium right under the nose of the harbourmaster."

"You went to Randall's warehouse," he said flatly. "Of course you did. And were you discovered? No one saw you enter or leave? You were not followed?"

"That is not your concern."

"Do you think I ask you these questions out of idle interest?" he said. "I worry for your safety. That you endanger—"

"You forget yourself, Inspector," she snapped. "You are not my keeper. Nor are you to tell me where I may go and with whom I may speak. I will not abide it. I may take risks, but those risks are mine to take. My life is my own."

In the firelight, his expression had gone fierce. "If you refuse to think of yourself, perhaps you might think of those who care about you and how they should live with it if something were to happen to you."

Indignation flared within her. "Your work puts you in danger every day, does it not?" she said. "Yet because you are a man, you think yourself impervious, whilst a woman such as I must be coddled and dissuaded lest she do harm to herself."

"I know I'm not impervious," he said. "I've seen my share of death, in Africa, in the Fens—hell, in the rookeries last night. I could have been killed when I was shot. I nearly lost my leg as it was. You think I believe myself superior to you? Madam, I have seen the indiscrimination of death, and I couldn't forgive myself if anything were to—" He stopped. "Do you understand me? I could not forgive myself."

She stilled, caught in place by a strange apprehension. The person before her was not the same she had met that first dreary morning at the docks. He had told her once that his only passion was to see a case well solved, and she had thought him cold and pitiless. But she sensed in him now an undercurrent of emotion, perhaps even of deep feeling, and it frightened her.

She rose. "I should ask you to leave," she said.

He rose as well. "Is that what you wish?"

She did not answer him. The word was caught in her throat, but she could not find the air to say it. He stood directly before her, perhaps knowing she would not speak, for if she did, she would betray herself.

From somewhere below them, glass shattered spectacularly, followed by raised voices. He stepped back.

"What on earth?" she said.

He had already turned and was taking the stairs down ahead of her. At the bottom, they found Emily in the foyer, her hands fluttering about her heart.

"Emily, is everything all right?" Catriona exclaimed, then looked beyond her into the parlour. Hughes was crouched on the floor, examining an object surrounded by shards of glass. Cold night air had flooded the room.

"It came in through the window. Broke the glass!" Hughes said as he rose. "I heard someone running towards the street."

Marlowe glanced at Catriona for only a moment before heading out the door. Through the windows, she watched him stride along the footpath and disappear around the corner of the square.

She entered the parlour, cautious of her footing as she made her way across the glittering Persian rug to where Hughes stood.

"Be careful, miss," the butler said as she bent to retrieve the object that had flown through the window. "Ah, what a mess."

It was a small parcel not unlike those she had seen in the warehouse that morning. A sense of déjà vu overcame her, and she watched her fingers move as if of their own accord to loosen the twine and unwrap the paper. For one mortifying second, she expected to see dark opium inside, but it was only a plain masonry brick.

Her relief was momentary, for on the inside of the paper was scrawled a message:

*MIND YOUR BUSINESS.*

The world tilted around her. She rose. The inspector could not be allowed to see this. He had asked if anyone had seen her at the warehouse that morning, and indeed, several people had. Perhaps she had even been followed home, for how else could anyone have known where to find her?

She folded the paper into a tight square and tucked it into her sleeve, then handed the brick to Emily and said, "Dispose of this, please. If the inspector asks, you are to tell him you have used the paper for the stove. Do you understand?"

"Yes, miss," Emily said, taking the brick from her and leaving the room at once. Not for the first time, Catriona found herself grateful for the uncurious nature of her maid.

She turned to the butler. "And you, Hughes, did you see anyone loitering about in the street?"

"No, miss," he said. "I was stoking the fire in the study. I heard some footsteps, perhaps."

"One person or more, could you tell?"

"I think only one," he said. He had recovered his usual deportment, but his expression was one of deep concern, and she understood at once that he had seen the message.

"Someone disgruntled at one of the stories in the *Messenger*, I expect," she said, though her tone was unconvincing. "Papa must be told this was the act of mischievous youths. It is not worth working himself up over, not with his heart."

Hughes said nothing in response, only nodded, then glanced at the doorway to the returned Emily, who had fetched a broom and dustpan.

Marlowe was back within ten minutes, and Catriona stepped out carefully, though Emily had already swept up the worst of the mess, to join him in the foyer.

"A brick," he said tonelessly in response to her explanation.

"Yes, Inspector," she said, "a plain masonry brick with no distinguishing qualities."

"Let me see it, please." He held out his hand as if she might produce it from thin air.

"I instructed my maid to dispose of it," she said. "I found the sight of it most vexing."

He levelled a disbelieving look on her but did not press her further. "And your man saw nothing?"

"Indeed, only heard footsteps retreating after the fact. Some youths have been engaging in mischief in the square recently. I suspect one felt particularly emboldened this evening. I gather you did not catch him."

"No." He turned to glance into the parlour, where Hughes had drawn the curtains over the broken window. "Blended in with the crowd at the street, if he went that way. Perhaps your neighbours saw something."

"It is quite late in the evening, Inspector," Catriona said. "I do appreciate your diligence, but if you wish to canvass the square, might tomorrow not be more appropriate? But then, tomorrow is the funeral for Lord Ashford. Do you plan to attend?"

"Of course," he said.

"The day after, then."

"You expect me to drop it."

"I do," she said with satisfaction. "Are there not more serious crimes afoot in this city?"

He had inhaled as if to reply, but she reached out and touched his arm, and the gesture cut him off.

"Before I forget," she said, reaching into her pocket, "you must take the warehouse key. I have no further need of it. I have confirmed all I wish to know of that affair."

He took the proffered key from her. "Have you?" he said.

Before she could think of a tactful way to evade the question, she was rescued by the fortuitous timing of her papa, who burst into the house and turned immediately towards the parlour with an expression somewhere between furious and bewildered.

Having spotted their guest, Sir Frederick cut off his initial exclamation and composed himself. “Ah,” he said, nodding to Marlowe. “Good evening, Inspector. Now will someone tell me what in God’s name has happened to my parlour window?”

# CHAPTER 20

The morning of the funeral had dawned gloomy and grey, much like the prevailing mood of the household. Having dressed in black paramatta for the occasion, Catriona descended the stairs to find the parlour doors open, and standing within was Sir Frederick, staring out the broken window towards the square, his stony expression reflected back at her in the remaining glass.

"Papa?" she said, at once overcome with a chill as she entered the draughty room.

He turned to face her, and the queer expression left his face immediately, replaced by something kindly and sad. "My dear," he said, "for a moment, standing there, you reminded me so much of your mama. Strange how years pass in an instant."

She joined him at the window. As the mourners were not set

to arrive for several hours, the street in front of the Turner house was still empty. The air outside smelled of rain, cold and earthy. She did not look forward to the procession. As she always did in the hours before any planned unpleasantness, Catriona felt as if time were at once suspended and flowing too quickly.

"It seems just yesterday," Sir Frederick said, having turned to look out the window again, "that we disembarked at the port. You clung to my hand as though I could protect you from anything, yet now it so often seems you are the one who looks after me."

"Papa, we look after each other as we always have and always shall," she said quickly, feeling apprehensive and not knowing why, and wanting to move on from the topic.

"Forgive me, my dear," Sir Frederick said. He patted her arm affectionately. "In those dark days after we came to England, Ashford was there for me like a brother. And now we must say good-bye to him too. I suppose that is the nature of time, yet I feel our losses keenly today—like a chill that has worked its way into my bones."

She glanced up at him. In the morning light, his profile was striking, the aquiline nose and defined chin familiar. Sometimes she still saw him as the strong and youthful father of her childhood, a commanding presence upon whom she could always rely.

She had not noticed it until now, or she had noticed it without realising what it meant, that the years had changed him. His hair, once black and full, had gone steely, and his blue eyes were surrounded by fine lines. Even the heart which once had spurred him across battlefields was beginning to fail him.

Like the grey sun rising wearily over the city, the realisation of his mortality had dawned on her. She could not speak for fear her voice might give away her sudden anxiety. But his hand remained gently on her arm, so she stood there with him by the broken window for some time, neither saying a word, until Hughes emerged from the study and announced pointedly that he had stoked the fire within if they wished to warm themselves, and perhaps it was best the parlour doors be kept shut for now.

"It feels so odd," Beth said, "as though Papa might appear in the doorway any minute to chastise us all for being so glum."

Catriona and she were standing to one side of the Turner parlour, in which the mourners had gathered. The room was close and too warm, nearly suffocating with the smell of white lilies and damp overcoats.

"I can imagine that," Catriona said quietly, for although she knew Ashford lay in the casket only a few feet away, she felt a strange anticipation, as if they were all waiting for him to arrive before the event could begin.

"And the weather is certainly not cooperating," Beth said. "We shall be a sea of black umbrellas." She rose on her toes to peer above the heads of those around them, engaged in a quiet hum of conversation. "Oh, where on earth is Nate? He told me he would be down shortly, and instead he has left me here to host all alone, the traitor."

From within the crowd emerged Bancroft, hat in hand. In anticipation of their imminent departure into the rain, most of the men still wore their coats and gloves, though all had removed their hats out of respect.

He stood before Beth and inclined his head, then said, voice low, "My apologies, but the vicar has arrived," and extended his arm towards her.

"Thank you, Henry," Beth said. She turned to Catriona. "I see I must make my rounds. Excuse me."

"Of course."

As Beth and Bancroft made their way across the room, Catriona stepped back into the doorway between the parlour and the library. Her papa was in the opposite corner, near the casket, speaking with a group of men she recognised as his old military comrades.

She felt suddenly very alone, for it had occurred to her that the killer might well be in the room. What was it Marlowe had said, that murder was almost always an intimate affair? The villain could be any one of them, a monster lurking behind a familiar face. Was he basking in the grief he had caused or even, perhaps, attempting to assuage his guilt?

She fought in vain the urge to turn and leave the crowded parlour, but when finally she gave in and did step back, someone was already there behind her.

"Miserable day for a funeral," Nate said.

Upon hearing his voice, she felt immediately reassured. The strange panic that had made her want to flee dissipated at once. But she had not seen him since Monday evening at the paper, and when she turned to look up at him now, he was paler, with dark shadows under his eyes. She wanted to ask him whether he was all right, but she knew he would insist he was, and the exchange would only annoy them both.

"Beth is very cross with you for abandoning her down here," she said instead.

He was looking over the room. "She and Bancroft appear to have the situation well in hand," he replied.

She followed the direction of his gaze to where the two stood in conversation with the vicar and his family. The imposing Vera Parsons appeared to direct the conversation with characteristic authority. Yet although Beth was nodding along to whatever she was saying, she was looking not at her but up at Bancroft, on whose arm her gloved hand rested, with a complacent expression of almost childlike trust.

The thought struck Catriona suddenly and impersonally: Beth had always looked to others for guidance, and now that her father was gone, Bancroft was the one to whom she would turn. It was a weakness that could hardly be held against her, and Catriona felt helpless and angry, angry at whoever had killed dear Ashford and angry at herself for her uncharitable thoughts.

"It is you, my lord," she said coldly, "not Mr Bancroft, with whom all these people wish to speak."

Nate turned to her, but whatever he wanted to say he left unsaid. Once he would have sniped back at her, and it would have become a quarrel, yet now he only watched her, and the moment stretched out, neither saying a word, until her anger faded, replaced by an almost desperate need to be consoled.

She allowed her hand to fall between them, and his fingers clasped hers. She felt all was forgiven, as it always was eventually, as it always had been since they were children, slighting each other as children did. Such was the nature of time, as her papa had said that morning by the window, and now she felt them too, all the years that had passed in an instant.

A shift in the atmosphere of the room, a rise and sudden hush in voices, signalled that the procession was soon to begin.

Nate released her hand and stepped away. "See you at the church," he said, and that was that. He had gone to join her papa and the other pallbearers.

Catriona was alone again, and she looked across the parlour to Beth, who, though she stood with Vera and Jessamine Parsons, the vicar having gone out ahead to instruct the waiting coachmen, had the look of one needing rescue. Catriona went to her at once, and Beth took her arm and allowed herself to be steered into the foyer.

"I shall never be ready to say good-bye," Beth said at last, as though she had only just realised it, and the two stood watching as ahead of them, the pallbearers proceeded through the door, down the front steps, and towards the hearse in the street, the casket carried feet first, as was the custom, so the dead could not look back.

At the cemetery, Catriona moved closer to her papa under the umbrella in a futile attempt to escape the cold mist of rain. The interment following the funeral had been a much smaller affair comprising only family and friends, but even then, Ashford had touched the lives of many. Old comrades, neighbours from the square, and police colleagues had gathered around the grave. Yet one absence struck her, and she found herself idly scanning the crowd in hopes of spotting him.

It was a ways off, standing under a lone pine, that she finally caught sight of Marlowe, and she muttered an excuse to her papa and stepped away. Marlowe watched her as she approached, her shoes sticking in the wet ground with each step, and wordlessly extended his umbrella over her once she had come to stand beside him.

"Do you not care to join us, Inspector?" she said.

He had already turned from her to resume his surveillance of those gathered around the grave. "Sometimes one observes best from a distance," he said.

"You think the killer may be here," she said with resignation. "I concede the same thought has crossed my mind."

Before she could elaborate, lightning arced across the dark sky overhead, starkly illuminating the tableau around the grave, followed immediately by a roar of thunder. It had startled her, and she realised she had unconsciously moved to stand closer to him.

"They say a clap of thunder means the soul of the departed has ascended to heaven," she remarked, having taken the slightest step back away. "A pretty thought, do you agree?"

"Not for those buried on a sunny day," he replied.

She did not know what to say to that, so she said nothing. However, she had come to understand that Marlowe would not speak just for the sake of speaking, and the longer the ensuing silence stretched out between them, the more she felt he was somehow teasing her, until she could stand it no longer.

"Do tell me how the killer might give himself away, Inspector," she finally said. "I am familiar with many gathered here and have noticed nothing out of the ordinary so far."

"No?" he said. She glanced up at him, but he had not turned towards her, still watching the mourners with a dispassionate expression.

"Clearly you feel otherwise," she said, irritated by the idea that he had noticed something she had not. "You must say whatever it is you wish to say."

"We are unlikely to agree on the matter," he replied.

"How can you know so?"

"Fine," he said. "Your friend the new Lord Ashford doesn't look well."

"He is stricken with grief," she exclaimed indignantly. "Have you no sympathy for him?"

"My sympathy or lack thereof is irrelevant to the question of his guilt."

"Hardly," she said. "And I know you are not so unfeeling."

He turned to look at her impassively. She had said it as a challenge. Standing in his presence again, she could not help but recall the evening prior, their halting conversation in the drawing room, and now the space between them felt inescapably charged.

"You do not know these people as I do," she continued.

"Perhaps you don't know them as well as you think."

"How convenient it must be to believe yourself so impartial." She spoke with forced lightness. "But perhaps you will take my advice: If you are to remain in London amongst people such as these, you might find it benefits you to play their game a little. To use honey rather than vinegar."

"I am not," he replied.

"Not what?"

"To remain in London. My secondment is temporary."

He was still watching her closely. She turned from him. This information had caused a strange sinking feeling inside her, as if she had been let down somehow.

"Oh," she said tonelessly. "You wish to leave us so soon?"

"After the case is closed."

"Then I am happy for you. Of course, why stay?" she said. "Perhaps someone in Birmingham anxiously awaits your return."

He did not reply immediately, and she kept her attention determinedly on the gathering at the grave, though she knew he was still watching her. How foolish, she had thought as soon as she said it.

"You mean to learn whether I have an attachment?" he said.

"Have you?"

"No," he replied—and then, "Are you glad to hear it?"

Her cheeks coloured despite the cold. She felt relieved, as if a great misunderstanding had been averted, and when again she glanced up at him, the corner of his mouth had quirked a little. She realised she had never really seen him smile.

"Inspector," she said, "you know how well I like having my curiosity satisfied."

He gave a quick exhale, like a laugh, and she allowed herself to relax.

In the ensuing silence, which was more comfortable, she looked out over the mourners with renewed interest. Her papa was engaged in conversation with Colonel and Mrs Isaacs, and across from them, Beth and Bancroft spoke with someone Catriona thought she recognised as a distant Turner cousin. The vicar and Mrs Parsons were also nearby, the latter casting a watchful eye over her daughter, who had gone to stand with Nate near the grave.

At the sight of that mound of fresh earth, like a scar in the grassy clearing, Catriona's mouth flooded with a metallic taste. How long would it be before she could remember Ashford fondly rather than recalling those terrifying final moments? Her black dress felt constricting, the back of her neck flushed with a cold sweat, and she wished suddenly to be anywhere but at the cemetery.

An unexpected flash of white drew her attention to a knoll beyond the gathering. She thought at first that it had been a bolt of lightning, but in the absence of thunder afterwards, she looked closer, peering through the mist of rain.

There it was again: A solitary female figure stood under a great lone willow tree, her face obscured by its bare branches.

"Inspector," Catriona said, having reached out to grasp his arm in surprise, "who is that woman?"

He followed her gaze. "In the crowd?" he said.

"No, behind that willow tree," she exclaimed. But whoever it was had disappeared. "I cannot see her now. It was as though she were watching in secret."

Marlowe held his umbrella out for her to take. "Excuse me," he said at once, then headed in the direction she had indicated. As he went, he signalled to the policemen gathered by the grave, who followed.

Lightning again arced overhead, and the rain intensified from a mist to a cold downpour, prompting the gathering to disperse towards the coaches. Her papa was looking for her, and she knew she must join him now.

The search would turn up nothing, perhaps an imprint in the dirt, a few muddy footprints, but nothing of substance. Catriona understood somehow that the woman, whoever she was, had known she had been spotted and fled at once. She was beginning to doubt she had seen anyone there at all.

Fire crackling in the hearth behind her, Catriona stood before the new parlour window.

That evening had been one of practicalities. Upon their return from the cemetery that afternoon, her papa had first withdrawn to his study, then set off for the Flag. The restless melancholy which seemed to have afflicted him worried her, but she remembered the same from the months after her mama died. It was, she understood, his way of coping with grief.

Having been left to languish in the drawing room as Hughes oversaw the replacement of the window, Catriona was relieved when the tradesmen at last departed, and she proceeded into the restored parlour and basked in the sanctity and warmth of her home. The last of the winter chill had been driven from the room, and the unblemished glass looked out onto the square gardens, over which darkness had fallen.

A warm bath and supper were calling, but Catriona remained

where she stood, wishing to enjoy her quiet solitude a moment longer. She was thus placed precisely to see a familiar figure racing around the street corner and up the footpath. She flung open the front door before the unexpected visitor had a chance to rush down the stairs to the servants' entrance.

"Miss!" It was Anna, the Turners' maid. "Oh, thank goodness. Please, you must come quickly."

"Anna, what on earth is the matter?"

"Miss Turner said I must fetch help at once," the maid called up, wringing her hands, her face twisted with uncertainty.

Catriona stilled. Panic ricocheted through her, followed by a resolute coldness, a sense of inevitability. She stepped out, down the steps to the footpath, and took the maid by the shoulders. "Tell me what has happened," she said.

"It's Mr Turner," the maid said. "His lordship. He's had some kind of fit. Miss Turner can't wake him."

"Anna, listen to me," Catriona said. "Run to the Isaacs' and ask to see the colonel. Use the front door. Do not allow yourself to be turned away. Tell him everything. Do you understand?"

"Yes, miss."

"Go immediately. I will join Miss Turner."

The maid rushed off towards the opposite end of the square, her little shoes clicking rapidly along the cobblestones. Catriona hesitated. She thought she must tell someone, but the thought disappeared quickly. She raced around the corner of the gardens to the Turner house, where the door was ajar, spilling light out onto the street.

The lower floor, which had held a crowd of mourners earlier that day, was now deserted, though the air still held the faintest smell of lilies.

"Beth!" Catriona cried, already halfway up the main staircase.

The reply was muted by distance, and she knew they must be in Nate's bedroom. She was out of breath by the time she reached the second floor and raced down the hallway. Inside, Bethany was kneeling on the carpet with his head in her lap.

Catriona flung herself down next to them. "Good God, what's happened to him?" she cried.

Nate's eyes were closed, his lips almost blue. He was dead, she acknowledged for one paralysing moment, and her breath rushed out of her lungs and the floor melted away beneath her. Then his chest rose.

"I heard the most startling crash." Bethany was shaking, pressing a hand to his forehead and stroking his hair back as a mother would. "I came up and he was lying here, barely breathing!" She cut herself off with a choking gasp. There was movement in the hallway behind them, the sound of water running.

"Anna is fetching Colonel Isaacs," Catriona said. Her voice sounded as if it had come from far away. "He will know what to do."

In the doorway, Jones had appeared with a washbasin, and he strode purposefully across the carpet and threw its contents over Nate. The splash of cold water was enough to shock Catriona as well, and she held his hand as he blinked awake.

"Darling, can you hear me?" Beth was saying.

He did not reply. His eyes were unfocussed.

Catriona felt along his wrist. His sleeve was already rolled up, and when she found his pulse, it was racing under her fingertips, but his skin was distressingly cold. It was then that she noticed it, a spot of blood on his arm.

Such an innocuous thing. A little pinprick.

She bit down hard on the inside of her mouth, clawing against the strange faint feeling that threatened to overwhelm her. Blackness had closed in, narrowing the world to the torturously slow rising and falling of his chest. The hot fire in the hearth threw shadows over them, and the carpet was dotted with little shards of brown glass, as if a bottle had been dropped and shattered.

His eyes had closed again. Beth was shaking him, screaming at him, an animal sound, but Catriona barely heard her. She was grasping his wrist so tightly that the bones in her fingers hurt.

Footsteps sounded in the hallway.

"Move aside, ladies," someone instructed. It was Colonel Isaacs, who had arrived and followed Anna up to the room, carrying his medical bag with him. He knelt on the carpet beside them and leaned over Nate, lifting one of his eyelids and saying, "There now, can you hear me?"

"His arm," Catriona said. "Colonel, has he taken something?"

Isaacs glanced aside to her. "Miss Winters," he said, his tone gentle but authoritative, "fetch more water, and quickly, please. We must keep him conscious."

He took the limp arm from her grasp and slung it over his shoulder, then gestured for Jones to take the other, and together they pulled Nate up, his knees dragging across the floor between them. Beth had backed away and stood with her hands clasped over her heart, her face flushed and streaked with tears.

"He must be made to stand," the colonel instructed. "Miss Turner, how often does your brother take morphine?"

Catriona had stepped back towards the doorway. Somehow, the washbasin had made its way into her hands, but she did not remember taking it. Her feet felt clumsy and numb as she turned and stumbled into the hallway.

How blind she had been. How blind and oblivious!

She knew where the bath was, but she was moving so slowly. She blinked and she was back in the doorway of the room, the basin sloshing with cold water now, but something had trapped her at the threshold, some force rooting her to the spot. From the hallway behind, Anna pushed past her into the room, a stack of clean towels tucked under one arm, and took the basin as she did so.

Catriona wanted to flee. The sight of Nate like this repelled her—head lolling, eyes glassy, mouth slack. She could not step forwards, and yet she could not turn and run. All her months of confusion over him, the roses that had bloomed and wilted in the garden, the letters unwritten and unsent, all of it to end up here?

She was no longer in the hallway. She felt as if she were back in the opium den, in the cold river air, caught in that heady smoke and its rapturous ascent. She saw the weakness in Nate now, and she accepted it as she had accepted all his faults: determinedly, unconditionally. It was not repulsion but fear that petrified her, fear and resignation, because she had realised she must love him after all, and it was too late.

She grasped for the door frame. The lapping of the river had faded, the grey dreariness replaced by firelight and sound.

She closed her eyes and crossed the threshold.

# CHAPTER 21

Night had trudged wearily into early morning.

Morphine suppresses the function of the nervous system, Colonel Isaacs had explained. A strong dose may slow the breathing to the point of death. If injected, the drug wears off within hours, so one must be forced to maintain consciousness until the crisis has passed.

Catriona sat perched at the edge of the bed in which Nate, slumped back against the pillows, blinked awake from a restless sleep. The colour had returned to his face, and his eyes were the eyes she knew again, no longer frighteningly devoid of awareness.

She reached out and brushed his hair back from his forehead. "Sleep now, Nate."

"I tried so hard—to stop," he said. "I tried to leave off it in the country, take a little less each day." He looked away from her. "But

I had got too used to it. I thought I would die. It was a compulsion."

"Everything will be all right now," she said, because it felt like what she should say.

"You pity me," he said. It was almost a groan, and his mouth twisted. "I see it."

"Shh." She took his hand in hers. "Try to sleep."

She looked away from him, over to the window, where snow fell gently, and closed her eyes. The house was very quiet now, the only house in the square in which the lamps were still lit. She did not have to wait long before his breathing evened out again. He had barely been awake in the first place, and she wondered if perhaps, the following day, he might remember the conversation as a dream.

From the doorway behind her, a shadow stretched out long across the room.

"Kitty, the nurse from St Thomas is here," Beth said.

Catriona released his hand and rose to join her in the hallway, where stood a young woman with dark hair and eyes. She was striking, Catriona thought, even beautiful, though when she observed her more closely, she could not pinpoint why she had thought so. A certain irregularity of the features, perhaps, which, when taken as a whole, were pleasing.

"Miss Miriam Fabian," Bethany said. "Miss Fabian, my dearest friend, Miss Catriona Winters."

"Miss Fabian, good evening," Catriona said, regretting how unfeeling she sounded, shivering with a deep bone-coldness she could not shake. "Or morning, I suppose."

"Colonel Isaacs has explained the situation to me," Miss Fabian said, her manner gentle but direct. "Miss Turner, did you know your brother had been taking morphine?"

"No," Beth said. "But I knew… I suppose there's no point in trying to keep it secret now." She had folded her hands tightly before her, fingers clasped. "This past summer, my father discovered my brother had been visiting an opium den in the East End."

Catriona felt for the wall behind her, suddenly very aware of the possibility that she might faint, but she said nothing, only listened as Beth continued.

"After that, Papa sent him away to the country for a while. When he came back, I supposed that had been the end of it, but I see now that he never gave it up, not really."

"Morphine is highly addicting, Miss Turner," Miss Fabian said, her dark brows drawing together. "If your brother is to recover, he must be completely withdrawn from it. Your intervention tonight likely saved his life."

Bethany gave a little gasp and reached out, and Catriona took her arm. "Forgive me, Miss Fabian," she finally said. "The past week has been trying for our family."

"The colonel told me of your loss," Miss Fabian said. "My sincerest condolences."

"Thank you," Beth said, and when she continued, it was with her familiar rehearsed courtesy. "I do so appreciate your coming to us at this hour of the night."

"Perhaps I might see to your brother now," Miss Fabian said, and gestured with her briefcase to the doorway behind them.

"Yes, please go in," Beth said. "I apologise for the state of the room. Be careful of the glass. Our maid has not had a chance to clear it up."

"Of course," Miss Fabian said, then nodded to them and went inside, leaving them alone in the hallway.

Beth closed the door ever so slightly behind her. Through the gap, Miss Fabian had moved to Nate's bedside and withdrawn from her bag a stethoscope with which she began to listen to his heart or breathing. Catriona looked away.

Neither spoke for a time. Their silence conveyed their shared understanding, a grim realisation that the order of their lives had nearly been upended once again, and the same could happen at any time, through no fault of their own, with no warning.

"Did you know all this time?" Catriona finally asked her. She felt it had come out like an accusation, though that wasn't how she had intended it.

"Papa was determined not to let it get out," Beth said. "The only reason I knew at all was because I overheard a commotion one night this past summer." She stepped aside slightly, away from the door, as if she were about to tell a secret. "Someone brought Nate home—practically left him on the doorstep. Papa tried to call after her, but she fled in a coach."

"A lady?" Catriona said.

"I never saw her. I assumed she was a..." Her face coloured. "A woman of low virtue."

"Oh," Catriona said. "I see."

She did not quite believe Nate kept company with prostituted women. She had flattered herself into believing she and he related to one another on the same level, intellectually and perhaps even emotionally. But did such behaviour not betray a sort of disdain for all women, a belief they were nothing more than commodities to be bought and sold?

"The next day," Bethany continued, ignorant of the inner turmoil into which she had thrown her friend, "Nate was off on the first train to Ashford, and that was that. Papa and I never really spoke of it afterwards." She reached out to take Catriona's hand again. "When you and I went to Limehouse last week and saw the men in that den, it frightened me to think my brother could have ended up that way. I felt such relief at the thought that he had been cured. But I should have known better than to believe it could be given up so easily."

Catriona forced herself to focus on Beth, on her doe-like eyes, full of sorrow and doubt. "Morphine can be got from any chemist," she said. "It would have been so much simpler than stealing away to the East End, and easier to hide. You cannot blame yourself for not seeing it."

"But I do," Beth said. "Nate is my brother, my only remaining family. I couldn't live with myself if…" She had cast her eyes downwards, her voice going quiet. "When Mama died, I thought he was very strong. Papa and I were set completely adrift, but Nate preferred to press on. Yet I look back now, and I think something must have broken in him then, some imperceptible fracture, and now the infection has finally set in."

Catriona felt compelled to reach out to her. Bethany looked suddenly so young, so utterly lost, as if she had become a child again, the girl Catriona had met so many years earlier. Beth had taken her into her circle as if she were a stray animal, a quiet dark creature she felt she must nurture into society. Catriona had been so envious of her then. She had thought Beth had everything—a living mother, a father not broken by grief. Now Beth had nothing at all.

Beth clung to her, and Catriona, feeling paralysed but finally somehow useful, patted her shoulder gently, over her hair, which, in the commotion, had come loose from its pins and fallen down her back in blond disarray.

"I feel I do not know him anymore," Beth whispered. "All this loss, this keeping of secrets from each other…"

The sound of footsteps on the back stairs caused them to spring apart. They moved aside to allow Anna to pass into the bedroom with a broom and dustpan. Catriona knew not what she might say to reassure her friend. As the silence stretched out, broken by the intermittent sound of glass being swept carefully across the carpet, she could only hold her hand.

"Henry means to visit me this evening," Beth said suddenly, as if she had only just remembered. "How shall I receive him here?" She looked around as though a hurricane had torn through the house, though in truth, it looked the same as it always had.

"You plan to keep this from him?" Catriona said.

"I know it would be wrong, but he disapproves of my brother enough as it is." Beth had straightened again, her voice regaining its familiar expressiveness. "The discovery of what Nate has been up to may be the last nail in the coffin of their civil acquaintance."

"Perhaps Mr Bancroft will surprise you," Catriona said, though she felt privately that it was unlikely. She had seen the disgust that twitched across his expression every time he and Nate were forced to interact, and she knew the feeling was mutual. "Surely he is not heartless."

"I know he would do anything for me, even play nice with my brother," Beth said. "But I don't wish to tell him, not yet."

"Perhaps you could meet at his place instead."

"Unchaperoned!" Beth cried, her hand flying to her collar.

"No, of course not. A silly idea," Catriona said quickly.

"His office in town would suit," Beth finally concluded, "yet he will protest my going all that way."

"You might tell him we are to dine out together, so it is more convenient for you to meet him there beforehand," Catriona suggested.

Beth regarded her with a satisfied expression. "Kitty, you are a most excellent liar," she said, "and I mean that as a compliment. I shall write him later this morning. Will you meet me at his office? I know he will insist on escorting me after otherwise."

"Of course," Catriona said. "But now you must rest. It's been such a long night. All will be well, dear Beth."

"Yes, not to worry," Bethany said as if trying to convince herself. "Miss Fabian is here to take care of us."

Catriona had slipped inside quietly, tiptoed up the stairs, and collapsed, boneless, into her bed without bothering to undress. She suspected her papa had returned home sometime earlier, as the house was quiet and dark. No one had been waiting up for her, so she realised that while Emily must have noticed her absence, she had covered for her, as she had done before, without even having been asked. Perhaps she had seen her rushing out across the square. Catriona sometimes wondered what her maid must think of her, especially lately.

She turned to lie on her back, staring up at the ceiling, across which, thrown into shadow by the streetlamps below, snowflakes drifted softly. So this was the reason Nate had left so suddenly that past summer, without so much as a good-bye to her. She had been so ignorant. That night in the darkroom, and even at the funeral, had she not sensed that something was entirely wrong with him?

And this, she now knew, was how Ashford had come to learn of the opium den in Limehouse.

Beth had said it was a woman who brought Nate home that night. She had not seen her, but her father would have done. He may even have spoken with her. A woman of low virtue? Perhaps, Catriona acknowledged reluctantly, that sick feeling of betrayal, of being stupid and small, lurching up in her throat again. What must Ashford have thought upon seeing his son in such a state? Catriona tried to picture it, the coach pulling up alongside the footpath in the darkness, the silhouette of an unknown woman just barely visible inside, her pale slender hand extended towards the latch.

A strange restlessness was stirring in her, like the feeling of grasping at something just out of reach. In that predawn hour, as she lay awake, exhausted but unable to sleep, disparate threads had begun to weave themselves together.

The morning Stratton was murdered, Catriona had come upon Ashford speaking to a woman she now knew as Madame Leung. She had witnessed him alighting from a cab one night later that week, farewelling someone—and having, as she later learned from her papa, to pay the coachman extra to take the woman on to her destination. She remembered the mournful way in which Madame Leung had stood by the Limehouse Cut, reflected like a ghost in the murky water, and that unknown watcher disappearing behind the willow tree at the cemetery.

Catriona sat up quickly, almost violently, her heart racing. Had she not perceived it from the start, in that dreary laneway, where Ashford and Madame Leung had stood, heads bowed together, voices low, as if they shared a great secret?

The following morning, Catriona paced in the drawing room. She had fallen asleep just as the first light crept up over the city and awoken several hours later, sluggish but aflame with purpose. She had to confirm her suspicions for herself, but she did not wish to go back to Limehouse alone, especially not after the harrowing warning of the brick hurled through her parlour window.

She halted, feeling paralysed by indecision, and, as if on cue, a knock at the door downstairs derailed her thoughts. Hearing a familiar voice, she proceeded out to the top of the stairs and looked down to see Marlowe standing in the entryway, Hughes having admitted him.

"Inspector, good morning," she called down.

Hughes bowed and departed. He had no doubt become used

to the comings and goings of the police of late.

"Found yourself in the neighbourhood?" Catriona said as she reached the bottom step.

Marlowe removed his hat and ran a hand through his dark hair. It was a white morning, pristine and quiet, and Catriona found herself idly noticing the way the light reflected in his eyes.

"I meant to speak with Lord Ashford," he said, "to allay my suspicions about the night of his father's murder. But I was turned away at the door by one Miss Fabian. Flu in the house, apparently. I thought to confirm you and your father are well."

"Perfectly well," she said. "Thank you for your concern."

He raised a brow. "I see your parlour window is repaired."

"Yes," she said, turning towards the room and gesturing for him to accompany her. Upon seeing him, she had been struck by a most marvellous idea. "Do come in. It is so terribly cold out. You must warm yourself by our fire, and perhaps some tea?"

"If you insist, thank you," he said, and shrugged out of his coat and hung it on the stand. They proceeded into the parlour, where Catriona rang the bell.

"Your timing is excellent," she began, lowering herself to the settee, and he sat in the armchair across from her. "I wished to discuss with you the identity of the woman the late Lord Ashford was seeing. His...paramour." Her face went hot. "I gather you have made no progress on that front."

"No," he said. "The constables were unable to track down the woman you saw at the cemetery."

"No matter," she said. "I believe I have uncovered her identity, but I wish to confirm it, and I should like you to accompany me."

"You should?" he said.

"Have I stunned you?"

He leaned forwards in the armchair. "Frankly? I had come to assume you would ask forgiveness rather than permission."

"I ask neither, simply your presence," she returned, annoyed. "But if you wish to lord that over me…"

"No," he said. "I will accompany you."

She felt a little surge of triumph, then hesitated. "You might wish to hear where first."

"Because I shall regret it once I do?"

"Perhaps," she said. "Limehouse, and I have stipulations."

"Of course you have."

"You must promise not to ask questions until we're through, and you must allow me, when we arrive, to do all the talking."

"One wonders why I'm needed at all," he said drily.

She gave him a pretty smile. "For the pleasure of your company, of course."

"My company," he said, "or my revolver?"

"Inspector, do you wish to come with me or not?"

"Now that I know where you intend to go, you give me little choice."

"I give you every choice," she said indignantly, "and I rather wish not to be treated as an obligation."

In the parlour doorway, Emily had appeared, carrying a tray of tea and biscuits, and cleared her throat gently before entering. This necessitated a pause in the conversation—and well that it did, thought

Catriona, as she required a moment to compose herself.

"Thank you, Emily," she said calmly after the maid had set the tray down on the low table. "That will be all."

As Emily departed, Catriona busied herself with preparing the tea. She knew Marlowe was watching her, tracking her with his stormy eyes. She felt entirely conscious of herself.

"I've been misunderstood," he finally said. "Miss Winters, I don't think of you as an obligation. Far from it."

She paused. At his words, a curious hot feeling had crept up inside her, a little thrill, unexpected in its intensity. "I see," she said, and set down the teapot.

"Then Limehouse it is," he said, "with no questions until we're through."

She looked across at him. How different this was from their last meeting in the parlour, when the floor had glittered with shards of broken glass, the air haunted by the cold night rushing in. Now it was daytime, and warm, and she felt for one surreal moment as if he fit in perfectly, as if they had sat there together before.

"Thank you, Inspector," she finally said, then shot him a glance as she added, "I rather thought I might have to do a little more to convince you."

"Oh?" he said, like a laugh. "I've given in too easily."

"Another time, perhaps." She gestured towards the teacups. "Now, how will you take yours? I can even offer you sugar."

# CHAPTER 22

Owing perhaps to his innately inspectorial bearing, Catriona thought, Marlowe had convinced a cabbie to take them as far as Whitechapel. The remaining walk of a half hour had been cold and damp. Mist rose from the streets, filthy with melting snow, and deepened to a white fog the nearer they drew to the river.

They spoke little. Catriona glanced once at Marlowe walking beside her, as they passed the weary chapel at the corner before the Limehouse Basin, and thought only that bringing him along with her was surely what Ashford would have wanted her to do. He would have told Marlowe about Madame Leung himself, she suspected, if only he had got the chance.

The door at the den opened without protest, the smoky warm air spilling out past them as they entered.

Madame Leung glanced up from the small book she had been reading and rose at once. "Miss Winters, good morning," she said, inquisitiveness creasing her brow. "Victor is away, I am afraid."

"Good morning, madam," Catriona said, though in the strange atmosphere inside the den, time seemed to bend into neither day nor night. Marlowe had closed the door behind them, plunging the space back into semidarkness. Curtains blocked off the smoking room; Catriona could not tell by sound whether they were alone. "In fact, it is you I have come to see. Might we speak privately?"

Madame Leung looked pointedly over Catriona's shoulder, awaiting an introduction. True to his word, Marlowe had said nothing.

"Mr Marlowe," Catriona said, "a colleague of…" She stopped herself. "Of someone with whom I believe you were acquainted."

For the briefest moment, so quickly Catriona would have missed it had she not been looking for a sign of recognition, the practised, mild expression with which the den madam regarded her shattered, replaced by something hurt and afraid. Then her face went blank again, and she said, "Come with me. We can talk upstairs."

Catriona glanced back at Marlowe, who gave her a significant look and gestured for her to go on ahead. The two followed Madame Leung through the smoking room, Catriona staring determinedly upwards to avoid the unpleasant sensation of shame and pity she had felt previously upon seeing those within, and up the back stairs.

The room they entered was familiar. It was the one in which Catriona had awoken on her last visit. The hearth, then crackling with fire, was now cold. Madame Leung gestured to the settee. Catriona sat, and Madame Leung sat across from her, just as they had been positioned then. Perhaps to keep from interjecting, Marlowe stood some distance away, by the window, looking out to the barges below, though Catriona knew he would hear every word.

"I know why you have come, Miss Winters," Madame Leung said. "I suppose it was only a matter of time. To think we kept it a secret so well, and now he has died, it will all come spilling out."

Catriona hesitated before replying. She felt relieved, even vindicated, having been correct in piecing together the little clues which had led her to Madame Leung. But she felt also a curious sort of discomfort at this confirmation that Ashford had been leading a secret life for several months.

"You knew the late Lord Ashford," she said finally.

Madame Leung only nodded.

"You knew him well?" she asked. But she did not need a reply. The answer was there in the sorrowful eyes of the woman across from her. Catriona felt compelled to comfort her somehow, but she did not know her well enough to know what to say to her, and regardless, the hurt went too deep. She said, "It was you who brought his son home that night this past summer."

Madame Leung looked away, into the empty hearth. "It was foolish of me," she said. "A foolish impulse. But in that young man I saw something of my own son. I wanted to protect him from the life that awaited him if he continued down that path. I have seen it often enough."

"So you put him in a cab and ensured he made it home."

"I thought that would be the end of it," Madame Leung said. "But Lord Ashford found me somehow. He must have tracked down the coachman. It would not have been difficult; only a few venture into Limehouse at night. We began a correspondence."

Catriona looked over to the window, where Marlowe stood, his back to them. Now that she had confirmed her theory, she knew not how to proceed. She thought of what Tsang had said about her bringing the police to his doorstep. She had done it after all, but little did he know his own associate had done so long before.

She could not speak. She felt overwhelmed by the secrets Ashford had kept, by the idea that he was a different man than she had thought him to be, having seen the weakness in his son and simply sent him away. And she felt guilty, guilty because she had approached the woman before her as an interrogator rather than as a friend.

Marlowe had turned to watch her now, and she knew he must have seen it in her eyes, a desperate, almost pleading doubt. His expression was unreadable, but at last he approached them and sat beside her on the settee, and something inside her relaxed. He looked away from her to Madame Leung.

"My condolences on your loss, madam," he began. "Forgive my insensitivity, but Lord Ashford was murdered, and we must find his killer."

"I understand, Mr Marlowe," Madame Leung said. "Ask me whatever you must. He would have wanted me to answer."

"He was the head of criminal investigations with the police," Marlowe said. "Surely you came to learn as much. Were you not afraid he would arrest you, put you out of business?"

"In truth," she said, "perhaps I hoped for it. I have wanted to leave this place for a long while. Seeing such misery, I have found it more and more difficult to live with myself and the role I play here."

"Then why continue?" he said.

"For Victor," she said. "Mr Tsang, the proprietor of this establishment. He acquired it for me, intended as a way for me to support myself after he went back to Hong Kong. He left behind a prosperous business to escort me to England, you see. I think he felt it was his duty, one last thing he could do for my son, my dear Desmond. As boys, they were like brothers."

"And it was Tsang who decided to sell opium to your patrons?" Marlowe said.

"The blame is not his alone," Madame Leung said. "Earlier this year, someone approached him with the arrangement. The hardships of his youth have made Victor ruthless. He saw an opportunity. I believe he wants what is best for me, but he has no qualms about hastening these men to their deaths."

"Madame Leung," Catriona interjected, "after Lord Stratton was found, Lord Ashford spoke with you in the laneway outside. I saw you together briefly. I thought he was questioning you. Now I realise you knew one another."

"Lord Ashford wished to learn the source of the opium trade in Limehouse," Madame Leung said. "In the months after we met, I had promised to help him figure it out in exchange for immunity from prosecution for Victor. I thought with the opium supply cut off, we would be free of this place, and we could move on."

"And what was it you spoke of that morning in the laneway?" Marlowe said.

"Something I had seen," Madame Leung replied. "Several nights before, I had awoken to find men moving packets of opium into our downstairs rooms. This was not unusual. But that night, I followed them in secret. I discovered the opium had been stored in a warehouse off Narrow Street."

"I know the warehouse of which you speak," Catriona said. "So you were acting as an informant, and you told Lord Ashford of all you had seen? Madame Leung, I believe your information about the warehouse did allow him to track down the supplier."

"It did? He never told me so," Madame Leung said.

"He never got the chance," Catriona said. "He must have checked property records to see who owned the warehouse. He met with the man last Friday and was killed later that night."

"Then you know who it was that killed him?"

"The warehouse owner has an alibi," Marlowe said. "He fled town before the killing. But if he was your supplier, your trade here will come to its natural end."

Madame Leung said nothing. Perhaps it was relief Catriona saw in her face, but more likely it was doubt. Limehouse seemed to exist under a cloud of smoke and mist from which none could escape, not its inhabitants, not those who had passed through for only a moment.

"Madame Leung," she said, "I've come today because I hoped you might know something which would help us find the killer. But also because I wish to extend my sincerest friendship to you. I thought I saw you yesterday at the interment."

Madame Leung looked up. "I wanted only to know he had been

laid to rest, to say good-bye one last time," she said. She levelled her dark eyes on Catriona. "We had to keep our relationship a secret. If Victor found out, he would have seen it as a grave betrayal."

Though perhaps Madame Leung had not meant it as such, Catriona thought, her words were a warning. Catriona had become overconfident, and the realisation of it chilled her.

She had learned all she wished to learn of the den and of what Ashford had been up to in the months before his death, she decided, and moved to stand, but Madame Leung reached out and caught her wrist. The movement was so sudden, so desperate, that Catriona was shocked into stillness, risen halfway from the settee.

"Miss Winters," Madame Leung said, "that morning in the laneway, his lordship asked me to marry him."

Catriona said nothing, only lowered herself again, anxious because she suspected she knew what was coming. Had Ashford made promises, promises Madame Leung would expect kept on his behalf? Catriona felt deeply embarrassed for both of them. She regretted coming at all.

"I see," she finally said.

Madame Leung withdrew her hand as if she had, in that instant, perceived everything Catriona thought of her. "I told him no," she said quickly. "That was the last time we spoke."

"But why?" was all Catriona could think to say.

"Madam, you must understand, I have a husband—or I had. He was a cruel man." She lowered her eyes. "After my son passed, there was nothing left for me in Hong Kong. I felt as though I were drowning. So I came to England for a new life, and I wanted nothing more in the world than to marry Lord Ashford, but I would have dishonoured him by accepting his proposal."

Catriona was silent, struck at once by the cruelty of her own assumptions. She had entirely misunderstood Madame Leung. She did not want money. She wanted only for someone else to acknowledge that the affection in which Lord Ashford had held her was real. She glanced to Marlowe, who had risen wordlessly and gone to the window.

"Though Lord Ashford knew my reasons, my reply hurt him deeply," Madame Leung continued. "I wish I had stopped him from leaving that day. Perhaps, if I had, everything might have turned out differently." She looked down. Her hands, folded in her lap, were pale and still.

For a moment, despite the vast differences between them, Catriona was reminded of her father. The woman before her exuded the same strength, that of having endured sorrows, like a rocky promontory which, though weathered by storms, still stood.

They spoke little after that. Hesitantly, Catriona extended a hand towards her. Madame Leung reached out and took it, and they sat for some time in companionable silence. Perhaps one day Ashford would have introduced them, Catriona realised, and perhaps, now that he was no longer with them, he would wish her to ensure the connection was maintained.

She said as much to Marlowe after the two had departed, leaving the warm den for the chill of a rapidly falling dusk.

"You think Miss Turner should like to meet her?" he replied.

"They have already met, though neither knows so," Catriona

replied. "When Detective Whitby saw me here last week, it was Bethany who accompanied me."

The look he shot her was incredulous. "For what purpose?"

"I think she wanted to see what had drawn her brother here. But I didn't know about that at the time. Then, I supposed she just wanted a little thrill."

In the small courtyard outside the den, a woman was wringing out the washing. She did not look up at them as they passed. From the docks beyond came the sounds of whipping sails and the lapping river. The place did not feel as alien to Catriona as once it had. Its inhabitants were people like her, there but for the grace of God.

"Is that what this is for you too, a little thrill?" he said without looking at her. He had not said it with disdain but as if he were dismissing her, which was worse. "These past two weeks, looking into the murders," he said. "Why do you do it?"

"Why do you?" she said. She knew what his answer would be, that it was his job. But that much was obvious. The explanation she wanted went deeper than that. She wanted to know what drove him, whether it was the same insatiable, restless curiosity which drove her.

They had reached the laneway, in which a cart clattered by. His hand went out in front of her as if to stop her from stepping in its path, and they waited for it to pass, standing close in the narrow space beside the stone wall of the courtyard. She looked up at him to find him watching her, and she was struck by him, by the realisation of all that had changed in the past two weeks.

"I think it was not so very far from this spot that we first met,

Inspector," she said.

"No, not so far," he replied. His hand still hovered there between her and the laneway, though the cart had now turned a corner and was gone.

She imagined it suddenly and intensely, as if it had come from somewhere outside her own mind—that his hand might close the distance to her waist, that there in the cold mist, he might draw her towards him.

The thought was gone as quickly as it had come. She stepped back, as did he.

"Shall we, madam?" he said, having already turned from her. "I think we have a long walk ahead."

Catriona paused at the entrance to the Holt & Bancroft Steam Shipping Company building, an imposing grey facade in the Gothic Revival style, overlooking the Strand. She and Marlowe had parted ways at Charing Cross station, he heading in to Scotland Yard and she to meet with Bethany and help her maintain her ruse for Bancroft.

All she had discovered during her visit with Madame Leung rushed through her mind. She was anxious to share it with Beth, but she knew not the right time or place to do so. Certainly not then and there.

Upon entering, she was directed by a clerk to the office of Henry Bancroft, at the end of a corridor on the third floor. Inside, he and Bethany sat a careful distance from one another on a sofa beneath an iron-framed window in which, lit by the streetlamps below, snow had begun to fall. The scene was picturesque; Catriona was sorry to interrupt.

Bancroft saw her and rose immediately, and Bethany followed.

"There you are!" she cried out. "Good evening."

"Good evening to you both," Catriona said.

"Hard at work today, Miss Winters?" Bancroft said.

"Always," she replied. "I have been chasing up a story at the port."

"Oh?" he said, pushing his spectacles to the bridge of his nose. "Perhaps I can be of assistance. Care to share?"

Catriona realised quite suddenly that she had risked bringing up the exact subject Beth was trying to avoid. "Not quite yet," she said at last. "But when the time comes, I might just take you up on that offer. I hope I haven't interrupted you two?"

"No," Bethany said. "I was just telling Henry how much I look forward to getting out now, having been cooped up all this week. Papa always enjoyed an evening in town."

"I shall not keep you," Bancroft said. "Might our clerk hail you a cab?"

"No, I think we shall walk," Bethany said. "I find this chill most invigorating. Good evening, darling."

"Ladies," Bancroft said, and gave a small bow.

As they stepped out into the cool night, Bethany turned her face to the sky. For a moment, as the snow dotted her cheeks and eyelashes, her expression was one of almost blissful calm. Then her brow creased, and she ran a hand over her face.

"That was not a lie, you know," she said. "I cannot stand being at home anymore. But that reminds me, Miss Fabian told me Inspector Marlowe stopped by this morning. I went to the window in time to see him admitted at your house. Does he still suspect Nate?"

Catriona fought the strange guilt that had arisen within her. She and Marlowe had not spoken further on his suspicion of Nate. In fact, she had determinedly avoided thinking of Nate all day—avoided thinking of him in that den, sprawled out mindlessly like those other men inside.

She swallowed and said, "I think perhaps it would be best if Nate spoke with him directly, to answer his questions, as a matter of procedure. But I really cannot believe he might think Nate responsible. The very idea is preposterous."

"I cannot bear it, this suspicion hanging over our heads," Beth said quietly. "And Nate is hardly capable of speaking with anyone right now. Miss Fabian had me dispose of half our medicines, even the laudanum. There is opium in everything these days. I would never have thought about it."

"No, of course not," Catriona said. "Colonel Isaacs was right to recommend her to you."

"Nate is fortunate, though he might not feel so very well now," Beth said. "I think leaving off morphine is an unpleasant affair. Miss Fabian has told me as much."

The two continued along the Strand towards the Underground station. Catriona was glad for the silence and for the walk, as the city, with its lights and sounds, was a much different environment than the desolate East End.

"She was in Afghanistan this summer, did you know?" Beth said. "A field hospital in Kandahar. She must have seen a great deal of suffering. It makes our lives here seem inconsequential."

"I had wondered how Colonel Isaacs knew her," Catriona said. "He holds her in high esteem, I believe."

"As do I," Beth said. "She is the very measure of calmness, understanding, and competence—whereas I must have come across to her as entirely lacking in substance."

"How could you think that of yourself?" Catriona said.

"No need to be offended for me, Kitty," Beth said, taking her arm. "I have been sheltered. In this very city are those who live in chronic poverty, and here I am, sad because I feel confined by my own privilege. My greatest trials will be choosing a dinner menu, or hiring a governess, or calling upon a tiresome acquaintance. No, there is so much more one might offer to the world than that. I admire Miss Fabian greatly, and I think I envy her a little too."

Catriona glanced at her as they walked. She understood Beth entirely, thinking of Marlowe, her earliest impressions of whom had been characterised by the same peculiar envy, keen as a knife. For he occupied a role she had wished for herself: the determined sleuth, resurrectionist of deeply buried secrets.

As if having read her mind, Beth said, "And now I should ask what progress the inspector has made in his inquiry. Are you his confidante? You must have some news to share."

"We did speak awhile today," Catriona said. "But your father dealt with so very many people. Tracking them all down to question them may take him some time."

"I think I regret his having been turned away," Beth said, her eyebrows drawing together. "I should have liked to ask him what steps he is taking to find the man who killed my father, and if I might help in some way. I keep thinking over these past few weeks, wondering if I might have seen something out of place without even knowing it."

They continued on that topic for some time. Catriona sensed Beth would grasp at anything to avoid speaking of her brother, and the conversation soon shifted to those who had been at the funeral the previous day, then to what a shame it was that Beth would be unable to attend any social events over the winter months, being in full mourning.

Inwardly, her thoughts returned to the woman who had been at the interment in secret, Jingyi Leung, and how she might tell Beth about her. Several times, the words fluttered in her mouth only for her to swallow them again, knowing the timing was not right. Not now, when her role in the events of that summer would be tied up in so many anxieties about Nate.

Further inwardly, Catriona thought of whomever it was who had killed Ashford. She thought of it with every stranger she passed, every man who tipped his hat at them. She imagined that faceless figure fleeing Scotland Yard into the night, the sin having been committed, the pistol still smoking in his hand. That very evening, he was there with them on the Strand, or slinking through the rookeries, or hosting in the parlours of high society.

Did he marvel at the dark secret he harboured? Did those who knew him look into his eyes and see it there—the shadow of death?

Did they recognise it?

Would she?

# CHAPTER 23

The following morning saw the arrival of a telegram from Boston. Having joined her papa at the breakfast table, Catriona took the proffered note from Hughes and stared at it. Her first sensation was worry, as a telegram suggested a matter of some urgency. Her second was guilt. It was a message from Sidney, thoughts of whom she had entirely avoided since her last letter to him.

"What is it, my dear?" Sir Frederick said, glancing up from his papers.

"Sidney Hampstead, Papa," she said. "He has heard about Lord Ashford and sends his condolences."

"How thoughtful. I assume his apprenticeship is going well."

"Yes, I believe so," she said. "His letters make it sound so very—edifying."

As edifying as living in the shadow of one's father could be, she thought but did not say, and the thought surprised her. "Papa, if I'm not needed at the paper today, I think I shall call on the Turners," she said instead. "You heard Nathaniel has been under the weather?"

"Flu, is it?" Sir Frederick said. He had set down his paper with a huff, evidently displeased at what he had read, and put his napkin on the table. "He sent me a note yesterday to apologise for his absence at the office, but in truth, I think it for the best he's forced to take a few days off. After your mama died, I too thought to ignore my grief and push on, but it catches up to one eventually!"

"You might follow your own advice, Papa," Catriona said. "You have lost your dearest friend."

"Ah, Catriona," said Sir Frederick, "the more losses one grieves, the better one learns to weather the storm of sorrow. Though, of course, I still feel it keenly sometimes, rattling the windows of the soul."

Catriona had poured her tea and stirred it in silence. Across the long table, Sir Frederick had turned to the frosty window and stared into the garden beyond, white and bare.

Breakfast was the only meal Catriona and her papa shared with any regularity. But there were mornings she felt so very lonely, sitting across from him, that she thought it might be best for them both if she began breakfasting in bed as other ladies did. Yet other mornings she felt that in the silence beyond that loneliness lived a shared understanding, an understanding of all they had withstood together, and to give that up would be an abandonment.

Sir Frederick turned from the window. "You will understand when you are older," he said, then rose decisively. "But now I am off to meet with our advertisers. Please do send my best to the Turners. You might have Mrs Travers share her receipt for that restorative soup she so often foists upon me!"

Catriona had crossed the square and begun to ascend the steps at the Turner house when the door flew open and out strode Bancroft, nearly bowling her over.

"Good heavens, Mr Bancroft, are you quite all right?" she said, somewhat offended, having grabbed hold of the entry pillar to stay upright.

"Miss Winters, my apologies," he said. He reached out as if to ensure he had caused no damage, then withdrew his hand just as abruptly. "Please excuse me. I must be going."

"Good day!" she called after him.

"Yes, good day," he returned. He had already descended and, walking briskly, was halfway to the corner of the square.

The door had been left ajar in the commotion, and Catriona pushed it open to find Bethany already there in the entryway, her cheeks streaked with tears.

"Beth, what on earth is the matter?" she cried out.

Beth struggled to speak. "Oh, Kitty, Henry and I have had the most distressing row," she said. "I think I have behaved—abominably!"

Catriona stepped forwards and ushered her to the stairs to sit. "You must tell me about it," she said.

"He showed up without warning," Beth said. She had sunk to

the third step. "I think he must have known something was wrong from my demeanour yesterday. I thought I couldn't lie to him anymore. I told him the truth of everything that has happened with Nate."

"And he admonished you?" Catriona said.

"No. But I could see it in his face—a sort of…disdain, I think. I felt such anger then, such resentment. I thought I must compel him to speak his true feelings or I could never bear to look at him again. I told him, surely he remembers how it feels to lose a father? It was not so very long ago that his own passed away."

Beth had been speaking very quickly, but now she paused, glancing towards the door through which Bancroft had fled. "I know I shouldn't have said it. The wound is still raw for him. It was cruel of me to bring it up," she said. "He said if I believe I can compare his situation to that of my brother, perhaps the differences between us are too great to overcome. He has had to fight for everything, whereas Nate has had it all handed to him."

Catriona listened in silence, giving little nods where necessary. She did not say what she thought, which was that on this point in particular, she sympathised with Bancroft.

"I told him if he thought so little of Nate, surely he must think little of me as well," Beth said, "and if he asked me to choose between him and my brother, he would regret asking."

"Oh dear," Catriona said.

Beth dropped her face into her hands. "He rose and left without another word. Is our engagement broken?"

"Couples must often have differences of opinion," Catriona

said, feeling a little out of her depth, "and you both have been under quite a lot of stress."

"Oh, he caught me in such a foul mood in the first place!" Bethany exclaimed. "I could barely sleep last night with Nate so unwell. I feel as though nothing is within my control. Sometimes I want to throw open the windows and scream myself hoarse. I think I am coming undone."

"You and Mr Bancroft will mend things," Catriona said, more hesitantly than she had intended to. She had never seen Beth like this before, and it frightened her. "But you must try to rest now. Let me take care of you both, you and Nate."

"Do you think he could have done it?" Beth said. The words had rushed from her suddenly.

"What?"

"Nate. Do you think he could have killed our father?"

"Why do you ask that?" Catriona said. She felt stunned, put on the spot. "Did Mr Bancroft accuse him?"

"He and Papa were always at odds. I think of this secret he has been keeping. And it is violent, is it not? Towards his own person, yet he was capable of it—to pierce the skin with a needle, drive down the piston…"

"You really believe he did it?" Catriona said. For a moment, she thought Beth would not answer, and that would in itself be an answer.

"No. No, of course not," Beth finally said. "Yet the suspicion has been planted, and I cannot uproot it."

"Marlowe will clear him of it, Beth. There are so many others who could have done it, people your father was investigating, criminals with form."

Beth would not meet her eyes. She stared ahead, and Catriona could not read her expression. There was only her profile, the dark lashes, the upturned nose, behind a gold curtain of hair come loose from its plait.

"I dream about him so often now. Papa," she said. "And in my dreams he calls for me the same way he did when I ran too far from him as a child, as though some unutterable danger were lying in wait…"

Her voice had gone breathy and strange. The house had fallen silent around them, Catriona realised, so silent that it chilled her. She rose at once on the steps.

"Take my arm, Beth," she said, feeling panicked and not knowing why. "You must rest awhile now, and then you will feel better. Shall we go upstairs?"

Catriona stood in the hallway on the second floor, suspended in place. The atmosphere in the home was so tense that it was like another world inside, grey and dreary. More dreary even than the morning of the funeral, because at least then the place had been full of people. Now it was empty, and Catriona felt, for the second time that day, awfully alone.

Beth had gone to bed without further protest, and though Catriona had assured her she would stay and look in on Nate until Miss Fabian returned, in truth she dreaded seeing him, and she had busied herself for some time collecting a tray of tea from the kitchens before she worked up the nerve to climb the stairs.

She knocked at his bedroom door, which was ajar, and called out quietly, "Nate, may I come in?"

There was no answer, but when she opened it he was awake after all, slumped in an armchair by the fire. He turned and, as if having only noticed her then, said, "Oh. Kitty."

"How are you?" she said, going into the room.

"Never better," he replied tonelessly. A blanket was draped around his shoulders and across his lap, though the fire burned hotly, part of it collapsing in the grate with a shower of sparks.

"Goodness, it's very warm in here," she said.

"Is it?"

She set the tray on the low table and extended a hand towards him, but he flinched from her, and she paused, her hand hanging uselessly in the air between them.

After a moment, he turned to her again. "I wish you wouldn't see me like this," he said.

She brushed his hair back from the sheen of sweat across his forehead and lay her hand there for a moment. "You're burning," she said. "Perhaps I should open a window—and would you not be more comfortable in bed?"

"No, I can't bear lying down another minute. I feel as though I'm trying to escape myself," he said.

She went to the window and pushed it open, and the snowy air rushed in. The collar of her dress felt tight against her neck, and her face was hot. She felt so nervous, so unlike herself, that she regretted coming at all.

"Will you have some tea, at least?" she said, turning back to him.

"It's really no use," he said. "I can't tolerate anything."

She went to sit in the armchair across from him, perched at its edge, and folded her hands carefully in her lap. "Nate," she said, "you must get well again."

He shot her a sullen, almost resentful look. "I know I've done this to myself," he said. "I've tried to stop. You must think me some kind of fiend to keep going back to it."

He breathed as if he were about to say something else, but instead he swallowed and went silent. She knew what it was he had meant to say. She could see it in his eyes: that if only he could take it again, one last time, it might be a little easier.

"Tell me how I can help you," she said.

"Don't look at me that way, Kitty, please."

"How?"

"As if you fear me," he said, and closed his eyes and leaned against the wing of the armchair.

Catriona understood it keenly now, the reason Bancroft had left in such a hurry earlier. Suspicion had permeated the walls of the house like a creeping damp one could not help but breathe in. She told herself Nate could not have killed his father, not him, no matter how many other secrets he had kept.

"Nate?" she said.

He did not look at her, and for a moment, she hoped he had fallen asleep. But his jaw was clenched tightly, and his knuckles were white on the arms of the chair as he murmured, "Hmm?"

She sat forwards and said, "I think you must tell me where you were that night."

Having disembarked at Charing Cross, Catriona headed out to the street and cut determinedly through the afternoon crowd.

It had not been long before Miss Fabian arrived and, after quickly surveying her charge, sent Catriona down to the kitchens for ice. Only when she returned did Catriona understand that Nate must have been keeping his composure for her sake. Miss Fabian had taken the ice from her in the doorway and left her standing there in the corridor, and Catriona had whirled away at once so she did not have to see him as he was—shaking, delirious, retching over a washbasin.

She paused at the street corner and made the dash across during a break in traffic. Her destination was tucked down a laneway off Pall Mall, not so busy at that hour of the day. The bell hanging above the door rang as she opened it and entered, then approached the counter. The air had a medicinal smell. The chemist beyond, a portly man of perhaps fifty years, set down his mortar and pestle and turned to face her.

"How might I help you, ma'am?" he said genially.

"Good afternoon, sir," she said. "I hoped you might provide me with some information."

"For yourself, or perhaps a child?" he said. He gestured to the shelf behind him, on which stood an assortment of glass bottles in various colours. "We stock paregoric, chlorodyne, and a variety of quieteners for young children."

"Not medical information," she said, "but thank you. I wished to ask if you might recall a customer you served the evening of Friday last."

The chemist lowered his spectacles on his nose and regarded her frankly. "Afraid I cannot disclose that, ma'am. My customers expect discretion."

"Yes, of course," she said, and reached into her reticule. "I can pay you for your trouble."

His sceptical expression forced her to change tack quickly.

"But in fact, I…" She took a breath, withdrew her hand, and steeled herself. "This is most embarrassing. I shall come right out and say it. I think my husband has been unfaithful to me."

"Ah," the chemist said, turning to stare determinedly at the shelf behind him. "We do, of course, carry remedies for…social diseases…"

"No!" she cried out. "That is, thank you indeed, but I meant only that I wish to confirm his whereabouts on the night in question." She continued quickly. "You see, my friend says she saw him in the company of another woman at nine o'clock, yet he insists he was here, making a purchase. So you would be doing a great service to us both in confirming his story."

The chemist gave a relieved sigh, that of an unpleasantness having been avoided. "Nine o'clock last Friday, you say?"

"Yes," she said. "Perhaps you recall him? Tall, blond, dark eyes…?"

"You may indeed put your mind at ease, ma'am," he said. "I recall him only because I was just about to close for the night, and he had an unusual order. A number of chemical solutions used for photography, I believe, and a bottle of morphine."

"Yes, that would have been him," she said. "And have you got a record of the time the purchase was made?"

"Let me check." He reached below the counter to withdraw a ledger, which he flipped through, bending over it and pressing his spectacles back against his eyes. His finger landed on one line, and he straightened. "I accepted the payment at five minutes before nine, precisely. I keep very strict records, you understand."

"Thank you indeed, good sir," she said. "You have been most helpful."

"My pleasure," he said. A wistful expression had crossed his face, and he tucked the ledger back away, then exclaimed, "The jealousies of young love! I remember them well. Good afternoon, ma'am."

"Good afternoon," Catriona said, and turned to leave.

She emerged onto the footpath and stepped aside, bracing herself against the building. Relief had flooded through her with such force that she had to catch her breath.

If Nate had been at the pharmacy at five before, there was no conceivable way he could have got back to Scotland Yard by the time the clock struck nine. The distance between the two points was too great to cover in that span, even if he had caught a hansom on Pall Mall.

Catriona knew at once what she must do. A purple dusk was falling, and the lamplighter was making his way down the street, but the information she had could not wait. She felt the familiar triumph of having landed on something the police had not. Marlowe was perhaps so stuck on Nate being the killer that the inquiry had stalled, with no further suspects. It was time to disabuse him of his suspicions.

# CHAPTER 24

Catriona found Marlowe seated in his office, lit by a single lamp at the corner of his desk. Its surface was covered with documents, some also stacked in boxes on the floor.

"Inspector, good evening," she said from the doorway.

He rose at once. "Miss Winters," he said. "To what do I owe the pleasure? Come in."

She proceeded to the desk but did not sit, instead facing him as she said frankly, "I came to speak with you about Nathaniel, Lord Ashford."

Marlowe narrowed his eyes. "What about him?"

"If I were to tell you without a shadow of a doubt that he cannot have killed his father, would you drop your suspicions?" she said.

"You believe it, or you know it for a fact?"

"For a fact," she said. "I have verified his alibi for the night in question. He does some work for our paper, as you may know. He was purchasing photographic supplies at a pharmacy off Pall Mall. I spoke with the chemist personally to confirm the purchase was made just before nine o'clock. He could not have returned here and committed the killing in time."

He set down the sheaf of papers he had been holding loosely. "I would rather you had told me before going there yourself. But then," he said, "if it turned out he was lying, I suppose you never would have told me at all."

"Then you might be thankful I have been spared the dilemma," she said. "Now will you tell me whom else you suspect?"

He closed his eyes and pressed his fingers to the bridge of his nose. "The murder was personal and premeditated. The killer would have had to carry a pistol into Lord Ashford's office. I have looked through old cases, even questioned convicts with known associates on the outside, but in all honesty, madam, we have no serious suspects."

"Then we have missed something, some grudge or personal dispute that drove the other party to violence," she said.

She felt frustrated with him, with herself—even, absurdly, with Ashford and the secrets he had taken with him to the grave. She crossed her arms, suddenly self-conscious. This was what her papa had spoken of, that strange dirty feeling of digging into the personal life of someone she had held dear.

"The late Lord Ashford was secretive," she continued. "His

clandestine relationship with Madame Leung would have remained so had I not been placed fortuitously to discover it."

As she spoke, she had paced to the other side of the office and back again, and his impassive gaze followed her.

"That was the reason he brought you here, Inspector," she continued. She was thinking aloud, hoping he might interject. "Because his investigation into the opium trade was tied up with his personal life, he needed a colleague who would remain loyal only to him. But surely he took someone else into his confidence. You might speak to my papa about the men at their club. He could certainly get you in the door. I know not how else to help you..." She trailed off, distracted by a glance down at the books and papers which covered his desk. "All these documents, what are they?"

"The contents of Alan Randall's office," he said. "The man kept volumes—contracts, shipping manifests, financial records, correspondence, all going back years."

"May I see?" she said. At his gesture, she went to join him on the other side of the desk. "Do you really think he killed Stratton, then?"

"Off the record? Almost certainly," he said, watching her leaf through the pages. "Amongst his correspondence we found a blackmail letter. The final draft, I gather. Stratton instructed Randall to meet him at the docks the night he was murdered."

"Have we not got an extradition treaty with France?" she said. "Can Randall be brought into custody there?"

"The gendarmerie in Calais have been notified, but he may already have fled beyond the French border," Marlowe said.

She turned over a page, a financial document of some kind. The back of it was blank. She was not sure what she was looking for. "You know," she said, and shot Marlowe a significant look, "alerting the public could help you in apprehending him."

"As soon as the information is ready to print, you shall be the first to hear it," he said.

This did not quite satisfy her, but she wasn't in the mood to argue about it. The bustle of the Yard was muted by the long corridor outside his office, which felt quiet and even cosy. Catriona was reminded of the feeling of having snuck away during a ball, just barely able to hear music and conversation from another room.

"A pity Randall was scared off," Marlowe said. "I doubt Lord Ashford even knew of his connection to Stratton when he visited his office. It was a poor coincidence."

"Yet Lord Ashford was killed so shortly afterwards," Catriona said, still turning the pages idly. "I have long suspected he must have taken something with him from Randall's office when he left that afternoon, and the clerk confirmed as much. He thought it might have been a letter or a contract. I believe it was evidence of some kind. Yet the night Lord Ashford was killed, his desk was empty."

"You think the killer took whatever it was when he fled," Marlowe said.

"I do. The clerk said before meeting him at the train station, Randall met with someone else. But whom? Perhaps when it comes to the opium trade in Limehouse, Randall is not the head of the serpent," she said. Having reached for a familiar ledger, she perched at the edge of the desk, pulled off her gloves to more easily turn the pages, and began to flip through it.

"A police auditor will need to comb through all of this," he said. "It may take days or more."

"This is the ledger I saw," she said, turning it to show him the jagged edge where she had torn out the page. "When he returned, I thought Randall would somehow sense I had done it. But I hid the deception well, I suppose."

"You do," he said. "Hide it well, whatever you're thinking."

She looked up at him where he stood beside her, facing her. "Really?" she said. "Sometimes I fear my feelings must be written plainly upon my face."

"You fear it?"

"Do you not?" she said. "That someone might, with a glance, perceive your innermost thoughts?"

"Sometimes I wish it," he said.

"So you might be spared having to express yourself?" She closed the ledger and set it on the desk between them. "Perhaps you and I are not so dissimilar, Inspector."

He reached down to take it but instead stopped, his hand still set on it, and said, "You need not call me that, you know."

"What—Inspector?" she said, thrown off. "I suppose, were you my acquaintance, I would call you Mr Marlowe. Or perhaps I should call you by your Christian name?"

"You should call me whatever you wish," he said.

A surreal feeling fluttered in her chest. It was her heart racing, she realised, though she did not know why. "Then you must call me by my name, as well," she said—and then, very quickly, "but perhaps not in company, or people will talk."

"No, and God forbid that, Catriona," he said, his voice low.

He had not looked away from her as he said it, and she gave a hitching little laugh, almost a gasp. It was she who felt she must look away, as if he had scandalised her, as if she risked revealing a great secret she only now realised she had been keeping. She glanced down at the desk on which she was perched, down to the ledger where her bare hand rested alongside his.

In the corner of her vision, his chest rose and fell, but he said nothing more. Some force had riveted her to the spot. She felt quite suddenly as though she were watching from outside herself, as though the sliver of space between her hand and his were the Rubicon and, without knowing when or why, with a movement of her little finger, she had somehow crossed it.

He stilled at the contact. Immediate regret surged through her, but she made herself look up at him instead of withdrawing. It was fear he must see in her eyes now, she knew, fear and a desperate, hesitant hope. For the briefest flicker of a second, his gaze fell to her lips, and he swallowed. Then his thumb brushed over the back of her hand, across her fingers, slowly, intentionally.

Footsteps sounded in the corridor. Marlowe stepped back at once, and Catriona turned to see Detective Whitby rushing into view and bracing himself to a stop in the doorway.

"Excuse me, sir!" he exclaimed, out of breath. "Robbery in Waterloo, sir."

"Coming," Marlowe said. "Have the coach ready."

Whitby gave a sharp nod and raced off, his boots pounding back down the corridor until the sound faded into silence.

Catriona waited for Marlowe to say something, anything. But he said nothing, and she knew what she was waiting for would never come. She had been clutching her gloves in her right hand, in her lap, and she pulled them back on roughly. That the silk was now creased only annoyed her further.

"Do go," she said archly. "I can see myself out."

He sighed—in resignation? Or perhaps in disappointment, in her or in himself. He stepped past her and out of the office without another word.

Late that night, when the household had retired, Catriona sat by the window in her bedroom, writing in her diary. She did not wish to think about all that had transpired that day, so instead she made herself focus on the two murders.

A dark suspicion had begun to wrap its tendrils around her heart. Marlowe believed Randall had almost certainly killed Stratton. Yet the actions of the antiquities dealer the night he fled town left Catriona with questions. His clerk had said he went to meet someone before catching his train to Dover, and that he kept a flat for a woman. Had he sought her out to say good-bye?

As pretty a thought as that was, she felt a more likely scenario was that whatever document Ashford had taken from the office that afternoon had in fact proven the involvement of someone else in the opium scheme, and Randall, conceding the jig was up, had gone to warn him. It was thus, she believed, that person who had gone to Scotland Yard and murdered Ashford, then taken the incriminating document from the desk as he fled to cover his tracks.

Her pen had drifted to stillness on the page. She looked out into the darkness of the square. Across the gardens, through the bare trees, the drawing room at the Turner house was illuminated, its curtains parted just enough for her to see within, where Beth and Bancroft sat on the settee by a dying fire. They had reconciled after all; his arms encircled her, her hands clasped between them.

Catriona looked determinedly away. She had never seen the two alone together, she realised, not without the pretences one kept up in company. How odd it felt. How odd indeed, and how strangely confronting, that her dearest friend could suddenly feel like a stranger.

She turned the pages of her diary absently, her thoughts having drifted, despite her best efforts, from the murders back to Marlowe and that lamplit office. Her fingers closed on a loose note, and she glanced down, almost surprised to see the warning which had been hurled into her parlour only a few nights before. She never had been very good at it, minding her business.

The hand was of a striking character, quick strokes and sharp angles. A thousand scenarios swirled in her mind, a thousand paths all leading to a dead end, a body drifting by the docks, a man bleeding out from a gunshot to the heart. The head of the serpent, whoever he was, knew her and knew she was hunting for him—knew where she slept at night, having apparently tracked her home somehow. Could she ever sleep again, knowing he was coiled unseen in the dark, watching her, waiting for the moment to strike?

# CHAPTER 25

At the breakfast table the following morning, Hughes presented Catriona with two letters.

"My dear, you are diligent in your correspondence lately," Sir Frederick said, having barely glanced up from his papers.

"This one is from Lady Stratton, Papa," Catriona replied. She pried off the seal and scanned the contents. "She says the police have finished looking over her house, and she is having it packed up so she might return to her family in America. She wishes to meet with me before her departure."

"Still no news from the police on who killed her husband?"

"Nothing I can tell her just yet, and nothing we can print, I'm afraid, but Inspector Marlowe said he would let me know at the earliest opportunity. Perhaps I should prepare a story ahead of time," she said, then waited for an objection from her papa.

He said nothing, only turned the page, then raised his teacup to his lips but did not drink, reading intently. She realised he had not really been listening to her. She chose to take his silence as a tacit approval. She set the first letter down and turned her attention to the second, the envelope of which bore no return address. The blank space unsettled her, and she could not help but think back to her fears of the previous night, that someone was keeping track of her enquiries, waiting for the moment she, like Icarus ascending towards the fiery sun, strayed too close to the truth.

She read the letter.

"Everything all right, my dear?" Sir Frederick said.

"Quite all right, Papa," she said automatically. "It is one of the ladies from the lecture I attended last week. I think perhaps I shall visit with her this evening."

Her papa nodded absently and turned back to his papers, but Catriona sat still with the letter in her hand. Everything was most certainly not quite all right. The letter was in fact from Madame Leung, writing to inform her that the den had received another clandestine delivery of opium the previous night.

Her suspicions had been correct. Tsang could not have arranged another supplier so soon, she was certain. A third player in the scheme had likely taken over where Randall had left off. She decided at once to write Tsang. He would meet with her willingly, even eagerly. Of that she had no doubt, and she would use the opportunity to gather more information.

"Perhaps it would be best if you stayed home today, Catriona,"

Sir Frederick said suddenly, peering intently across the table at her.

His words had wrenched her from her thoughts, and she realised she had been staring unblinkingly out the window, still holding the letter. She set it down at once.

"Even our Lord rested on the seventh day, you know," he continued. "I am going in to the office anyway and will manage well enough."

"But I really must write that story on the man they will charge in the Stratton case," she said. "I wish to have it ready to print at a moment's notice. No, I shall come in with you."

"If you insist, my dear," he said, but the unusual concern in his expression gave her pause. Perhaps the strange turn in her demeanour had worried him. That was how her mama had been sometimes, staring out the window in their sitting room, which had overlooked Castries and the bay below.

"But that reminds me, Papa," she said, forcing herself away from the memory. "Inspector Marlowe wishes to speak with the members of your club. In case any of them knows anything, you see."

"I suppose he is overturning every rock in hopes something comes crawling from underneath," Sir Frederick said, lips curling in distaste. "I can have him admitted as my guest if he will be discreet in his questioning."

"He will," she said without hesitation.

Sir Frederick narrowed his eyes. "One hopes your detective inspector will make some progress on the case soon," he said.

She stilled, butter knife paused halfway across her toast. "He is hardly my detective inspector, Papa," she replied mildly.

"Is he not?" he said. "I doubt he devotes such time to every journalist. Police contacts are good for our business, Catriona, but try not to lead the man on too much."

"Good heavens, do you think me heartless?" she exclaimed a little breathlessly, a little too quickly.

"Hardly," he said. "And perhaps that is my point."

She forced her face into a placid expression, feeling mortified, as if he had somehow read her mind and seen the thing she had been hiding from herself. Her papa had never attempted to direct her attentions, at least not obviously, and because of that, she had, she now realised, deluded herself into the belief that he would be satisfied with any suitor of her choosing. He had seemed content enough with the idea of Sidney Hampstead, after all.

But this gentle warning, implied if not stated outright, had left her with a cold, empty feeling—and a resignation that he was right to have given it. Of course, Sir Frederick had the same ambitions for her that any father should have for his daughter: that she marry well, perhaps even above her station, and in so doing elevate them both further in society. She had been acting like a selfish, rebellious child, Catriona decided, wanting something only because she had thought she could not have it. All of that would end now.

"You need not worry on his account, Papa," she finally said, making her voice light. "I doubt Inspector Marlowe thinks of me as anything but a thorn in his side, if he thinks of me at all."

Sir Frederick only raised a brow and returned to his paper, then said, without looking back up at her, "You may as well write him to join me at my club for supper tonight. He is to meet me at the doors at eight."

At the *Messenger* offices that evening, Catriona read back the last few sentences of her article, which urged the public to report any sightings of erstwhile antiquities dealer Alan Randall to the police immediately. To her right lay a sketch of him, a faithful likeness, she having spent the better part of an hour with their illustrator, instructing him from her recollection as to the exact slant of the mouth and angle of the eyebrows.

She set down her pencil on the desk with finality. Through the windows, dusk had fallen with a spectacular misty red sunset. The man with whom her father had been meeting tipped his hat to her as he passed through the bullpen and departed, and Sir Frederick lingered in his office doorway as the reporters packed up and trickled out for the evening. As always, they tried to cajole her papa into accompanying them to a nearby pub, and as always, he commended each man on his work for the day and declined the invitation—but not without hinting that he might just join them in future.

Once the office was empty, he approached her desk. "How is your story coming along, my dear?" he said, looking down at her work.

"Very well, Papa," she said. "Perhaps when you meet with the inspector tonight, you might convince him of the importance of printing it."

"No doubt I shall bring it up," he said, then swung his hat onto his head and looked to the doorway. "In fact, I should head out or risk keeping him waiting at my club. Can I walk you to the station?"

"No, thank you," Catriona said. "My friend is to meet me here presently. In the meantime, I think I shall go over the story once more."

Sir Frederick shot her a strange, almost appraising look. "How you remind me of myself at your age, nose always to the grindstone," he said, then glanced away again. "But I suppose I have no one but myself to blame for that."

She thought perhaps this was one of those times where her papa spoke without requiring her reply. She said nothing, but she could not help wondering whether he regretted allowing her to assist him at the office, whether he had assumed she would tire of the novelty quickly and be eager to return to days of needlepoint and pianoforte. Had he realised now that she would not give it up happily, and was he perhaps thinking of how to approach the uncomfortable conversation in which he would put her back in her place?

Some time later, she stood by the window, watching him head off in the street below, pulling his coat tight in the cold, his breath rising in a mist from under the brim of his hat. Then he was gone, having disappeared around the corner, but Catriona remained standing there, her hand resting on the ledge. She was not looking at anything in particular now, only waiting for the sound of someone approaching from the stairwell.

She thought she heard footsteps, and she turned to greet her visitor, but there was no one. She resumed her waiting.

Catriona had written Tsang to request he meet her there at

eight, by which time she had known the upper floors would be deserted. But she had received no reply. Just as she had once left him to wonder whether she would take him up on his invitation to the Café Royal, he had now done the same to her. She could not help but doubt herself. Perhaps she had been too confident in her ability to charm him.

She was sure she heard footsteps now. She turned again, and in the frosted glass window in the door, his silhouette appeared. She stepped forwards to greet him as he pulled it open.

"You are here after all," she said.

"Good evening, Miss Winters." He removed his hat and, at her gesture, followed her to the sitting area in her papa's office.

"Do take a seat," she said. "I should be hospitable and offer you something to drink. Do you like whiskey, or I could find some port?"

"Depends on whether I should keep a clear head," he said, sitting in one of the wingback chairs and setting his hat on the low table beside him. "Your note of this morning was very vague. To what do I owe the pleasure of your invitation?"

"I have some questions for you," she said, and turned from the shelf from which she had retrieved a carafe and two glasses. "Chief amongst which is whether you had someone hurl a brick through my parlour window last Wednesday."

"A brick?" he exclaimed, his eyebrows shooting up. "No, of course not. What a question. Well, do pour me that whiskey after all, madam. It appears I shall need it."

Either he was a very good actor, she thought, or he was telling the truth. She poured two glasses and handed him one. "To your health," she said, and raised hers.

He was looking around the room, at the corner of her papa's desk, where she had left her report and its accompanying illustration for him to approve the following morning. "A handsome sketch," he said.

"Not my work," she replied. "You should know I'm quite certain it was Randall who murdered Lord Stratton."

"Really?" he said flatly. "Never would have taken Randall for a killer."

"Stratton was blackmailing him. A scared animal will attack when backed into a corner."

"Hmm," he murmured noncommittally, swirling the whiskey in his glass.

"That was why I thought it might have been you—the brick, I mean," she continued. She went to sit in the armchair opposite him, where she leaned forwards. "I thought perhaps I had backed you into a corner, and you were trying to warn me away from Limehouse without getting your hands too dirty."

As she spoke, she watched him for a reaction, but there was none, only that mildly inquisitive expression she thought he must put on consciously.

"But it would have been too neat of an explanation," she said finally. "And besides, if you wanted to warn me off, you had ample opportunity to do so in person. I made myself quite vulnerable when last we met."

"You must know you have never been in any danger with me,"

he said. "I have never wanted to warn you off."

"Someone does," she said. "I think my last visit to Limehouse touched a nerve—but as Randall has left the country, who else could it have been?"

"You trust it was not me, I take it," he said.

"If not you, someone connected with your opium trade."

"My trade?" He gave a quick flash of teeth, not quite a smile. "You give me too much credit. I only sell what has already made its way onto British shores."

"Be that as it may, it has become clear to me that the scheme does not begin and end with you and Randall. Another party is surely involved, and he has threatened me. I must know who he is."

"Must you?" he said. "You might instead take the warning seriously and leave the matter alone."

"How convenient that would be for you."

"How convenient for us both," he said. He was still sitting back, one leg crossed over the other as if he were perfectly at ease, but something in the tone of the conversation had shifted, and inexplicably, Catriona felt a prickling sensation at the back of her neck, as if she were being watched.

"I should like my business to continue as usual," Tsang said. "And I imagine you should like not to meet the same fate Stratton apparently did after sticking his nose into matters that did not concern him."

"You paid Randall for the opium every two weeks, did you not?" Catriona said, pressing on. "If your business is, as you say, to continue as usual, surely you will have to make another payment soon."

"What are you getting at?"

"I must know who is selling you the opium," she said. "When the time comes for you to pay him or his next front man, I ask that you tell me."

"You ask too much," he replied immediately, then drained his glass and set it down.

"You will not even think about it?" she said. For a moment, she thought he was finished with her and would rise and depart, but he stayed, leaning forwards.

"What is there for me to think about?" he said. "On the one hand, I sabotage my own business interests. On the other, I give you information that will ultimately put you in danger. I see no upside."

"The day you came to my rescue," Catriona said, "afterwards, when I awoke, I had occasion to speak with Madame Leung. She told me you acquired the boarding house for her sake. Do you really think this is what she wishes, to have it play a role in a criminal scheme?"

"This criminal scheme, as you call it, is what gives her the life she enjoys. She may have scruples, but they disappear when it comes time to order new silks or brew a fine tea."

"Perhaps those things ease the guilt she feels," Catriona said.

"Why should she feel guilty?" he replied. "Do I hold a pistol to the heads of my patrons? No. They make their own choices—just as you did."

"It is hardly a choice if they are addicted," she said. "You may not have inflicted their weakness upon them, but you certainly take advantage of it."

"Did I take advantage of you that day?"

She breathed in and forced her hands, which had been gripping her glass so hard it might shatter, to relax. She was thinking of Nate, of course, which she had been trying so hard not to do. "I rather think I knew what I was getting into," she said.

"Everyone thinks that," he said, then rose at last. "I cannot give you what you ask, Miss Winters. Limehouse is not for you."

She rose as well. Desperately, she wanted to beg him, to explain why she needed so badly to know: because she suspected that whoever was behind the scheme had fired the shot that killed Ashford. But to tell him so would risk too much, not only for the integrity of the police inquiry but for Jingyi Leung, whose secrets she had promised to keep. She said only, "Perhaps you will come to regret denying me this."

"Perhaps," he said. "But I have made my decision."

"Then there is nothing more for us to say," she said, and turned abruptly. "I shall not keep you any longer, Mr Tsang. Let me see you out."

Neither spoke further. She accompanied him through the office, down the stairs, to the street, where she watched him from the doorway as he departed. Snow had begun to fall. She was disappointed in her failure and angry with him for standing in her way. She knew that even after she was home, she would think of him that night, returning to the laneways of Limehouse like a ghost in the briny mist.

He had reached the end of the street and was about to turn when she felt it again, that peculiar sensation of being watched. The door swung open soundlessly behind her, with a rush of air, and the scuffle of a shoe over the threshold had her turning. Before she could step aside or see who it was, an arm swung across her chest, pulling her back.

She struggled to cry out before the heavy hand clamped a rag over her mouth, cutting her off. She pulled ineffectually at the arm, the heavy dark fabric of the coat, but it was solid and strong, too strong for her to fight. When she gasped at last for air, her senses flooded with the sweet-bitter taste of ether, and the world spun. A bright pain bloomed out behind her eyes. The snow fell as pinpricks over her face.

In the distance, someone was shouting. Footsteps rang out over the cobblestones. Waves crashed against a ridge.

Oblivion.

# CHAPTER 26

"Miss Winters, can you hear me?"

Catriona blinked awake in an unfamiliar bed, lying atop starched sheets. A gas sconce shone dimly overhead, glinting off pale green wall tiles. Someone stood there, looking down at her. The person was familiar. It was the nurse she had met at the Turners', Miss Fabian.

"Where am I?" she said. Her throat felt scratchy and dry.

"St Thomas Hospital," Miss Fabian said. A small crease in her forehead was all that betrayed her concern; she spoke calmly and matter of factly. "A gentleman brought you in, saying you had been assaulted outside your office. Look into the lamplight so I may examine your pupils, please."

"Where is he, the gentleman?" Catriona was struggling to sit up, but Miss Fabian placed a hand firmly to her chest, and she relented and lay back, allowing the nurse to turn her face gently towards the lamp.

"He left a few minutes ago as you began to wake," Miss Fabian said.

It must have been Tsang who brought her in, she realised. He had heard the commotion and turned back to investigate, and thank God he had, as who knew what might have become of her otherwise?

"Miss Winters, I think the police should be sent for," Miss Fabian said. She hesitated, then produced a note from her apron and held it out. "This was tucked into your collar."

Catriona took it from her and unfolded it. She recognised the hand at once, the same determined angular script from the paper that had been wrapped around the brick.

*LAST WARNING.*

"Do you know who did this to you?" Miss Fabian said.

"No," Catriona said. She was having trouble thinking past the insistent pain behind her eyes, still stuck on the image of a set of gloved fingers tucking the note into her dress, directly against her neck. "The man who brought me in, did he mention seeing anything?"

"He said you were alone on the doorstep of your office when he found you," Miss Fabian said. "Please allow me to send for a constable at once."

"No, I do not wish to involve the police," Catriona exclaimed quickly, nearly reaching out to stop her. "I should like only to go home."

"I cannot in good conscience advise it," Miss Fabian said. "But nor can I keep you here against your will. Can I send word to anyone for you? You may still become disoriented."

"To my residence, please," Catriona said. "Our butler will come to escort me."

"Of course," Miss Fabian said. "Try to rest in the meantime. I'm sorry this has happened to you."

The nurse left, pulling a thin curtain closed around the bed as she did. Catriona turned to face away from the lamp but did not sleep, instead staring into nothingness. Last she remembered, she had been standing in the doorway at the street, watching Tsang retreat in the snow. She could remember nothing after that, only the cold rag closing over her mouth, held in place by a strong hand.

Someone had come upon her, subduing her before she could fight back. He must have entered the building at some point, she realised, and waited in the stairwell for his opportunity to strike. Yet he had come prepared with a note to leave on her person. Surely that meant he had not intended to kill her?

She knew the attacker was the man who had killed Ashford, a murder he had not hesitated to commit. So why go through the trouble of continually warning her away? Perhaps he knew she was nowhere close to unmasking him. Perhaps he simply wanted to show her what he was capable of when pushed. Or perhaps he had a conscience after all.

She was so bone tired, so infinitely weary. Her mouth still tasted of chloroform, and unless she focussed very hard, which only worsened the pain in her head, the world tilted ever so slowly around her.

"Kitty, thank God," someone was saying.

She had fallen asleep without realising it. Minutes had felt like seconds, and as she blinked awake, her face was hot, her eyes bleary. He swam into view before her, the lamplight glinting off his hair. "Nate. How did you…?"

"I was out in the square when the messenger arrived. Miss Fabian has told me what happened."

"Oh," she said tonelessly. She could not very well blame Miss Fabian for telling the truth, though she wished she had not. She sat up a little and looked at Nate more carefully, having realised suddenly that he was recovered. The colour was back in his face, and he had shaved. "But you are looking so well now, dear Nate."

He sat on the bed before her and took her hand. Once she might have thrilled at that, but now she felt he were treating her as he would a child. "Kitty, listen to me," he said. "The police must be sent for immediately. Why-ever should you not wish to see this man caught and apprehended at once?"

"Of course I wish him caught," she said, firmly withdrawing her hand from his. "I will tell the police when I see fit."

He shot her a disbelieving look. "Is this about your enquiries into Stratton?"

"Not entirely."

"Then what the hell else is it about?" His voice had risen. He caught himself, lowering it as he said, "My God, you could have been killed."

"But I was not," she replied. She knew that were she in his position, she would find that sort of response infuriating, yet it was all she could think to say. She did not wish to justify herself.

"That is hardly the point," he said. "Tell me who is encouraging you in this nonsense. Not that wretched policeman you consort with, surely."

"Is that what this is about?" she exclaimed. "Your jealousy of my professional acquaintances? I wish you hadn't come. Now you think you have the right to demand I explain myself to you."

"I do demand it, because the thought of something happening to you makes me sick to death," he snapped. "Do you understand that I love you? Do I not have the right to protect you—from yourself, if necessary?"

Catriona sat stiffly, her hands tense in her lap. He had nearly snarled the words at her, but now, as if having suddenly become conscious of his behaviour, he leaned back and rose, his shadow stretching tall on the curtain. She was forced to look up at him.

"I suppose you plan to keep this from your father," he said, and then, when she did not answer, "I should tell him myself. He might have better luck at reining you in."

"I do not wish to be reined in," she said, "and I think you're being a little hypocritical!"

"Think what you like. I would rather be subjected to your ire than stand by whilst you throw yourself directly in the path of whatever madman is out there."

"You make me sound unbearably naive," she said. Something cold and defiant had dawned inside her, and the words flew out before she could stop them: "It is not I who has been off playing De Quincey whilst the man who murdered his father roams free."

He stepped back further, as if she had struck him. His face went blank. "You can be extraordinarily cruel sometimes, you know," he said.

She regretted it at once. She sagged back against the pillow, every ounce of fight having left her instantly. When she looked up at him again, she knew it was with an awful, pitiful expression. "Forgive me, Nate," she begged him. "Please. It was badly said."

He gave a measured sigh and closed his eyes in a long blink. For a moment, she was sure he would leave her, pull back the curtain and simply walk away. Instead he lowered himself so he was kneeling beside the bed, so they were face to face, and took her hand again.

"Perhaps we should take some time away from the city," he said, "somewhere without so much to distract us."

"You want to leave London?" she said.

"We could go anywhere you like—California, or Australia, or the West Indies," he said. "A place beside the ocean, where you could feel the sun on your face, and we could be happy."

His hands were warm around hers, his expression so fiercely sincere that she felt ashamed of herself, ashamed that her first feeling upon hearing his proposal, and it was a sort of proposal, even if he had not said the words, was not elation but something unrecognisable and frightening.

It was a realisation, a realisation that wherever they went, they would be running, not from the dreariness of London but from themselves. After her mama died, Catriona and her papa had left

St Lucia forever, but a ghost had crossed the ocean with them. It would be the same now. She could not outrun the thing she was trying to flee. It was herself, her own nature, and a restless, hungry dissatisfaction that threatened to consume her.

"Say something," Nate said. "Tell me what I must do to make you say yes."

"It sounds so very pretty," she said. "A pretty dream."

He let go of her hand and rose. It was a rejection, and he knew so. He looked away from her, to the opening in the curtain and beyond it. "You're tired," he said. "It can wait. I'll flag down a cab."

Later that night, Catriona sat in the drawing room, her legs tucked up under her nightgown, staring out the window into the square. When a coach pulled up and out stepped her papa, she hoped he would go past the room without seeing her. She had lit no candles; she sat in the dark.

From downstairs came the sound of the door opening, then the hushed voices of Hughes and Sir Frederick. It was very late, nearing three in the morning. How had the inspector gone with his questioning at the club, she wondered?

"Catriona?" It was her papa, standing in the doorway. She had not heard him come up the stairs.

"Hello, Papa," she said. She had lowered her legs to the floor and sat with her back straight, hands folded placidly in her lap. "How was your club tonight?"

"Forget that," Sir Frederick said, and strode into the room to stand facing her before the dark, empty fireplace. "Hughes told me you were in hospital this evening. Are you quite all right?"

"It was nothing. I simply fainted," she said. "A little embarrassing, really. My friend insisted I see a doctor, but as you see, I am perfectly well now."

"You have been pushing yourself too hard lately," he said, having barely let her finish, as if, whilst ascending the stairs, he had already decided what he would say. "All this running around. Tomorrow you will stay home and rest. I will not hear otherwise."

She knew what this meant. He was finding a way to extricate her from the place she had made for herself at the *Messenger*, and he was doing so under the guise of his fatherly concern for her, against which she could not possibly argue. To do so would once have been her first instinct. She surprised herself by saying simply, "Of course, Papa."

He sighed a long sigh, perhaps in relief, and lowered himself to the armchair across from her. In the faint light from the window, he looked suddenly very old.

"Please, Papa, there's no need to worry yourself," she said—and then, feeling she must change the subject at once, "but you must tell me how the inspector got on with his enquiries at your club."

Sir Frederick surveyed her carefully. Then, apparently having decided the matter was settled to his satisfaction, he replied, "I admit I may have underestimated him. Did you know he was a lieutenant in the navy?"

"Oh?" she said. She recalled what little he had told her of his past. She had never asked his rank, as perhaps she should have done. But then, that changed nothing now. She hardly knew him.

"He asked me to introduce him as such rather than as an inspector—to put people at ease, I gather," her papa said. "After all, one rather wishes not to be interrogated by the police whilst socialising."

"Hmm, quite," she said. "And did the lieutenant find out anything useful?"

Her papa raised a brow. "He spoke very naturally with several people over the course of the evening. But I gather it was not much help to the inquiry," he said. "I have come to understand that Ashford was very secretive, even amongst his friends. But then, I can hardly begrudge a man his privacy."

"I imagine even ruling out suspects was helpful," she said.

"In that case, I suppose I should take it as a compliment that the inspector has not asked where I was at that fateful hour," Sir Frederick said.

"Not directly," Catriona said. "Perhaps, when he went there to seek you out that night, he confirmed your whereabouts with the club staff."

"I had not thought of that," he said. "I was there, of course, all evening, waiting on Ashford, unaware he would never join us again." He glanced out to the square, in the direction, she knew, of the Turner house, the windows of which were dark.

Catriona waited for her papa to say something more. Several seconds passed before he did.

"But it is quite late now." He rose abruptly and brushed his hands together. "Please get yourself to bed, and in the morning, we shall ask Mrs Travers to make those Liège waffles you so used to enjoy, and perhaps some hot cocoa."

"That sounds nice, Papa," Catriona said. "I think you may be right that some rest will do me good."

"Excellent. You must allow your papa to believe he is looking after you every once in a while. Now good night, my dear."

"Good night," she said.

Once he had departed, she turned to face the window again. She had tried to sleep but could not. It was not the memory of the cold hand clamped over her mouth which frightened her; it was what she had seen upon returning home and looking into the mirror. Her mama, waiting there in her reflection.

Catriona had recoiled from the sight as if burned, and she could not shake it. Just as she had that night on the ridge in St Lucia, she felt it now, a sense that events were tumbling inevitably towards a terrible end. She had already accepted it: She would either catch the killer or, in the process, set herself up neatly as his next victim.

And she had accepted too that all of this was not because she felt an obligation towards Lady Stratton, or because she wanted justice for the murdered Lord Ashford, or even because she wanted to prove herself as a journalist. It was because of a compulsion she could not deny, because waiting at the end of every risk she took was the answer to a question she had asked ever since that night with her mama on the ridge.

The killer repulsed her. His sins were too grave for forgiveness. And yet, secretly, did the idea of him thrill her too? Did she anticipate it with every part of her being, the moment she would come face to face with death at last?

# CHAPTER 27

After breakfast the next morning, Sir Frederick headed in to the newspaper offices, leaving Catriona to roam listlessly about the house. She had already taken a bath and dressed for the day. She had even acquiesced to Emily tugging the dreaded comb, scalding from the stove, through her hair to tame the curls before piling them all up on her head once more. Part of her suspected the maid was under instructions from her papa to keep her from leaving, by force if necessary.

Catriona had finally settled on a book to read and had curled up in front of the fire in the drawing room like a pampered cat when she was rescued from her leisure by the sound of the front door opening. She set the book down at once and rushed out to the top of the stairs to find Beth in the foyer, holding a bouquet of flowers.

"Beth, good morning," Catriona said as she descended the stairs to join her. Hughes had taken her coat and bonnet and departed with a bow and a promise that refreshments would be sent up.

Once he had disappeared down the back stairs, Bethany reached out to embrace Catriona. "Nate told us he retrieved you from hospital yesterday, you poor thing," she exclaimed. "I thought to come by and see how you are feeling."

"You are too kind," Catriona said.

As they parted, Beth extended the bouquet, white mountain ash and asphodels, towards her. "These are from Henry, with his well wishes," she said. "He does try."

"Oh, how thoughtful," Catriona said. "You must give him my thanks. But in all honesty, I am perfectly fine. No need to worry."

"Kitty, you must allow people to fuss over you when given the opportunity," Beth said, raising a finger as though chastising her. "Especially men. It makes them feel so important."

"I shall keep that in mind," Catriona said, and together they started up the stairs. At the top, she handed the pretty flowers off to a passing Emily, and they went in to the drawing room and were seated on the settee.

"Papa insisted I stay home today," Catriona said. "Yet I find I cannot stand the thought of things happening at the office without me."

"Perhaps you might get used to it," Beth said. "A husband will expect you to give up the paper, after all." She was looking not at Catriona but at the low table by the armchair, and she said, as if to change the subject, "Is that *Endymion* you were reading?"

"I had just barely started," Catriona said.

"Hardly worth the bother. I found it dreadfully myopic," Beth remarked with a vague little wave. Catriona had sensed her friend was in a poor mood, and perhaps she had visited in an effort to shake herself of it. She wondered whether Beth and Bancroft were not so reconciled as they appeared, but it was too personal a question to ask, not directly.

Their conversation had stuttered to a halt, each occupied by her own thoughts. Catriona finally said, "I suppose a husband would expect me to give it up after all. The paper."

"And what does Sidney think of it?" Beth said.

"Nothing at all, I expect," Catriona said. "But that reminds me, he sent a telegram with his condolences. I forgot to tell you, with everything that has happened."

"How kind of him," Beth said. "He is such a good friend."

"Yes, a very good friend." Catriona suddenly regretted having presented the opportunity to bring Sidney up, as Beth had taken on a familiar expression that suggested she would interrogate the topic further than was desirable.

"But I expected you might think of him as a little more than that…?" she prompted.

"I know it hasn't been so long since he left," Catriona said, "but perhaps I am a different person now. I struggle to imagine what we might have in common when he returns, if he does."

"I think I understand," Beth said. "I was so sure about Henry once. When he and I met, he had just started taking on more responsibilities with the company. But then his father passed away, and he had to shoulder so much so quickly, and perhaps it has changed him."

The turn in the conversation surprised Catriona, who had expected Beth to pounce at the slightest suggestion that she and Sidney might not be compatible. Instead, she realised with some relief that Beth had not wanted to talk about Sidney at all. She had been looking for a way to express her own anxieties, and perhaps now Catriona would get her answer as to whether the couple had in fact made peace with one another.

"He has always been reserved," Beth continued, "but he was never like that with me. He used to smile more often. I thought we made each other happy."

"It has been such a difficult year for you both," Catriona said. "But the next will be better."

"God willing," Beth said. She gave Catriona a strange smile, one that did not reach her eyes and disappeared quickly. "I think ours has been an inauspicious engagement."

They were interrupted by the sound of light footsteps on the stairs, which preceded Emily into the room. The maid set down a tray of tea and biscuits before departing, and the two ladies were quiet for a moment longer. As Catriona held her teacup, absently watching the steam rise, Beth spoke again.

"I have been thinking of Lady Stratton and her late husband, of what secrets he was keeping from her. It makes me wonder if every marriage must be like that."

"Surely we all have a few secrets," Catriona said.

"Not me," Beth said. "I could hardly bear keeping the secret about Nate, and when I did finally tell Henry, I think it disturbed him, the idea that I had hidden something from him. For a moment, he looked at me as though I were a stranger. No, I am not made for secrets, and he has realised it now."

Catriona glanced from Beth to the window, to the gloomy sky. It was neither raining nor snowing, the heavy grey clouds suspended indecisively. "Perhaps it shocks them to realise we have our own lives, our own inner selves. But I suppose marriage ends that," she said, and then, without thinking, "I could not bear someone knowing everything about me."

Beth reached out as if to touch her hand, but she stopped herself. "I wish you wouldn't say such things," she said with a fierce little expression. "It makes me so very sad to think of you alone."

"I am not alone," Catriona replied quickly, almost defensively. "I have Papa and you and our friends, and I have the paper…"

"Kitty," Beth said, interrupting her, and something about the careful way she had said it, as if she had taken a breath and were about to plunge into the depths, made Catriona fall silent. Beth said, "I have seen the way he looks at you."

"Who," Catriona said, "Sidney?"

"No, not Sidney."

Catriona didn't know what to say. She couldn't deny it. A feeling like vertigo swam in her, a lukewarm sort of shame.

"I suppose I was pretending not to see it," Beth continued. "But I think Nate has always loved you, ever since we were children." She reached across and did take her hand then, her expression gentle, saintlike. "I'm not angry with you. It's myself I'm angry with, for being so jealous. I hated the thought that you two might share a secret, and I was to be left out."

"It was never like that," Catriona said quietly.

"I know. And in truth, I always believed he would move on," Beth said. "Nate never holds an attachment long. But then, how could he? No one will ever compare to you."

Catriona felt she must say something, anything, but the sound that came out when she tried to speak was more like a pained gasp, and she snapped her mouth shut again.

"Really, nothing should make me happier than the happiness of my brother and my dearest friend," Beth said. "And I do wish that for you, every happiness in the world."

"I feel as though I have wronged you," Catriona finally said.

"It is I who has wronged you," Beth replied, "pushing you towards Sidney when I knew your heart was not in it. I was afraid you and Nate would hurt each other irreparably, and then everything would change."

"I've never meant to hurt him."

"Nor he you," Beth said. "Not intentionally. He thinks he must prove himself deserving of you, that if only you believe in him, he will better himself. But the thing Nate is looking for cannot be found in another person. And I know you, Kitty, well enough to know you have only ever believed in yourself."

"I..." Catriona choked out. She felt as though she had been pushed and were falling, grasping for something to hold on to, some way to explain a thing she could not explain even to herself. "I know

I have always been a—hard woman."

"I do not say this to hurt you," Beth said. She was gripping Catriona's hand tightly, and when she spoke again, it was with unexpected intensity. "I love you, Kitty. More than I love anyone else, I think. But Nate frightens me so very much sometimes. He needs someone to protect him, and in the end, the one who needs you is the one you must love the most."

Catriona focussed on the dull burning pain in her throat as if it were an anchor. She forced herself to take one long breath. There it was again, retrieved from its shelf inside her, the little box in which her feelings must be locked back away for as long as it would take her to forget them. She withdrew her hand carefully.

"You will not have cause to worry for long," she said at last, her voice now calm and weightless. "Nate sees a wall and batters himself against it in the hope that whatever lies beyond will be worth the fight. But there is nothing in me for him or for anyone. He will realise it, sooner or later. And I shall be relieved for him when he does."

Beth regarded her for a long moment, her face twisting from a wince to something gentle and pitying. "You say that now," she said. "But one day you will meet someone who is your equal, and you will understand each other, and it will not feel like a fight to be won."

Catriona said nothing. She felt as if she couldn't get enough air, as if she might faint. Beth had such a hopeful expression, like a mother encouraging a child to walk. Catriona did not want to disappoint her. Beth had always believed they would accompany each other through life as sisters. They would become wives and then mothers, and their own daughters would play together as they once had done. It was a shimmering future that dissolved through her fingers the more tightly Catriona tried to hold on to it. It was not to be, and she knew so even if Beth did not.

At last the burning in her throat faded, and the shameful feeling was gone, replaced by cold certainty.

"Thank you for calling on me, Beth," she said, then rose, and Beth had no choice but to rise as well. "I think I must be tired after all."

Catriona had spent the rest of the day in that warm stupor so characteristic of being immersed in a book. She had abandoned Endymion Ferrars for one of her oldest friends, Captain Nemo. Yet at the very moment the *Nautilus* came under attack by the giant devilfish, the sound of a male throat being cleared jolted her from her reverie.

It was Hughes, standing in the doorway of the drawing room. Catriona shot up in her chair, startled. She had not heard him come up.

"Excuse me, miss," he said, "but a gentleman is downstairs."

"Put him off, please," she replied without thinking much of it. "I am otherwise engaged."

"He says you will wish to speak with him."

"Who is he?" She set her book down in her lap.

"One Victor Tsang," he said. "He asks me to tell you he has thought further on your request."

"I see," Catriona said. Annoyance had quickly transformed into intrigue. "Have him wait in the parlour, please. I shall join him presently."

Hughes nodded and disappeared back down the stairs, but Catriona did not rise at once to descend. She composed herself, smoothed out the wrinkles in her dress, and tucked a few loose curls back into their high bun. Tsang had once said it was fate that had brought them together. Had it been fate when he turned back in the snow and found her lying unconscious in the street, or when he rescued her as she fled the warehouse at the docks? Had it been fate when he caught her as she fell that first day in the opium den?

She rose. No, it had not been fate, she decided. She had made her own decisions, and he had made his, and now it was time for each of them to make one more.

She paused halfway down the stairs to watch him where he stood in the parlour. He seemed to absorb every shadow and flicker of firelight in the room, like the focal point of a painting.

"You look better than when I saw you last, Miss Winters," he said as she joined him.

"I must thank you for once again coming to my rescue," she said. She lowered herself to the settee, and he sat across from her. "I dare not imagine what might have become of me otherwise. You saw nothing of the man who attacked me?"

"No," he said. "I thought I heard you cry out, but by the time I reached you, he was nearly out of sight. I could not very well leave you lying there to pursue him. Did he intend to kill you, do you think?"

The cavalier way he had asked it might once have offended her. Now she had come to understand this was just his manner, and besides, the question was one she had already asked herself.

"If he wanted me dead," she said, "he could have killed me right there easily enough. A knife through the ribs and it would have been over quickly and quietly. No, I think his intent was to frighten me off, not to hurt me."

"And has he succeeded?"

"I think you know he has not," she said. "So have you come to check in on me? You could have stayed a little at the hospital last night instead of disappearing at the first opportunity."

His only reaction was the slightest quirk of a brow. "I thought that nurse might send for the police," he said. "Better to stay out of their way."

"Of course," she replied, folding her hands in her lap. "And now that you have confirmed I am unharmed after all, you have discharged your duty."

She had said it as a challenge, expecting a quick rapier reply, but he remained silent, and it was only then that she realised the change in him. He had always, at least with her, masked an innate wariness with affectations, a languid gesture, an indolent smile. All that was gone now. He sat forwards, predatorial.

He said, "Madame Leung has told me everything."

Catriona stilled. Even her heart had stopped. He was telling her so only because she had betrayed him too, she was sure, and whatever retribution he had paid Madame Leung he would now also pay her. Perhaps he had killed her, she thought. Perhaps she was already adrift in the river.

"I see," she said.

"Do you?" he returned. It was an accusation, but a half-hearted one. He leaned back in the armchair. "It should not have surprised me to hear you brought the police to my establishment after all. But then, I suppose they already had me in their sights, as Madame Leung has apparently been conspiring against me for months now."

"Can you not see how she loves you?" Catriona said fiercely. "As if you were her own son. What you call conspiracy has been her way of trying to protect you."

"I am not to be protected from my own ambitions," he said.

"Then the police should be the least of your worries. You are playing a dangerous game with dangerous people."

"It is an even match, madam," he said. "Do you think because we have civilised conversations, because I can act like a gentleman, I would hesitate to kill to get what I want?"

"Are you threatening me?" she said. "There is no point. I am not afraid of you or anyone."

"Perhaps you should be."

"Yes, I should be a great many things I am not," she said, and rose from the settee without knowing why.

She meant to dismiss him but instead found herself caught in place, that strange cold sense of resolution dawning within her. Behind him, in the dark window to the square, was her firelit reflection, but its eyes were not her eyes. Defiance melted into acceptance. She sat bonelessly back on the settee.

"But this is my nature," she said at last.

He rose—to leave, she knew, and she would let him, because she could not beg him to tell her what she needed to know. Her pride would not allow it. Instead, he crossed the room and knelt before her.

"I am not here to threaten you," he said.

She was too astonished to speak. His expression was earnest, the first real feeling she had perceived in him. He had taken her bare hands in his.

"I will give you the information you seek," he said, "and you will tell your friend in the police, and that will be the end of it—for us both. Madame Leung will make a new start here. And I…"

"You are leaving London," she said.

"This city is not for me," he replied. "It took me too long to see it, but I have seen it now. She is too old and canny for me to master her. But not to worry, Miss Winters. The world is a vast and wonderful place. I hear the view over San Francisco Bay is spectacular."

He held her hands a moment longer, then released them, and he stood abruptly. She rose with him. From his jacket he produced an envelope, which he handed to her. "Inside is fifty pounds," he said. "This must be left in the wall box at the address noted there, on Kemble Street, by midnight."

"I understand," she said. "You do not know what this means to me."

"I do," he said, "just as I know I should not bother warning you against your plans. Like Pandora, you will pry open the box regardless of what evils lurk inside."

He stepped back, and she drew the envelope towards herself.

This was it, the chance she had been waiting for, and she willed herself to feel the triumph she had anticipated. But instead there was nothing, only that empty dread, that feeling of an impending end.

"Now, as much as I should like to," he said, "I will not watch this scenario play out. I am leaving for Southampton. Tomorrow I set sail for America."

"Then we shall not see each other again," she said.

"Miss me, will you?" It had returned, the indolent smile. "Our paths diverge now, but what a pleasant companion you have been whilst we shared the road."

He turned to depart, but she reached for him, her fingers brushing his sleeve. He stopped.

"You are a good man," she said.

"Am I?" For barely more than a blink, his expression had faltered. "I have never thought so. In fact, I know otherwise. But even a bad man can do a good thing."

Catriona nodded. She withdrew her hand.

"This is good-bye, Miss Winters," he said.

"Yes," she said. "Good-bye, Mr Tsang. And good luck."

He bowed deeply, a man in whom, though she had not known him, not really, and never would, she felt she had found a kindred spirit. Then he turned from her and departed, and she watched from the window as he made his way down the street and, at last, was gone.

# CHAPTER 28

Catriona rapped on the door at No. 9. She had been forced, with such little time before midnight, to make a choice between the Yard and his residence. She gathered Marlowe often worked late, but some inner sense had guided her to Islington, and from the faint lamplight spilling out under the door, she knew she had chosen correctly.

He opened it, and before he could speak, she held up a hand and said, "Let me in, please, and you must listen without protest. We have so very little time."

He stepped back without a word, his cold eyes unreadable. She knew he was thinking, always thinking, but she could not tell what. She crossed the threshold, and in the room, the window was open to the street below. A paraffin lamp flickered dimly on the table, and a trunk lay alongside the bed, his clothes folded neatly inside.

He was leaving. She understood it suddenly and impersonally, and the gnawing pain of disillusionment clawed its way up inside her. She forced herself to breathe. There was no time for all this now.

From the window, two reflections watched her. He was there, waiting for her to explain. But it was not her he stood behind. The face was not her face, and in her ears was a constant pounding sound, the constancy of waves against a ridge, and she could hardly bear it any longer. She pulled her arms tightly across her chest, reaching blindly inside her for that little box, and at last she found it, and turned the lock, and she was herself again.

She whirled and told him all she must: her conversations with Tsang, the assault of the night before, the envelope that was to be left in the wall box. It all left her in a rush until she trailed off lamely and waited for him to reply.

His eyes were not unreadable now. They were the grey of storm clouds, of an ironclad hull lashed by the sea, and he said, "I cannot believe you've kept this from me."

She uncrossed her arms. "If you must scold me, do it later," she said. "I'm telling you now, and now there's no time."

His mouth had gone into a hard line, and a muscle tensed in his jaw. He stepped back, turned to the doorway, and then turned to her again. "I'll flag down a patrolman on my way and have him send word to Scotland Yard," he said. "You are to stay here."

"I will not be ordered about!" she exclaimed.

"I'm not ordering you," he said. "I am begging you. Let me

handle this. Promise me you'll stay here tonight."

She would not answer him, and they stood there as if caught in a lamplit tableau, neither moving, neither willing to cede a step.

Finally, he exhaled and said, "Give me the envelope."

She held it against her chest. "No," she said.

"Give it to me, Catriona!" He extended his hand towards her. "For once, do not argue."

His voice was commanding, and she responded automatically. The envelope was gone from her hand before she could stop it. As soon as she realised what had happened, she was furious with herself. Her face went hot, but she could not very well snatch it back from him.

"Lock the door when I leave," he said. "Open it for no one."

He turned to go, pulling his jacket and revolver from on top of the bureau, but when he opened the door, she breathed in as if to speak, and he stopped at the threshold and turned back to her. She said nothing. She knew not what she had meant to say. A hundred protests were at the tip of her tongue, but, absurdly, the only thing she wanted to tell him was to be careful, and she could not find the words to do so.

As the door swung closed behind him, she went across to the window. In a matter of minutes, he strode out into the street below, hailed a cab, and disappeared inside. The horses kicked up slush behind them, and the coach clattered off down the rutted road and out of sight around the corner.

She paced, her shoes clicking on the hollow floorboards, and her reflection paced alongside her. Marlowe would be at the address, which was in Westminster, in twenty minutes at most. Cutting it close, but he would make it before midnight and lie in wait until someone arrived to claim the money from the wall box, and she would drive herself mad pacing.

A train rattled by distantly outside. Someone was smoking in another room, and the acrid smell scratched at her throat. The flat felt empty and cold. She closed the window, and in the quiet, she sat at the little table next to it and watched the flame in the lamp. A minute went by, then two, then three.

She turned down the lamp till it sputtered out. She could still make it if she left now.

The Strand was not deserted at that hour of the night, though the crowd were mostly men, and as Catriona alighted her cab and almost submerged her shoe in a cold puddle along the footpath, she felt it again, that peculiar prickling feeling of being watched. She drew her coat tighter around her, dashed between horses and coaches across the road, and slipped down a laneway.

Kemble Street lay ahead. She had instructed the coachman to let her off at the opposite corner so she could approach undetected. As she neared the mouth of the laneway, she pressed herself back into the shadows against the brick wall alongside. The snow was falling thickly now, and she squinted through it to see. Across the street was an unassuming rundown townhouse, one in a row of such houses. Even so close to the Strand, this area was destitute.

Distantly, echoingly, the bells at King's College were ringing midnight. Marlowe must already have placed the envelope in the wall box and was also waiting nearby, but she could not see him. Perhaps the money would not even be claimed that night. It was a possibility she had not thought of.

She felt suspended in place, listening to a bark of laughter from the Strand, wheels and hoofbeats in the street, whistling from an upstairs window—and footsteps behind her, as fleeting as a butterfly. She whirled. The laneway was empty. Her nerves and the memory of that cold hand closing over her mouth were making her paranoid.

From the end of Kemble Street, glass shattered across brick, and Catriona raised her hand to stifle a gasp. It was only a bottle tossed aside by a group of drunken young men. She forced herself to take a deep breath, focussing on the hot mist against her glove. When she looked back to the road, he was there in the laneway across from her.

In quick succession, there was recognition in his eyes, then frustration, then resignation. Marlowe took a step towards her.

It had been a mistake for her to come. She realised it too late; she had distracted him. From the laneway behind him emerged a dark figure, and a warning surged up in her throat—too late, too late. With the whipping crack of a pistol against his head, Marlowe crumpled to the ground.

She thought she must have cried out, but there was only the silence and the snow. She could not move, paralysed against that brick wall. Marlowe had gone completely still, sprawled half over the street, and Catriona bit down inside her mouth to fight the horrifying faint feeling that swam through her. Blood seeped darkly through his hair, over his closed eyes, and onto the snow.

"You across the street, come out. Slowly now." It was a male voice, cold and familiar.

Catriona reached out blindly for the wall. A streetlamp shone sickly yellow in her eyes, and she realised she had stepped forwards.

"I so hoped you would listen to my warnings," the man said. Every sound in the city had fallen to a hush. It was only them, the world narrowed down to that dark street.

"Step into the light," Catriona said. It had come out as barely more than a whisper, but when again she spoke, the words tore at her throat. "Show me your face!"

A movement, a step forwards. "This was the only way you would ever stop," he said, "and now it is too late for us both."

His dark shoe appeared, then his coat, then his hat, and he raised his head so his face was not in shadow any longer. Light glinted off his spectacles. Catriona stumbled back. The sharp features of Henry Bancroft were visible at last.

"No," she said, but her voice came out weakly. She swallowed and pressed a hand to her chest. "No, this is a mistake."

"If only you knew how I have tried to avoid this," he said. He had stepped forwards again but stopped himself, stopped and shook his head, then raised his hand, which held the pistol, and levelled it at her. He said, "You leave me no choice, Miss Winters. I shall regret this."

# CHAPTER 29

"Stop!" Catriona cried. She had thrown her hands up before her, her entire body pierced by panic. "Bethany will never forgive you if you do this. You will end up in prison."

"I gave you so many chances to back off," Bancroft said. "Do you think I wish to kill you? I know what your death will do to her."

"Then you must think of her now," Catriona said. Everything in her was screaming to flee. Instead, she took the slightest step forwards.

"These past two weeks, I have thought of nothing but her," Bancroft said.

"You were thinking of her when you killed her father?"

He had lowered the pistol slightly, just enough that she was no longer staring down the barrel. "I really had no choice," he said.

"He had tracked down my shipping contract with Randall and figured out everything."

"It was you who imported the opium," she said.

"Randall approached me with the proposal after my father died. He was an old friend of mine, you see, always full of ideas but without the resources to carry them out. He knew my father had mismanaged the company. Holt & Bancroft was in dire straits."

"He gave you an opportunity to rectify that," she said. She glanced down to where Marlowe lay in the street between them, still unconscious, perhaps even dead. At the memory of that pistol cracking against his skull, her mouth flooded with a coppery taste.

"The risk was low," Bancroft said. "Persian opium is of high quality, higher than Indian, but Randall needed a way to get it into the country and sell it at a profit. My ships go uninspected through the ports; a few false manifests and we could avoid customs altogether."

"Lord Ashford uncovered your operation," she said. "Why kill him? Smuggling is not a capital crime. You would have paid a fine, if that."

"Are you to be my confessor, Miss Winters?" he said. "So be it. God knows, after you're gone, I shall take all this to my grave." He had lowered the pistol fully now. "No, smuggling is not a capital crime. But murder is."

"Murder," she said tonelessly.

"Of Lord Stratton, of course."

"But—no, it was Randall who did it. He was being blackmailed."

"Yes, and he thought he ought to pay Stratton off, as if he

would keep quiet about it. No, I know his type. He would come back for more. Either way, Randall could not be trusted to handle the matter, so I told him I would take care of it."

"It was you who met Lord Stratton at the docks that night," she said.

"Yes, and I did what Randall would not have done."

"But why? Stratton needed the money, that was all."

"No," Bancroft said with unexpected venom. "They're all the same, men like him, born into centuries of unearned wealth. They think they're entitled to it, as if anyone who works his way up in society is taking something that doesn't belong to him. Even as he descended to blackmail, Stratton regarded me with that smirk of satisfaction, as if he were doing me a favour by deigning to speak with me. You know what I mean, Miss Winters. Because we're not like them."

She took another small step forwards, just close enough. Marlowe was still alive. He was breathing. His hand had twitched, fingers splayed across the snow. Catriona looked up quickly. Bancroft could not be allowed to notice.

"It was so easy," he said. He was not even looking at her, not really. "He never expected it. I shoved him, and he hit his head on the dock, and that was that. He was quiet."

She knew she must keep him talking somehow. Marlowe had said he would flag down a patrolman. Surely the police were en route? "And you pushed him into the river," she said, "where he drowned."

"I misjudged the tides. Thought his body would be gone by

morning. But he was still there, drifting…" His lip curled in distaste. "Maybe I frightened Randall when he saw what I was willing to do. At the slightest hint of trouble, he told Ashford everything. At least he had the decency to warn me once he had. I assured him there was no need to panic; I would handle it all. But by the next day, he had fled. Suppose he thought I would come after him next, poor bastard."

"You would have done," she said. The words had flown out. She knew not what had come over her. Her hands clenched into fists at her sides. "You're going to kill me as you killed Lord Ashford. How could you, Mr Bancroft? He was so fond of you. Surely you could have explained Stratton provoked you."

"I did. Ashford and I had a very reasonable conversation. He suggested perhaps Stratton had attacked me, and I killed him in self-defence, or it was an accident. I would spend some time in prison and lose the company, but I would keep my life."

"That wasn't enough for you?"

"Of course not. The company is everything to me," he said. "Everything aside from Bethany, and her father would never have allowed me to marry her then. So you see, I was thinking of her when I did it. It was a mercy, a bullet to the heart, a very quick way to go."

"You were not there as he died, Mr Bancroft. I held him in my arms, and his last thought was of Bethany too. My God, he was trying to warn me about you." Her hands were shaking. Even her voice trembled. "She will never forgive you," she said.

"She will never know," he replied, then raised the pistol again, but his eyes darted from her to Marlowe, who had staggered up on his hands and knees.

Catriona cast herself onto the snow next to him, throwing a hand up frantically between them and the pistol. "Mr Bancroft, please!" she cried, and his face twisted with something like cold disdain. He hesitated before turning from her and glancing down either end of the empty street.

Marlowe reached out blindly across the snow with one hand, the other clamped to his head. She grasped him by the shoulders and tried to help him rise, but he had already lost consciousness again, collapsing against her. She sank to her knees, struggling to hold him up.

"Inspector," she hissed fiercely. "Thomas!"

His head was at her collar, his eyes rolled back. She grasped his hand in hers—limp, useless.

"Mr Bancroft, I beg you, he needs a physician," she cried.

"You must see that is not an option," he said.

"Whatever you've done, it's over now! It can all be worked out. I know you're not so heartless as to kill us both in cold blood."

He glanced away once more and cursed under his breath. She could not tear her eyes from him, hoping that as long as he would have to face her when he did it, Henry Bancroft might not have it in him to murder her. He had begun pacing, his lamplit shadow crossing over them again and again.

Catriona stiffened. For a second, so quickly she thought she had imagined it, Marlowe had returned her grip on his hand.

She did not glance down at him, did not speak, did not even

breathe. She only kept her eyes on Bancroft, watching him stalk from one side of the street to the other. Marlowe pulled her hand towards him, slowly enough not to be noticed, until finally her gloved fingers landed on cold metal—the revolver, hidden beneath his coat, strapped to his side.

The world went into sharp focus.

Bancroft, having come to some decision, whirled to face them again. "Turn away now, Miss Winters," he said.

"No, please," Catriona whispered.

"Turn away! Let him go and turn away from me."

"You don't mean to do this."

"I do mean it. I've already made peace with it. You will be found dead here come morning, both of you. A murder-suicide. The inspector made advances towards you, and you rejected him, and he snapped. That will be the end of it." He raised the pistol and cocked it. Reflected off his spectacles, the lamplight obscured his eyes. "But look on the bright side, Miss Winters," he said. "It appears you got in a good hit before he shot you."

It was unbearable now, the waves roaring in her ears. She took a deep breath, night air flooding her lungs painfully, and grasped the revolver.

"Henry, no!"

Bancroft spun towards the mouth of the laneway, from which the little cry had come. Bethany stepped from the shadows and stood, illuminated, under a halo of lamplight.

Catriona did not hesitate. She withdrew the revolver, aimed it, and fired once. Bancroft dropped his pistol and staggered back. His hand flew to his shoulder.

"By God, you've shot me!" he screamed.

Catriona was still clutching the revolver, her hand cemented to it. The recoil had ricocheted back through her arm, and she had nearly thrown it out of surprise. She had not thought beyond that first shot, and she had missed. Bancroft was still alive.

In a flutter of footsteps, Beth raced out into the street, knelt to retrieve the pistol he had dropped, and stepped back, levelling it at him.

"Bethany, no," he said. "You must understand…"

"How dare you!" she cried. "I've heard everything. How dare you say you love me when it is you who has taken so much from me?"

"I do love you, Bethany," he said. "Just listen to me."

Beth did not reply. The pistol was shaking in her hands, her dark eyes wide and frantic—and hesitant. Her finger landed on the trigger, but Catriona knew it with almost prophetic certainty: She would not do it. And perhaps Bancroft knew so too. His face had gone chalky grey. He stepped back and sat heavily on the kerb of the footpath.

Bethany lowered the pistol.

"Halt!" someone yelled. At one end of the street, a coach had come careening to a stop, and from it rushed Detective Whitby, flanked by three others.

Catriona exhaled at last. She let the revolver fall to the snow, distantly aware of Marlowe against her, still alive, still breathing, and she closed her eyes and listened as the waves receded into silence.

. . .

The Yard was quiet in those strange hours between night and morning. In a room off the back hall, sitting side by side on a worn sofa, each holding an untouched cup of dark tea, Catriona and Bethany waited.

"I let him into our lives," Beth said at last, blinking rapidly. She was looking not at Catriona but straight ahead, at the wall across from them, over which there must once have been wallpaper but was now only bare plaster.

"You could not have known," Catriona said.

"He would have killed you," Bethany replied fiercely, whirling to face her, nearly upending her tea. "I should have fired that pistol when I had the chance. Papa taught me to shoot; it would have been over quickly. Now he shall be put to trial. But perhaps that's what he deserves—to be hanged."

Catriona said nothing. She was remembering the previous spring, when Beth had knelt next to her in the gardens, clasped her hands within hers, and said, her dark eyes full of a feeling that was neither hope nor trepidation, "Henry and I are to be married." Catriona had been happy for her, the bittersweet happiness of endings and beginnings.

No, she could not have known.

In the corridor beyond, several constables passed. One cast a glance through the open doorway, but none stopped, and their footsteps soon retreated.

"You saved our lives, Beth," Catriona said at last. It had not felt real, turning to see her dearest friend having stepped from the shadows, come to her rescue. "How did you know where to find us?"

"Oh," Beth said. Her face had gone a curious shade of pink. "I must apologise for that. After we parted earlier, I became consumed by guilt. I couldn't stop thinking of the harsh things I said to you, and finally I thought I must go across and tell you how sorry I was. But when I looked over, I saw Mr Tsang coming down the steps, and I thought, how odd. Before I could wonder about it any more, you headed out with such a severe expression that I knew something must be amiss. So I followed you."

"Beth!" Catriona exclaimed.

"I really am sorry, Kitty."

"You mustn't apologise. It's only that you've surprised me so greatly."

"I've surprised myself," Beth said. "I never leave the house at night, never alone. But it was such a strange feeling I had, so I didn't think. I just did it. I followed you on the train and then to that tenement and waited as you went inside, and at last I saw you and Inspector Marlowe in the window."

Catriona had been trying not to think of him, trying not to glance down to the bloody place by her collar where his head had lain. He had been hauled up onto a stretcher and taken directly to hospital; she had heard nothing of him since.

"Will he be all right, do you think?" Beth said.

Catriona could not reply. She was focussing on the burning in her throat and eyes, trying not to lose her composure because it would only upset Bethany further. A desolate, keen hopelessness, an understanding that she had realised something important, but she had realised it too late, had pierced her and would not let up.

Beth said, "I think you've become friends."

"Yes," Catriona said quietly.

Beth laid a hand gently over hers, which was shaking against the teacup. Her grip was warm and surprisingly strong, and she said only, with serene certainty, "There, all will be well."

Before Catriona could reply, if she would have replied at all, a constable came in to escort them to their interviews.

The hospital corridor was dimly lit, its quiet punctuated only by the occasional cough or murmur. After being questioned courteously but thoroughly by a detective sergeant whose name she could not now recall, an ordeal which had lasted till nearly four in the morning, Catriona had set out from the Yard into the chill dark, down a nearly deserted Parliament Street and across Westminster Bridge, where the Thames, unseen far below, lapped steadily.

Since its relocation in the previous decade to make way for the expansion of the Underground, St Thomas Hospital had stood along the riverfront, its wards facing the embankment. The institution was one with which Catriona had become only somewhat familiar, and very recently at that, but a nurse passing through the main pavilion, having noticed her pale, exhausted expression, had been kind enough to offer to guide her. The two now walked in silence, Catriona following a half step behind.

She had not thought about what she would say to Marlowe. He was alive, that much she had been told, but she had an awful picture of him as he had been on Kemble Street, his face deathly white beneath all that blood. Till that moment, she had imagined him to be somehow inured to the possibility of further injury. But he was only a man after all.

The nurse left her in the doorway of a ward similar to that in which she had awoken the previous night. How little time had passed, and everything was changed. The man who had assaulted her, the solid body trapping her in place, the hand clamped over her mouth so she could not scream—it had been Henry Bancroft, and the realisation was almost too much to bear. At the memory of his flowers still sitting prettily in their vase in the withdrawing room, she gave her head a shake and entered the ward.

The place was not entirely empty. She walked down a row of beds to the farthest, around which the curtain had been pulled halfway. Marlowe was there, lit barely by the few gaslights. The blood had been cleaned from his face and hair, and his jacket and vest had been removed, leaving only the white shirt, pulled open at the collar. His colour had returned a little. He lay asleep atop the starched sheets, legs stretched just over the end of the cot.

There it was again, the unguarded expression that made him seem much younger. Catriona lowered her hand, which she had raised to her collar without realising. Looking at him when he could not look back at her felt too intimate, almost voyeuristic. She turned away. He was alive; she had confirmed it for herself, and there was nothing more for her to do there now. She decided to leave, and she took a step.

"Catriona."

She stilled. When she turned again, he had half risen and was watching her. She held out a hand and darted forwards at once.

"As you were, Inspector," she said. "How are you feeling?"

"Not too poorly," he said. "A little concussed, apparently."

He allowed her to arrange the pillow so he might sit up fully, and once she had done so, she perched at the very edge of the bed. A strange trepidation had lodged itself in her throat. She wanted to tell him how sorry she was. She wanted to tell him, I feared you were dead, and I could not have forgiven myself if you were. But the feeling was too vast to express.

"I didn't mean to wake you," she said instead.

"I wasn't sleeping," he replied, and he said nothing else, only watched her when her hand rose, as if of its own accord, to the place behind his temple, her thumb hovering over the line of stitches that disappeared into his hair. She withdrew it quickly, without having touched him.

"It was my fault," she said, and her lip was trembling pitifully, shamefully. "My fault that you were injured. Because I was there and I distracted you."

"Had you not been, he might have killed me outright," Marlowe said. "What's done is done, and there's no point in your regretting it."

"Yet I do," she said. "All the times I spoke with him, with Mr Bancroft, I should have seen he was hiding such a terrible secret."

"We never do see it," he said. "Not in the ones we think we know."

She glanced down to her hands, folded placidly in her lap, not the sort of hands one might imagine to have held a revolver just hours earlier. Marlowe was right, of course. Bancroft had fooled them all, expertly and completely, and she could have killed him for it. But she would not think of him now, not if she could help it, and perhaps not ever again.

When Catriona looked back up to him, Marlowe had closed his eyes, only for a second, and gone pale once more. She knew it was time for her to leave, only she wished she might have had a better picture by which to remember him. She rose abruptly.

"I should not disturb you further," she said. "You must get some rest. I came only to see you were all right—and to say good-bye, I suppose."

His brows drew together, but she held up a hand before he could speak.

"I saw your trunk packed up," she explained quickly. She tried to smile but knew all she had managed was an empty, flickering thing. She turned from him. She was so determined to get away, so determined that he not see how inexplicably forlorn she felt, that she had already taken a step when his hand caught the sleeve of her dress.

"Catriona, I'm not leaving," he said. He exhaled, like a laugh, and his mouth quirked a little. "The trunk you saw, it was my things sent from Birmingham. The Met have offered me a permanent position."

"Oh," she said. Slowly, hesitantly, she lowered herself back to the bed. "So you are to stay in London?"

"I am," he said, and then, with an unexpectedly wry glance,

"Are you sorry to hear it?"

She had tried to force herself to distrust it, the hopeful feeling he had sparked in her. But it was too late, of course; her heart had already given a little leap.

"No," she said at last. "No, quite the opposite of that."

Happiness, happiness and relief, was bursting up through her. She smiled because she could not help it—and there it was, the thing she had not realised she was waiting for: Marlowe was smiling too, a boyish, crooked smile, like sunlight piercing a grey sky.

# CHAPTER 30

"Would you pass me that little angel, Papa?" Catriona said. "I have found the perfect branch for him at last."

From where she stood by the Christmas tree in the parlour, she held out a hand expectantly. Sir Frederick sat on the sofa in his slippers, reading the competition, the grey morning pouring through the window behind him and firelight from the hearth flickering across his steely face. Nearly three weeks had passed since that night on Kemble Street, and Catriona was still facing her consequences, as her papa was now somewhat loath to let her out of his sight.

He retrieved the silvery bauble from the pile of tissue paper on the cushion beside him and extended it towards her. Catriona busied herself with it for a moment, and only when she had finished and stood back to admire her handiwork did she realise her papa had looked up from his paper and was watching her, as perhaps he had been for some time, with a strange expression.

This was one of the rare occasions on which Catriona could tell exactly what he had been thinking: The expression was the one he wore when recalling her mama. She lowered herself to the armchair across from him. Although he had said nothing, she sensed there was indeed something he wished to tell her.

Since the fateful night, Sir Frederick had neither scolded her nor shown any outwards anger over the poor judgement which had led to her facing down a killer. But she had felt the wary way he watched her, as though she were a stranger to him.

He set his paper across his knees, gave her a frank, almost helpless look, and said, "I have made so many mistakes with you, Catriona."

She said nothing, feeling as though he had struck her. It might have hurt less if he had done, she thought. She could withstand the harsh judgement of anyone but her papa. She braced herself, clenching the arms of the chair tightly, and Sir Frederick must have thought she meant to protest, because he held a hand up to stop her.

"No," he said. "I have made the same mistakes I made with your mama. She frightened me, and I was only a young man who didn't know better. But I know better now. I indulged her when I should have used a firmer hand, and because of that I lost her. I cannot lose you too."

Catriona forced herself to look past him, out the window to where the snow glared white. Her expression had twisted awfully, she knew, and the burning brightness was the only thing preventing her from crumpling into tears.

Sir Frederick cleared his throat roughly. "You are not a child anymore," he said. "I have done my best without your mama here to set an example for you. But I see my best has been insufficient, and of late, where you are concerned, I have felt the sword of Damocles descending ever closer to my neck."

"Papa," she began.

"No, my dear," he said. "This behaviour, this traipsing around at all hours, associating with whomever you please, fascinating yourself with—with morbid subjects, it all ends now. It ends this instant. Do you understand?"

"Yes," she said quietly, though the voice, devoid of emotion, was not her own.

"I will not tolerate it any further!"

"Yes, I understand."

Sir Frederick sighed.

There was no more for either of them to say. It had been settled. Though everything in her was screaming to rise at once and quit the room, Catriona sat stiffly and perfectly still. Fleeing was what a child would have done, she knew, and it was true: She was not a child anymore. She could bear it, this straining pain of reaching for a thing that had already slipped from her grasp.

As though somehow sensing its occupants desperately needed rescue from one another, Hughes chose that moment to sweep into the parlour with the midmorning post. He presented several letters to Sir Frederick, who indeed appeared grateful for the distraction, and then brought the silver tray to Catriona.

The single envelope on it bore an assortment of stamps but no return address, and inside was a painted card. Colourful little houses stood on hills rising up from around a sandy bay, beyond which, through a narrow channel, lay an endless blue sea. San Francisco Bay and Golden Gate, read the handwritten caption beneath. There was no note.

She held it and closed her eyes for the briefest moment. She was not imagining a sunny city halfway across the world; she was remembering Limehouse and a cold, smoky room with a window overlooking the docks, and she was yearning for a freedom she would never feel again.

When she looked up, her papa was watching her.

"Sidney Hampstead?" he said, glancing pointedly, perhaps even hopefully, at the card in her lap.

"No." Catriona slid it gently back in its envelope. She would take it out again sometimes, only sometimes. "No one," she said. "Just a friend."

"I went to see him," Bethany said. "Henry."

Catriona looked up from her needlepoint. The drawing room was lit warmly by the fire, but the atmosphere had chilled at once. Beth sat in the armchair across from her, her cloth canvas lying forgotten in her lap. How long had she been sitting there, lost in her thoughts?

"Oh," Catriona replied.

"He seems changed somehow," Beth said. "Perhaps it's only because that place is so awful. But I wonder that I couldn't see it before, the coldness in his eyes."

Catriona set her work down on the cushion. She had tried to avoid picturing Bancroft in his cell at Newgate Prison, but now she could not help it. In her mind, he was haggard and unshaven, his spectacles had been broken, and the cell was very cold and dark. Perhaps it was not far off from reality. She did not ask.

"He says he still loves me," Beth said.

"Perhaps he does, in his own way."

"I went because I believed it would make me feel better to see him locked away like that, but I regret it. It only made me sad." She shook her head. "You must think me irrational."

"No," Catriona said. "No one expects you to forget whatever affection you had for him."

"It was not affection that caused my sadness." Beth looked across at her, and her dark eyes were so suddenly intense that she appeared more like her brother than herself. "It was that I realised I felt nothing for him, nothing at all. I made so many excuses for myself, all the reasons I should put off marrying him. But the real reason was the simplest: I didn't love him. I never did."

Had anyone else made such a confession, Catriona might have suspected she were lying, trying to convince herself of it as a way of coming to terms with a terrible reality. But Catriona knew Beth better than that, enough to see she had spoken the truth.

"You and Mr Bancroft were ill suited for each other," Catriona replied. "Of course you were."

"I would have married him anyway, you know, holding out hope that one day I might learn to feel something for him. But I think that day would never have come. No, in fact, I am certain of it." Beth folded her hands over her canvas. Her expression was calm and sure, and at last she continued. "I have visited lately with Miss Fabian. The nursing programme at St Thomas is accepting candidates in the new year—and I intend to enrol."

Catriona sat dumbly. She was too stunned to speak, but her hand had flown to her mouth to stifle a delighted gasp, and now she could not hide the smile that broke out behind her palm.

"Please do say something," Bethany said.

"I hardly know where to begin," Catriona said. Absurdly, tears pricked her eyes, but she blinked them away quickly. It was only jealousy, only that awful yearning to again be allowed to pursue her own ambitions. The feeling could be ignored. "I am so thrilled for you, Beth. You will make an excellent nurse."

"Yes, I believe I will," Beth said with a little smile of her own, one that remained for the rest of the evening, as she absently continued her needlepoint, whenever Catriona glanced across at her.

Later, when she was leaving, Catriona stopped halfway down the front steps. Nate stood against the iron fence of the square garden, watching her as if he had been waiting there. He put out his cigarette, and she proceeded across the street to him.

"Did you not wish to join us?" she said.

"I would have done, eventually." He glanced up to the window of the drawing room, though it was empty now, Beth having seen Catriona to the door and not yet returned to her spot. "She seems better these days," he said. "Bethany. She never talks about it, you know. Our father, and what happened. Maybe pretending is easiest.

Some days, hours will pass without my thinking of him, but then something reminds me, and…" He half turned from her, and when he spoke again, his voice was hoarse. "And I realise—oh, my father is gone after all."

The square was quiet in the snow, but distantly, coaches passed on Pelham Street. It was not so late in the evening; the windows of many of the neighbouring houses were still lit, enough to cast a dim glow over him through the darkness. Catriona recalled that first night he returned from the country, when they had faced one another and she had felt so keenly his months of absence. All she had wanted then was to have him for her own. She could become that girl again. She could want that life once more.

She laid a hand on his arm. "I miss him too," she said. "And I miss you."

He turned to her, his brows drawn together. The assuredness with which he had always approached her, the confidence he put on, had disappeared ever since that night in the hospital. All that remained was a weary, inextinguishable hope.

"I want us to stay in London," she said.

"Of course, whatever you wish." He clasped her hand in his, and she allowed him to draw her into his arms, press her forehead against his chest so he could bend to kiss the crown of her head. "I love you," he said. "I would do anything for you."

She nodded, told herself this was everything she wanted, and closed her eyes.

Catriona had decided she must visit Lady Stratton at last. The two had exchanged letters over the past few weeks as her ladyship supervised the packing up of her city home, and though the coming week-end would mark her departure to America, Catriona had put off seeing her for reasons she could not quite have articulated. Perhaps it was the suspicion that upon facing her directly, Lady Stratton would realise that her connection to Bancroft was indeed too close for comfort.

However, she arrived at the house in Piccadilly and was admitted immediately. She had worn lavender, a colour of half mourning, out of respect, but as expected, the Stratton house was still in full mourning, with any remaining mirrors covered and the staff all in black.

Lady Stratton awaited her in the parlour. Next to the settee was a bassinet in which lay her son. The nursemaid took him away quickly enough, as babies were not often kept out during social calls, but not so quickly that Catriona missed the unselfconscious doting expression his mother wore while cooing over him. Lady Stratton patted the empty spot on the settee next to her, and Catriona felt immediate relief at this signal that she was persona grata after all.

The footman had brought in tea, and Lady Stratton poured two cups and handed Catriona hers directly, then said without preamble, "I rather liked Mr Bancroft, you know. Upon making his acquaintance, I remember thinking how different he was to my husband. I thought, there is a man who knows how to make his own way in the world. Poor Miss Turner, to have been so deceived."

"She wished me to pass along her good-bye," Catriona said. "She felt she could not face you."

"Oh," Lady Stratton said, as if that had not occurred to her. And perhaps, Catriona thought, it had not. "I would very much have liked to tell her in person how sorry I am for what she is going through."

"That will be a great comfort to her," Catriona said. "I think she feared you might blame her in some way for what has happened."

"Blame her!" Lady Stratton exclaimed, and shot Catriona an unexpected wry look. "Miss Winters, if we women are to be held accountable for the sins of our men, heaven will be left entirely empty."

Catriona covered her smile by sipping her tea. She regretted that it had taken a murder, in fact two murders, for her to deepen her acquaintance with Lady Stratton. "So you are leaving us this week-end," she said, setting down her cup.

"I am," Lady Stratton said. "In truth, losing my husband has made me realise how alone I have been here. All those who pretended to be his friends deserted me when it really mattered—all but you. No, I have perceived a sort of blackness at the heart of this city, and I must raise my son in greener pastures than these."

"You must be so eager to see your family again."

The gentle, unpretentious expression that made Lady Stratton so pleasant to regard was back. "At the end of the day," she said, "our families are the most important part of our lives. Do you not agree?"

"I do, of course," Catriona said, though she and her papa had hardly spoken since his chastisement of her in the parlour, the two having exchanged nothing more than pleasantries for several days now. "I'm sure your parents will be overjoyed to be near their grandson."

"My mother tells me she has prepared the old nursery," Lady Stratton said. "Yes, I think this will be best for us both."

Some minutes passed in comfortable silence, Lady Stratton stirring more sugar into her tea and Catriona looking around the room, which was mostly bare of furniture. The paintings were gone too, though their ghosts remained in the darker rectangles of wallpaper unexposed to the sun.

When she looked back, Lady Stratton was staring somewhere past her tea, her hand having stilled with the spoon. She shook her head and looked up, regarding Catriona frankly as she said, "I must ask you something."

"Of course," Catriona said.

"One day, my son will wish to know about his father. He may even return here, and who knows what sorts of awful rumours people will remember? I feel I must prepare him somehow, but I know not what to tell him." She set her tea down on the low table and folded her hands in her lap as if bracing herself. "I believe it comes down to the simple question of whether my husband was a good man in the end."

Catriona too had gone still. She was thinking of Bancroft and how, just weeks earlier, she had thought he was a good man. She was thinking of him and Lord Stratton and Ashford and the tangled web they had left to be unravelled in their absence. And she thought of her own mother, her every memory of whom had been blackened by one final sin.

"I am asking for your judgement," Lady Stratton said, "for the question is one I cannot answer on my own."

Catriona forced herself to breathe and speak past the tension in her throat. "His lordship loved you, and he loved your son," she said. "I believe you know the answer in your heart."

Lady Stratton sighed and closed her eyes. For a moment, something like relief, so intense as to be painful, spilled across her expression. Then she drew herself up and faced Catriona again. "Atherton was the love of my life," she said, "and I will love him till my dying day. But I never knew him, not really. How well can you know someone, even someone you love with all your heart?"

Lady Stratton had reached across the space between them and clasped her hands warmly. She withdrew and gave her head a little shake before continuing with a rueful smile. "They say there's a skeleton in every house," she said. "None in mine, I thought. But it was there after all, locked away so tight I never heard it rattling behind the door."

Catriona said nothing, her hands still in her lap where Lady Stratton had left them. After a moment, her ladyship rose.

"I suppose this will be our farewell, Miss Winters," she said. "You have been such a good friend to me. I will write, and I hope you will reply."

"I will," Catriona said quietly as she rose too. "My lady, I wish you good health and all the best on your journey. And I wish you and your son all the happiness in the world."

For the first time in days, as Catriona made her way down the steps and out through the gate to the street, the white sun had burst through the clouds overhead.

She walked quickly, trying not to think of anything ugly, not Stratton lying still and dead at the docks, not Ashford gasping in that bloody chair in his office, and not that imagined cell at Newgate to which her thoughts had drifted so often of late. Murder was one of the only remaining crimes for which the sentence was hanging. It was almost too final, the thought of Bancroft hanging by his neck. But she thought of it nonetheless, not with vengefulness but with an icy, detached pity.

She forced air into her lungs until they burned. A walk was necessary, she decided as she cut through Green Park, bordered by the palace gardens to the south, where the snow was sparkling and new. She wandered aimlessly, or so she thought, on through St James and up Whitehall Place, distracting herself with the city around her, full of the stories of everyone she knew and would know and might never know at all.

The newspaper boys were out in force, promising all the news of the morning for a few pence. She weaved around them and through passing coaches to cross the wide street, and at the other side, she stopped, because in the shop window ahead was her reflection, her own dark eyes watching her. A few wild strands of her hair had come loose, her complexion made rosy by the walk, her expression mildly inquisitive, as if she had recognised an old friend.

She shook her head, took another step, and it was only then, as she reached the familiar arch, that she realised she knew where she was after all. It was Great Scotland Yard, and it had, of course, been her destination all along.

# FACT *vs* FICTION

Though the characters and events of this book are fictional, I have attempted to maintain historical accuracy where possible.

Opiate use, both recreational and medicinal, was rife in England in the nineteenth century. It was only in the later years of the Victorian era that social reformers began to protest the state of affairs, leading Parliament to act in 1868 and restrict the sale of opium to licensed pharmacists. This did little to curb its use. Laudanum, an opiate tincture, was a popular painkiller amongst all classes, and opiates were administered frequently and often indiscriminately to children as cough suppressants and sedatives. Whilst opiate use amongst the lower classes was seen as a sign of moral degradation, use amongst the upper classes was often viewed as little more than a bad habit.

It was not until the turn of the century that addiction began to be treated as a medical rather than moral problem. On that note, we have the Victorians to thank for the introduction of heroin. First synthesised in 1874, it was later introduced to the market by Bayer with the intent of capitalising on fears about the addictive nature of morphine. Heroin was advertised as a "non-addictive" substitute, available for purchase in pharmacies without a prescription.

Popular conceptions of the role of women in society underwent significant changes during the Victorian era, which spanned more than sixty years. The modern notion that women of the time were confined solely to the domestic sphere, forbidden from travelling alone or taking employment outside the home, is ahistorical. Amongst the lower classes, women worked out of necessity in factories, textile mills, and even heavy industry. In the latter half of the nineteenth century, women of the middle class, long employed as domestic servants, governesses, and schoolteachers, had begun to take positions as secretaries and sales assistants. Women also made headway in the medical professions, first as nurses and midwives, then as physicians and pharmacists.

Amongst the upper classes, women were afforded as much or as little freedom as their male relations allowed. No law prevented a woman from traversing the city alone; it was the threat of social censure which kept women in line. Women of all classes embraced advances in transportation, such as the expansion of the Underground system and the use of bicycles in warmer weather, to travel without the supervision of a male companion.

In England, women had been contributing to journalism since the late 1840s. Highly educated and ambitious, female journalists were almost exclusively of the upper middle and upper classes. They included such celebrated figures as novelist George Eliot and feminist and social reformer Frances Cobbe. In 1881, England would see its first female war correspondent in Lady Florence Dixie, reporting for the *Morning Post*. I believe Catriona would have admired and respected these women and would naturally have been attracted to this field of work.

# ABOUT *THE* AUTHOR

Isabella Duke lives and writes in Sydney, Australia. *A Skeleton in Every House* is her debut novel and the first in this series. For news on forthcoming books, visit her online at www.isabella-duke.com.

Printed in Great Britain
by Amazon

56067654R00209